UNFORGIVABLE

UNFORGIVABLE

JENN LESSMANN

UNFORGIVABLE
Published by FARMER'S DAUGHTER ARTS, LLC
Copyright © 2024

Cover Design by Get Covers
Editing by Sharon Stogner

ISBN: 979-8-9893324-2-7 (Paperback)
ISBN: 979-8-9893324-3-4 (eBook)

For more information visit: www.JennLessmann.com

For those who seek their own magic.

S tupid, cryptic prophesies never turn out the way anyone expects.

On the day I was born, my name appeared on the list.

The Gatekeeper gave her blessing: "She will be next." The following years should have been filled with training and preparations for taking on the honored position. A blessing and a curse.

Knowing it was inevitable didn't keep my parents from trying to stop it—*as if that ever worked*—and ruining my life in the process. They couldn't hide the Gatekeeper's pronouncement, so they hid me instead. Mom and Dad bound my Gift and altered my memory to cover their deception. *Couldn't have their daughter growing up knowing they'd dealt her our community's harshest sentence as a doomed protective measure.* They thought I wouldn't miss my Gift if I didn't remember having one. Better to be the family failure than trapped in the Gatehouse forever. No great power. No responsibility whatsoever.

Until everything went wrong, and I discovered the truth.

I was the last Gatekeeper, Gifted unlike any other.

The power I harnessed in fulfilling my destiny faded when I opened the Gate, letting magic and those who practiced it escape into the mundane world. The Gift I'd so recently

1

unbound apparently went with it, the price of saving the world. If I hadn't done it, the energy of that same magic would have destroyed us. The boundary around our community protected us for generations, but the population of Queen's Creek had outgrown its capacity to contain it. The Gate was never meant to last forever.

But our freedom brought fresh danger. Magic would follow the witches. Without the boundary to contain it, the energy would find us wherever we went, and so would the hunters.

This time, I didn't need a prophecy to identify me as the Chosen One. Someone had to go out and warn the witches who'd already left. While the elders debated over rewriting our covenants, I started packing. I had to get out before anyone could stop me. Not that I thought they would. Who better to navigate the mundane world than the only witch in town who'd grown up without a Gift?

Adam made things complicated.

"You could come with me," I said, avoiding his eyes as I shoved stuff into my backpack. A strand of purple hair dipped over my face, and I blew it back. It caught in my glasses.

Adam didn't need the invitation, but I hoped he'd take it. We still had so much catching up to do. In the week since I'd come home from my Wakening, I'd learned my father was missing, found him, lost him again, and destroyed the enchantment that hid Queen's Creek from the mundane world.

Too many things hid in the shadows these days.

He smiled, and I thought I might finally win one. But his eyes drifted away from me, taking in the open door to Gatekeeper's empty bedroom, the bare window in the living room, and the bridge on the other side leading back home. He shook his head.

Then, he kissed me. A familiar warmth flushed my face, and a memory hovered just out of reach, fuzzy around the edges. The feelings returned more quickly, but they were confusing without the memories to back them up. My heart raced, and I was dizzy when he pulled away.

"So you don't forget me this time," he said, tucking a stray hair back behind my ear.

I pressed my lips together, trying in vain to make them work again. Goddess bless him. He was good at that. My fingers twisted a copper curl behind his neck. I didn't want to leave him. It would be so much easier if he'd just come with me. I was about to say so again when my brother Thomas called my name from outside. Impeccable timing, as always.

"Better get going." Adam tapped the doorframe on his way back to the bridge. "And Cate? Happy Birthday."

"You have to stay?" It came out as more of an accusation than I'd intended.

"They need me here," he said, watching the tree line and the secret town of witches beyond it.

He was right. He'd been the last line of defense on the other side ever since he'd come home from his Wakening. It was selfish of me to try and pull the Guardian away when our community was vulnerable.

I sent one last text before pressing my phone, and my future, into Adam's hands. *Please, Goddess, let this message through.*

Then I left him behind again and caught the plane back to Chicago. It would be a temporary separation this time, but it still felt wrong. Somehow, our timing was always off.

1

My prayers were answered by the stack of boxes waiting in the middle of my dorm room. Well, by the presence of my bike leaning against them with a friendly note taped to the handlebars.

"Welcome back! Come by the café when you get a chance. I'm opening tomorrow.

-Brian"

I have wheels! Thank you, Mother, Maiden, and Crone. He got my text.

Queen's Creek was finally becoming part of the real world. A few weeks ago, the energy of the boundary spell would have interfered with the signal, and my message never would have passed the Gatehouse. Now, I could ride my bike to the electronics store, pick up a new phone, and call Adam to have Queen's Creek's first-ever long-distance conversation.

Instant communication at my fingertips. Tell me that isn't magic.

It was such a change from the snail mail I used to exchange with my dad. I'd tucked Dad's last letter into one of his notebooks and stuffed it back into my bag before I left the Gatehouse. There had to be more clues in there. Something that would explain his work and how to get him back. If I'd been able to call him before, things might have ended differently. Now, I had to cross my fingers and hope one of the mundane professors on campus had a side interest in alchemy and string theory. No one had mixed magic and math like Dad had. In the meantime, I had to trust that wherever he was—whenever he was—he was also working on the problem and trying to get home.

I pulled open the top box and started putting things back where they belonged. Thank the goddess Brian had convinced me to let him store my stuff for me. My friend and coworker had been much more confident in my return than I had been.

The door slammed open as I emptied the last box. My heart raced until I recognized the tearful face under bright red box braids. Not hunters. Just my roommate, coming back unexpectedly early from Spring Break.

Nyla dropped her duffle on my bed, her top bunk inconveniently high, and let out a deep sigh. Unfazed by my presence, she unpacked orange juice, vodka, and a broken heart.

"She said we could still be friends. Do you believe that shit?" she said, pulling down a couple of my mugs from the bookshelf that doubled as my kitchen storage. She split most of the bottle of vodka between them and topped them with just enough juice to give it color.

I took a sip, and my eyes watered. Maybe Nyla would mistake it for sympathy. Not that I wasn't sympathetic, but my friend was a serial monogamist. At the rate she was going through girlfriends, she was likely to run out of options before finals. "You're still friends with Emi," I said.

"Emi didn't break up with me in a text message while she was in Cancun with her apparently not-so-ex-boyfriend." Nyla slumped against the wall.

I sank into my desk chair. "Ouch."

"Yeah," Nyla said, sliding down the wall to sit on the floor. "Ouch."

"Do you want to talk about it?" I honestly didn't know what I wanted her to say. I had a lot of things to think about after my own Spring Break trip. None of them was going to be easy. But I couldn't exactly talk about those with my mundane roommate, no matter how much we'd shared over the last few years.

Nyla peered into her mug as if it held tea leaves instead of alcohol and OJ. Being neither spiritual nor aware of the presence of real witches in the world—much less in the room with her—she'd probably have smirked at the comparison. Like most of the theater department, Nyla had a deep understanding of superstitions, but like most of the other students at our university, she didn't believe in magic. She most likely expected a witch to wear a pointy hat and carry a broom, or at least to hang pentacles around their neck and paint their nails black.

When her pale screwdriver failed to answer my question, Nyla scrunched up her nose and answered herself. "No?"

I took another sip to keep from laughing. It burned. "You sure?"

She gulped back some of her drink and put the mug on the floor, nodding so violently her braids swung. "Yes."

This time, I did laugh. I felt some of the tension I'd carried back with me ease away.

Nyla smiled. Crossing her legs, she clasped her hands in her lap and straightened. "Really. I don't want to think about my Spring Breakup anymore. Tell me about your trip. You left early, didn't you? Is everything okay?"

It was my turn to consult my cup. There was so much I hadn't told her, and most of it I still couldn't talk about. I might have let magic out into the world, but I would not be the one to tell mundanes their fairy tales and nightmares were about to come true.

It was more important than ever to keep my heritage a secret. It wasn't just my safety at stake anymore. With the Gate down, everyone back home was unprotected. I couldn't be responsible for alerting the hunters.

But I owed her something. I'd left in such a hurry that I didn't say goodbye. I hadn't even been sure that I was coming back.

The easiest response was the most painful, but staying close to the truth was best. I couldn't think of a way to begin, so I just said the words. "I lost my father."

Nyla's smile melted away. Her posture softened as she leaned forward. "Oh, Cate. I'm so sorry. Tell me what you need."

I shook my head and held up the cup. "This is a great start."

"Well, aren't we a fun pair?" Nyla sank back against the wall.

We sat in silence for a few minutes, sipping our screwdrivers.

"How's everything going with the show?" I left in the middle of painting the set for the spring musical. If not for my family emergency, I'd have stayed with the student cast and crew to keep working on it. My roommate was head of the scenic design crew for the show and a few of our friends were in the cast.

Nyla's smile came back, lighting up her dark eyes. "Oh my god, you missed it! I can't believe you weren't there. Madi and Morgan threw down! Everybody thought they were going all *method*. You know, really getting into Katherine and Bianca. But, man. Wow. It got rough. I mean, my sister and I fight, but this was...so meta."

I raised an eyebrow. Madi and Morgan Edwards were

sisters in every sense of the word, born a year apart, legacy members of the same sorority, cast as ensemble members of every show on the main stage. This year, they'd been cast as Lilli Vanessi and Lois Lane in Kiss Me Kate. They were sisters, playing actresses, playing sisters in the show within the show. I didn't think I'd ever seen them disagree, much less argue in public. There had been a few passive-aggressive comments, but they were practically the same person.

Nyla giggled. It was a strange sound coming from my snarkiest friend. "Oh, man. They were so…Oh my god. You had to see it. I thought Madi was going to murder her!"

"What was it about?" I tried to picture it and failed. I kept coming back to the time Morgan caught Madi making out with her boyfriend. She'd said she was more hurt that her sister hadn't told her she was interested in him than that she'd acted on it. The girls got over it the same night. The boyfriend got ditched.

"You're not going to believe it. It's insane. They are insane." She swirled her cup and drank a little more of the mix.

When she didn't elaborate right away, I shifted in the chair and gestured for her to continue. "And? Come on, then. I am literally on the edge of my seat."

"She put a curse on her!" Nyla covered her mouth and stared at me with wide eyes.

2

y mind raced. They weren't witches. They couldn't have. They wouldn't know how. The magic had been contained back then. If you didn't have a Gift, and Madi and Morgan definitely did not, there was no way. What had they done? It had to be a joke. I forced a laugh. *Thank you, alcohol, for covering my slow response.* "She what? Who?"

"Morgan!" Nyla said, getting the hiccups from holding in her laughter. "She did some kind of spell. I guess she wanted the bigger role."

"Yeah, but a curse, though? Did she really think that would work?" I tried to sound more skeptical. *Magic? What? Nobody believes in magic here, right? No such thing.* I wasn't sure I was pulling it off, but Nyla had already sucked down most of a bottle of vodka, and she seemed to have missed any holes in my performance. There was a reason I only worked backstage.

"I don't know," Nyla said, almost gasping for air between the giggles and the hiccups.

"What happened?" I pressed.

Nyla snorted, bringing on another fit of giggles.

"Are you okay?" I asked, on the verge of cracking up myself. How much had she drunk before she came home?

Shifting against the wall, she took a ragged breath and let it out slowly. "Okay. Sorry. Yeah. I'm okay. O.K."

I waved her on. "You were saying? Morgan jinxed her sister or something?"

"Yeah, so—" Nyla sat up a little straighter and cleared her throat.

I mentally noted how far she was from the trash can. *Maybe I should grab it before I find out what she had for lunch.*

But then she burped and continued. "I don't know how long it's been going on, but apparently, the Greeks have gone Goth. Or their house has anyway. I don't know. Too many 90s horror flicks at film night, I think. Who knows what danger lurks in the sorority house, you know?"

I frowned. A mundane sisterhood might draw followers of the Goddess. Why hadn't I thought of it before? I came back to warn undercover witches about the energy we'd released and the hunters who might follow. Maybe finding them would be easier than I thought. If the sorority sisters were true practitioners of the Craft, they might have already felt a shift in the energy. Or maybe they really were just a bunch of mundanes playing pretend. How could I know for sure? "So, what, they watched The Craft and decided to call the quarters? That didn't work out so well in the movie."

Nyla swallowed the last of her vodka juice. "For real. They're psycho. Whatever. So, Morgan suddenly got all ambitious, and I don't know if she wants to be a witch or act in witch movies, but everything is crystals and chakras over there."

"And she put a curse on Madi?" I could barely get a spell to stick, and I'd lived with witchcraft my whole life. Maybe, if one of her *sisters* had a Gift...

"Madi says she did." Nyla shook her head, the gold beads

at the ends of her braids jangling. "I missed how it started, but the other night, I was working on the show drop, and I heard screaming coming from the girls' dressing room. Something about a hex bag, and 'You're trying to kill me!' and 'Why can't you just let me have this?' And the tears, girl. These actresses are so emotional."

"Wow."

"Yeah, wow."

I didn't know what to say, so I finished my drink. Nyla upended the vodka into my cup. "Whoa, whoa. What are you trying to do?"

"You got to catch up. I'm over here hiding from my feelings, and you barely look buzzed."

"So sorry. I'm a quiet drunk. Gonna probably pass out after this one." I yawned. I wasn't lying. It was already hitting me.

"Nope. Unacceptable. Your turn. Tell me about your trip. Share your trauma. I'm here for you." She adopted a straight-backed pose, psychiatrist mode activated. From anyone else, her playful tone might have hurt, but Nyla and I spoke fluent sarcasm and knew it hid real concern.

Still, I didn't have to let her off easily. I smirked. "You want me to bare my soul so you don't have to think about that text message?"

She examined her nails. "I don't know what you mean, but if I did, I would probably be hurt that you would bring up my recent heartbreak when I am clearly here to support you in yours."

I rolled my eyes, "You didn't even know—"

Nyla held up a hand and dropped her head. "Please, this is not about me. You're suffering. Let it out."

I sighed. "I went home. I hadn't been back in a while. My dad's gone. The whole place is different. Things, people, changed while I was away."

"It sucks to go home sometimes," Nyla agreed, dropping

the act.

"Yeah."

"Yeah."

"A text message, huh?" I said.

She shook her head. "Nah. Don't change the subject. Still not talking about it. You go. People change? That doesn't sound like it's about the grieving fam. Did you leave a boy back home, Cate Corey?"

My face warmed, and I doubt either of us thought it was the alcohol.

Nyla hooted. "Yes, girl! It's about time! Spill."

"I don't know what you mean," I said, mimicking her earlier escape.

"I will throw this mug at you." Nyla held it up.

I narrowed my eyes, contemplating the safety of my mug. "You wouldn't."

"I would. And it would be a shame." She turned the mug to get a closer look at it. "Such a fine example of what I can only assume was a good ten minutes of ceramics class."

"Hey, I made that when I was fourteen."

"Really?" She tilted her head, examining my work with new appreciation.

"Yes." I had actually been kind of proud of that one. It was the first one that had come out watertight. And it was prettier than Thomas's. In retrospect, I may have been influenced by my twin brother's muse-like magical Gift. Another thing I owed him, then. Maybe I should let her smash it. If nothing else, it might divert her from this line of questioning.

Nyla raised a perfectly shaped eyebrow. "They didn't have stores where you grew up?"

I started to defend my traditional upbringing, but she held up a hand, flashing her new manicure. "No, I'm genuinely curious. I'm imagining a picturesque small town with one stoplight. The kind of place jaded New York lawyers go to find true love in Hallmark holiday movies."

"There's no stoplight," I mumbled.

She held my mug out over the floor. "Tell me about the handsome woodcutter you left behind, or the childhood crockery gets it."

"He's not a woodcutter." *He's the Guardian of the Gate. But there is no Gate anymore.* "He's kind of…a security guard."

Her arm lowered. "Y'all don't have stoplights, but you have security guards? You get lots of burglaries in a place where everybody knows your name?"

"Adam keeps people safe," I said.

"I'll bet he does." She grinned, spinning the empty mug on her finger.

I rolled my eyes. "Please put that down."

"Well?" She set my mug back on its shelf. "Were you?"

"Was I what?" I stalled, pretending to straighten the mug. It was hard to think about Adam.

"Safe?" Nyla waggled her eyebrows.

I chewed my lip. I knew what she meant, and I could almost feel Adam's arms around me. But so much of what happened between us had been wrapped up in magic, in the literal source of magic for our community and the curse that bound me to it.

"We were…careful," I admitted.

Nyla swooned. "Be still my heart."

"I knew I couldn't stay." Going home had never been part of my plans. Maybe that would change now that the trip didn't have to be permanent.

"Sounds like a perfect spring fling," she said, lying flat on the floor and staring at the ceiling.

"It wasn't really the time. My father…"

Nyla sat up. "Shit. I'm sorry."

"It's fine." I wasn't sure where that sentence was going to end, anyway. We had lost him. There'd been a funeral. But he wasn't dead, and I still hoped I'd find a way to bring him back.

"No, for real. Are you okay?" She wasn't sober enough to understand the truth, but she wasn't drunk enough for me to explain it.

"I will be," I said, opting for truth-adjacent. "Right now, I'm just tired. It was a long flight."

Nyla smiled, glancing at her bag on my bunk. "I can take a hint."

The polite thing would have been to argue, "*No, wait. I didn't mean it like that…*" But I did mean it like that, and I was glad she understood. "Thanks," I said instead.

Nyla stood and tossed her bag on her dresser. Unzipping it, she dumped her clothes in the drawers and dug out her phone, scrolling through messages. "No problem. Your imaginary love life was a good distraction."

"Happy to help. Are you going to be okay?"

She tossed her hair and waved me off. "I'm fine. Her loss. Other fish. Whatever. Hey, there's a party off-campus. Sure you don't want to go make some bad decisions?"

I shook my head. The vodka was already making me drowsy. "Think I'm in for the night. You go."

I probably should have gone with her. There was nothing stopping me from making bad decisions all on my own.

3

When I had the room to myself again, I unpacked my backpack. I slumped back on my bed and stared at the tarot card my academic advisor had given me when I went on my unexpected leave of absence. *Strength.* I hadn't known the head of the Theater Department was a witch until I'd gone to tell her I was leaving. *Did she know what our lead actresses were up to?* She'd talked me out of dropping out and given me the card *for guidance.* Later, I discovered it was no ordinary divination tool. It was a charmed object.

It hadn't changed since I read it in the Gatehouse, but I knew if I asked a new question, it would shift again, showing me any card from her deck. There'd been no time to question it before. But even after studying the source of magic back home, I couldn't understand how this card reformed with each reading and seemed to give my nearly nonexistent skills a power boost. It was just one of many unanswered questions I still faced.

The answers I wanted right now had nothing to do with my advisor's secrets.

Why hasn't he called? I was being stupid. How was Adam

going to call me when he had my phone? Besides, I saw him a few hours ago. He didn't owe me anything. I was the one who left right as we were starting over. It was practically my fault he had to stay behind anyway. Not that he'd put up much of a fight. *That kiss good-bye, though.*

Draining the last of Nyla's vodka from my mug, I filled it halfway with water. I should have drunk it and gone to bed. Taken two aspirin.

The mint case that held my altar supplies was in my desk drawer, under a stack of post-its. I grabbed a tiny bell and a tea candle from the tin. The bell slipped from my fingers and rolled across the desk. It hit the ground before I could catch it. *I should put it away.*

Gathering it back up, I narrowly avoided bumping my head on the edge of the desk. It took two tries to light the match. *Probably a sign. I should go to bed.*

But I didn't.

What if he's in trouble?

He's probably fine.

Does he miss me?

This is a mistake.

Too late now.

The flame cast a faint glow in the darkened room, just enough to chase shadows across the water in the mug. My bare feet pressed into the floor, grounding me, even in the third-floor dorm. I propped the tarot card between the keys of my laptop behind the mug. The bell rang out three times as I held it over the water, cleansing my tools with the sound. I set it aside. Placing my hands flat on the desk on either side, I stared at my reflection in the dark computer screen.

The edges of my face wavered in the shadows as my eyes began to unfocus. My breath slowed. I swayed a little, my eyelids fluttering as I let my mind drift into a relaxed trance. *Thank you, alcohol.*

My head dipped over the mug. Shadows floated on the water, morphing with the flickering light. Shapes formed, dissolved, and mutated. I blew across the surface, sending ripples with my intention. *Show me Adam.*

The scrying I had done in the past had been fairly interpretive. Like reading the cards, most of what I saw was as much a reflection of my own thoughts and feelings as any kind of message from the Powers That Be. When you don't have a Gift for divination, you make do with peeking through shadows and making your best guess.

Whether it was the vodka or the charge I pulled from the charmed tarot card, this time was different. The shadows shifted, taking on more distinct shapes. They started to pull color, refracting the light from the candle as it bent through the water. I saw Adam as if I were looking through a window.

I watched the image in the cup tighten. It was still dark. There wasn't that much of a time difference, but if it was night here, it was later there. Adam's face came into focus, flickering in the candlelight. He smiled. It set the butterflies in my stomach dancing. I smiled back, even though there was no way he could see me. *There. I've seen him. He's fine. I should go to bed now.* It was wrong to spy on him.

Then he laughed. My eyes narrowed. It wasn't that I begrudged him a moment of levity after all we'd been through. I didn't. He deserved to be happy. But who was making him laugh in the dark of the night? *It's none of my business.*

I breathed across the water, the ripples adjusting the angle of my vision. Adam stood outside the ruined Gatehouse on the mundane side of the Creek. That was almost a shock in itself. It shouldn't have been. Nothing was stopping him from crossing the Creek and leaving the community. But he'd stayed behind when I left. He was a Guardian and always would be. Even without the Gate. *Especially without the Gate.* They needed him.

So what was he doing on the outside?

He held a star torch out in front of him, a glass jar with a heatless flame that probably shouldn't have worked on that side of the Creek. It wasn't bright enough to show much beyond the length of his arm, but I could make out the edges of the rough path that led through the woods. The shadows of the overhanging branches made patterns move across the dirt in a soft breeze.

Another breath and the ripples pulled back further, revealing the space unlit by Adam's light. Someone stood in front of him, just out of the trees. She wasn't cloaked like he was. His deep hood draped across his shoulders, looking no more out of place on him than the mundane hoodie she wore. I remembered how he'd wrapped that cloak around me once, using it to pull me closer. I'd finally felt safe.

But he'd never smiled at me like that. This was softer, sadder somehow. *Who was she? And why was he meeting her outside the community in the middle of the night?*

I tried to get a better look at her, but I'd asked to see Adam, and no matter how I shifted, that smile was the center of my vision. I needed to see from his perspective to get a look at her face.

My hands pressed into the desk. Visions are delicate things. The harder I tried to concentrate, the more I focused my eyes, the further away I seemed to get. Too much thought, too much effort between my intuition and me. *Too much alcohol.* The vision blurred.

"No!"

I hadn't meant to say it out loud. It shouldn't have mattered, anyway. Scrying mirrors only work one way. But before the water cleared, Adam looked up.

I panicked. Jumping back, I reflexively threw my hands

over the mug to block the connection. The mug tilted off balance, rolling into my lap, splashing water over the candle, my desk, and the keyboard.

"Shit!"

4

The morning sun streamed through the window with a violence worthy of the elder gods. In the light of day, I couldn't be sure of what I'd seen. I was drunk. For all I knew, I'd fallen asleep at the scrying mirror, and it was all a bad dream born of insecurity and alcohol.

It hadn't felt like a dream.

This is why we don't drink and do magic, Cate.

This, and the potentially relationship-ending consequences of spying. *Goddess, what a mistake that was.*

Had Adam seen me? How could I find out without asking him directly and revealing myself if he hadn't? Who was that girl? Was I overreacting?

Almost definitely. Too bad knowing that didn't make it stop.

Quit looking for problems when you have enough of them in front of you. Just buy a new phone and call him like the normal, unmagical girl you so desperately want to be.

But first, caffeine.

No one could've expected me to face the aggressive sunlight without caffeine. The problem was how to get it. My mother could have waved her hand and floated a can of Dr.

Pepper through the air, but I didn't have that power. I should have gotten out of bed. It would have taken two steps to reach the fridge. Maybe the headache was clouding my judgment, but I really thought I could reach it if I just stretched a little farther.

I was wrong.

I hit the floor hands first and rolled onto my back, knocking against the stack of boxes I'd unpacked before my roommate came home and got me wasted. Call it karma for ill-advised midnight magic or the unfortunate side effects of unexpected vodka. Maybe I deserved it.

Nyla made a snuffling sound from the top bunk and rolled over. That girl could sleep through the apocalypse.

I rolled my wrists and checked for breaks or sprains. I was definitely going to have a bruise on my shoulder. It didn't feel like I would need to visit to the university health center, where they mostly only tested you for pregnancy and lectured you about drinking too much anyway.

Back home, I would have hobbled over to the Healer's cottage and let Mom or her new apprentice apply a poultice. As it was, I was stuck with some half-dead herbs growing on my windowsill and whatever I had in the fridge.

The fridge. Right. The whole reason I was on the floor in the first place. Pushing myself up to my knees, I swung it open. Empty. Well, almost empty. We had two bottles of water, Nyla's leftover OJ, and a shriveled lemon. No caffeine.

Standing, I almost slipped on a piece of loose paper. Brian's note. *Come by the café.*

The promise of potentially free chai overpowered my desire to curl back up in a ball and wait for the pain to ease. But when I caught my reflection in the dark screen of my computer, I knew I had to work up to it.

The mug and candle from last night's misguided spell work taunted me from my desk. At least I'd shoved Nora's card in a drawer last night. After what Nyla told me about Madi and Morgan, I needed to be more careful about my craft.

I slipped out of the room to wash the sticky mugs in the hall bathroom, and when I snuck back in, Nyla snored softly from the top bunk. Even that gentle sound grated on my frayed nerves. I couldn't face the weekend crowd at the café like this. Between the hunters and the hangover, last night's mistake was going to haunt me.

Setting the mugs back on my desk, I shoved the candle aside to make room for my kettle. *No more magic.* But I was the daughter of a healer, so why shouldn't I make use of some very practical medical knowledge?

I snipped a sprig off the mostly dried rosemary plant and dropped it into my electric kettle with some bottled water. The tea would take the edge off this headache until I could get something stronger. While it steeped, I rubbed peppermint oil into my shoulder. The smell was vaguely medicinal, but it would fade. I hoped my fears would do the same.

5

Parking my bike outside the café, I ran through a few possible approaches in my head. This was going to be a great conversation: "Yes, I'd like one chai latte and my job back, please."

A little over a week ago, I quit my job without notice and essentially disappeared. I claimed a family emergency, but it probably looked like I just wanted to extend my Spring Break, especially now that I was back in time for classes.

It hadn't been a lie.

My return to campus was a near-miracle, but I wouldn't be able to stay if I didn't get my job back. I'd been using my savings for room and board, and the unplanned flight home had almost wiped me out. My advisor had protected my need-based scholarship by clearing my leave with the university, but the scholarship only covered tuition.

I should probably go see her tomorrow and thank her for that. Maybe we could also have a long overdue conversation about her secret identity, and she could tell me how to find any other witches still hiding in the broom closet.

The wind picked up as I snapped the lock on my bike, whipping my hair across my face. I shoved it behind my ears and headed inside. The weekend rush wouldn't start for a couple of hours, but a few study groups were already using the bigger tables and a couple of moms in athletic gear sat by the backdoor with packed strollers. A barista I didn't recognize wiped down the coffee server, her back to me. *Great, I've already been replaced.*

This complicated things a little. I had banked on a familiar face at the register to bolster my confidence or at least give me a reading on how my desertion had been received. I turned to the community board to buy myself some time.

A shadow of a girl blocked my way. Taller than me but more slender, she wore a faded black tank under a long-sleeved black fishnet shirt. Her tight jeans were also black, as were the chunky platform boots and the spiked belt low on her hips. Her long dark hair hung straight down her back, barely moving when she reached forward to post a flyer on the board. She was like a sketch come to life, all black and white lines.

I stepped aside as she backed up from the board, but her huge shoe caught my ankle anyway. I winced.

"Omigosh. Oh, I'm so sorry. I didn't mean to. Are you okay?" The words tumbled out in a high breathy whisper. She seemed to shrink into herself, although she would still have towered over me barefoot. Her eyes shone, and I worried tears would smudge the thick eyeliner.

I leaned on the rail under the board and rubbed my ankle. "No permanent damage."

She nodded solemnly. "Sorry."

The girl practically bolted for the door. Freshmen. She put all that energy into her look, and had none left over for human interaction. Maybe that was why she chose a style with so many spikes.

Satisfied that I hadn't lied about the state of my injury, I dropped the ragged hem of my jeans around my paint-splattered chucks and eyed the flyer she'd posted. A blurry gray-scale photocopy announced a coven meeting. A sketched pentacle and triple moons featured prominently. There was no date or address, but a QR code over a cauldron in the bottom corner promised more information. If I wanted to know what she was up to, I'd have to come back after I picked up a new phone.

I looked after the girl, who had left the door swinging and was already clomping across the street. She ducked her head against the wind and clutched the remaining flyers that threatened to rip from her fingers. On the other side, she put the pile down and stepped on it, carefully pulling out one page and attaching it to the streetlight with strips of duct tape from a roll she wore around her wrist and ripped off with her teeth. A strand of dark hair caught between black lips, and she shook her head to free it. When it didn't come loose, she took a visible breath. A pendant hanging low around her neck glowed despite the shadow of an overhanging tree. The next gust ruffled her hair like a shampoo commercial, leaving it smooth and shiny.

Before the Gate came down, I would have sworn I was seeing things, justified it as a trick of the light or a really good shampoo. But rationalizing evidence of magic was a mundane quality, and I knew better. Magic had been rare a few days ago, but it was no longer contained in my formerly enchanted hometown. What would happen if it found the witches who'd left before I did? Most of the people who'd left Queen's Creek had done so because their Gifts were weak enough to make an unmagical life preferable to one stained by jealousy. An influx of magical energy might change things for all of us—even if I hadn't felt anything yet. *Did that girl even realize what she was doing?*

Separating the secret witches from the social pagans might be harder than I'd thought. I added Goth Girl to my list of potential magic users, right under the Greeks Nyla mentioned.

"Good morning and welcome to—oh, hey, Cate. You're back," the barista called, her bored tone shifting mid-sentence. She pushed away from the counter she'd been leaning against when she recognized me. It took me a second to return the favor.

"Morgan?" I looked around for a sorority sister with a phone pointed at her. She had to be making some kind of video. None appeared. *Weird.* I never would have imagined her on that side of the bar. Of course, if I hadn't talked to Nyla last night, I'd never have imagined her trying to work a curse, either. With her honey ponytail and strawberry lipstick, she didn't exactly look like the kind of girl who'd respond to the newest flyer on the community board.

"We heard about your dad," she said, lowering her curled lashes. "I am so sorry for your loss."

I was so sick of that phrase. "You work here now?"

She pulled a large plastic cup from behind the espresso machine and sucked a vibrant green drink from the straw.

I raised an eyebrow. We definitely weren't allowed to keep drinks on the line. *Unless the manager has gotten a lot cooler over Spring Break.*

She saw me watching and tucked the cup into a low shelf. Glancing up at the security camera in the ceiling, she gave it the finger before turning back to me. "Yeah, you know. It's temporary. I'm saving up for a car. Mom and Dad bought one for Madi, but I guess they don't think I'm responsible enough or whatever. Anyway, my Uncle Dan said he'd match me if I could raise half. At least somebody cares about my safety."

I wanted to ask about how things were going with her sister (*Hex anybody lately?*), but before I had a chance, the door to the back room swung open.

"I knew they were watching," Morgan grumbled. She

glared at the camera even as a booming voice sounded from behind her.

"The prodigal barista returns!" The store manager laughed at his own joke. *So, not cooler.*

"You know that's actually kind of offensive, right? The prodigal son was an asshole," I said.

"I said what I said." Mark shifted his stance and crossed his arms.

And I've already messed this up.

"I'm sorry," I said. "It was a family emergency, and I didn't think…"

"No, you didn't think at all. Did you? One of the reasons I hired you in the first place was that you were available over breaks. What am I supposed to do when my whole staff takes off the same week to go party at the beach?" Mark did his best to look imposing, with some success. But I'd worked with him before he got the promotion. Somewhere under the overbearing attitude lay an overly ambitious teddy bear.

"It was a family emergency," I repeated.

"That's what Brian said. But you're back now, so I'm assuming whatever it was got resolved?" He wasn't really asking.

I nodded.

"Convenient."

I bit my tongue so hard I tasted copper.

"Her dad died. Lay off." Morgan glared at him like he'd done her personal injury.

My chest tightened. I wanted to scream that it wasn't true, but I couldn't explain what really happened. Morgan's unexpected support brought back complicated feelings I wanted to ignore. *It was my fault.*

She waited for the manager's response, apparently battle-ready despite our tenuous friendship. *Goddess, save me from a sorority girl with a savior complex.*

Mark looked from her to me, his full face softening. *Here it comes.*

"I'm sorry for your loss," he said, and he probably meant it. Just like everyone else who'd said it this week. I'd come halfway across the country but couldn't escape the pity or the guilt.

"Do you still need help?" I narrowly avoided side-eyeing the new barista, who'd stood down once she'd engaged Mark's sympathy.

The manager didn't even try to hide his disapproval of the new hire. He frowned as Morgan leaned back on the counter, picking at her nails. "If you've got time to lean, you got time to clean."

She rolled her eyes and picked up a rag, rubbing the same small circle on the counter. She kept watching him, even after he turned away.

The manager mumbled something about the unavailability of good help these days and crossed his arms. "Same schedule. Start tomorrow. Maybe you can show this one how it's done. Brian's been too easy on her."

"Thanks, Mark." I grinned. "Is he here?"

"He's on a ten." The manager tilted his head back toward the back room. "Go ahead back."

He tied his apron and stepped behind the counter, grabbing a fresh towel and instructing the unimpressed new barista on proper cleaning techniques. She crossed her arms, frowning.

Brian sat against the back wall with one foot propped against a pallet of coffee beans, scrolling his phone with one hand and drumming on his leg with the Sharpie in his other. He'd had a haircut since I last saw him. The line-up and low fade made him look older, and I hoped his Spring Break hadn't changed him as much as mine had. When he saw me, he looked up and pulled his earbuds out. The same old Bruno Mars song.

"Hey, you're back," he said, smiling.

"Just flew in yesterday," I said, stifling the dad joke.

Brian's wide lips twitched. "Say it."

I stared at the ceiling. Shaking my head, I met my friend's warm eyes. "And boy, are my arms tired."

"There she is!" He gave me a quick hug and then dropped back into his seat, pulling out Mark's desk chair for me as he went. The upholstered rolling chair was out of place in the narrow back room, but the store manager claimed he needed the support when making the week's order.

"Thanks." I sat in the chair and immediately lost my balance as the back dropped away, smacking the desk behind me. My cheeks burned, and I fumbled to find the lever that would lock it out of the recline position.

"You okay?" Brian asked.

Another question I was tired of hearing.

"Yeah, yeah. I'm good. Should have known he's taking naps back here," I said when I was finally settled.

Brian leaned forward, resting his elbows on his knees. His earbuds dangled around his neck. "No. I mean, are you okay?"

Our last conversation played out in my head. He didn't know anything about magic, but he'd been here when I found out my father was missing. I'd told Brian there was a family emergency, and I didn't know when (or if) I'd be able to come back. I couldn't tell him about what was really going on back home without breaking the covenant of secrecy. And I couldn't discuss my concerns about the hunters without explaining how magic came into our world. So, I lied.

"I will be," I said. "When I get some caffeine."

6

Something crashed in the front of the store. Brian bolted out of the back room, and I followed. Another crash sounded at the end of the bar as a plastic pitcher full of ice and smoothie mix hit the floor.

Every customer in the café stared at the bar, mixed expressions of fear and concern on most of their faces. Mark's broad back blocked my view of the new barista, but they weren't looking at him. A teenage boy pulled out his phone and nudged his friend, who did the same. "Coffee girl's lost her mind, man."

Morgan leaned over the counter and shrieked at the kid, then backed up, covering her face with her hands as she collapsed back against the ice machine.

Mark held up his hands. "Hey, hey, let's just calm down a little."

"Don't tell me to calm down!" Morgan screamed. She waved the ice scoop at him, and he stepped back.

What in Gaia's name had he done? I'd never liked Mark, but he'd never done anything to make me want to murder him with a tiny aluminum shovel.

"You're making a scene. Let's just take this down a notch,

okay?" His voice dropped, softer than I'd ever heard it, like he was soothing a wild animal.

"No! Leave me alone. I know what you're telling them. In your reports. You're working with them. Get away from me!" She backed into the counter, knocking a drawer of grinds on the floor. I wasn't sure how much farther away she expected Mark to get. He already stood at the opposite end of the counter from her.

Mark looked down and took a deep breath, his hands on his hips. When he looked up, his voice had lost its sympathetic tone. "I need you to get control of yourself, now. You're scaring the customers."

The customers had recovered from their initial shock, actually. Several of them held up their phones or had whispered conversations, pointing to whatever Morgan was doing at the end of the bar. Dismantling the espresso machine by the sound of it.

Brian tapped Mark on the shoulder. The store manager turned and gratefully stepped back to let him by.

"She's lost it. I'm calling the police." Mark patted his pockets and came up empty, a victim of his own rules. No phones behind the counter.

"Wait. Just gimme a minute," Brian said, squeezing past him in the narrow space at the end of the counter.

Mark shook his head. His breathing was heavy, but he looked more angry than afraid now that Brian's athletic frame stood between him and the rampaging girl. "That's a new machine."

"I know," Brian said calmly. "Just a minute."

Mark grumbled something about taking it out of her paycheck and pushed past me to the backroom. Morgan shrieked and slammed the drawer of coffee grinds back into the machine.

"What are you going to do?" I asked, grabbing Brian's arm.

He shrugged. "I don't know what's wrong with her, but getting her arrested will not make it better."

I looked back at the door Mark had gone through. I didn't think I could convince him not to make that call.

"They're watching us! Always watching. They'll see. You'll see. They know." The barista had given up on the espresso machine and was dumping ice out of the bin. She slammed the scoop into the ice, left it there, and raked her fingers through the bin, searching for something.

"Can you clear the room?" Brian nodded to the customers who were still watching. The ones closest to the back door had already grabbed their stuff. An older man shook his head and mouthed something that looked like "drugs" to the couple sitting near him as he stood to leave.

Grabbing a few free drink coupons from a drawer by the register, I shoved them in my back pocket. I pushed my hair out of my face and stepped out from behind the counter, summoning the voice I used to address the stage crew when managing a show. I tried not to think about the potentially viral videos already being made. "Okay, thank you all for coming in. As you can see, we have a situation…uhm…that requires our attention. So, if you'll all see your way out that door…"

Most didn't need to be told twice, but a few students lingered, laughing as they filmed whatever breakdown was happening behind the bar.

"You too, guys. Thanks for coming in. Have a nice day." I stepped between them and the counter, hopefully ruining their shot.

"Aww, come on," one of the guys whined, trying to hold his phone above my shoulder.

"No, really. Thank you so, so much for coming in today. Next one's on us." I pulled out a coupon and held it in front of the phone.

"Can I get one of those?" his friend asked.

"Absolutely. You know, these are also good at the one on Devon." I pointed down the street as I ushered them out the back door.

They took the hint and headed down the sidewalk. I locked the door behind them. Turning, I was just in time to catch a couple coming in the front door. Their eyes widened at the commotion from the bar, where Morgan was trying to make Brian understand something about illegal surveillance and secret shoppers who actually wanted to steal our identities.

"Sorry, we're closed. Try the one on Devon. Just at the end of the block. Thank you," I said, locking the front door, too.

The barista's hands shook. "No. No. They're watching us."

"Who's watching us?" Brian kept his distance.

"Them!" She pointed to the camera in the ceiling.

"You want to come over here? The couch is free." I gestured to the empty café.

"Hey, Morgan? Let's go sit down, okay? There's nobody here any more."

The barista's head popped up over the espresso machine like she was seeing the rest of the store for the first time. "They're gone?"

"Yep. All gone. See? The doors are locked and everything," I said.

She licked her lips and sniffed.

Brian started to put an arm around her to lead her out but thought better of it when she flinched. Instead, he came out and stood beside me, giving her space to get to the couch on her own.

Morgan followed him out, her eyes shifting rapidly as if she expected someone to jump out from the brightest corners of the room. She sank into the couch and hugged herself.

I went back behind the bar and got her a cup of water.

She squinted up at me when I held it out to her. "Who's she?"

"It's Cate," Brian said, confused. "From school? We all had Stagecraft together? She works here."

"No, she doesn't." Morgan rocked on the couch, her eyes darting just over my head.

Brian sat on the low coffee table in front of her. "She's been away for a while."

"She's one of them." Her eyes darted from me to him.

"One of who?"

"A witch," she whispered.

I bit my lip to hold in the panic. The way her eyes flicked around the room, never landing, reminded me of one of the crones back home. She saw things others couldn't. *Is she having a vision? What does she know?*

Brian only raised an eyebrow. "Morgan..."

I held out the cup. *New subject.* "Sure, you don't want some water?"

"That's not mine." She leaned back, pressing into the cushions to get farther away from me.

I stepped back.

"No, it's a fresh one," I said. "Do you want me to pour it in the one you were using? Where is it?"

Behind the bar, I stepped over a pile of cups and tried to avoid the grounds she'd dumped on the mats. I found her cup shoved back on a low shelf near the ice machine. When I reached for it, I knocked over a glass bottle sitting behind it. It was one of those little craft bottles you can get at the dollar store with a cork in it. There had been a wax seal on top, but it was broken. I held it up to the light. A few drops of liquid sparkled inside. It had an herbal smell, like lavender, but more earthy.

Brian was talking to Morgan in a low tone, and she seemed calmer. He caught my eye. I nodded at my hand, holding the bottle out of Morgan's sightline, and he came to the counter.

"What is that?" He glanced over his shoulder to make sure she wasn't listening. Her eyes drooped.

"I'm not sure. Is she taking anything?" Most herbs wouldn't cause a response like this on their own. *Where would she get hallucinogens? And why would she take them at work?*

It didn't make any sense.

"I don't know. She's only been working here a few days, and we haven't had a class together since freshman year. Where did you find that?"

"It was by her cup. I think she dosed her tea." I rattled the ice in the cup, looking for sediment that wasn't the green tea powder the café used.

"Why would she do that?"

Such a straight edge.

"I don't think this is the effect she thought it would have. It smells like St. John's wort. Some people use it for depression or anxiety, but I've never heard of a reaction like this." *Unless she mixed it with something?*

Brian looked at me with suspicion. *Was he reconsidering Morgan's witch accusation?* It was just a flash, but I felt compelled to explain myself.

"My mom has some in her herb garden." *Was that better?* "It's kind of a weed," I added.

He glanced back at Morgan. She'd tipped over sideways on the couch, her head on the arm, her legs drawn up.

There was a knock at the front door. A couple of police officers stood on the other side of the glass. "Damn it, Mark," Brian grumbled.

I dropped the bottle in my jacket pocket as the manager came out from the back.

"Had to do it," Mark said, avoiding Brian's eyes. He went to the door and let the officers in.

After taking our statements and checking out the mess

Morgan had made, the officers asked Mark if he wanted to press charges.

"She didn't break anything," Brian said. "It's just a mess. We can clean it up."

Mark frowned.

"Sir?" the cop said.

"Come on, man. She had a bad day," Brian said.

"I'll cover the rest of her shift," I offered. *Please, let them take her home to sleep it off instead of dragging her into a police station to rave about witchcraft.* The cops might not believe her, but she and I agreed on one thing. Anyone could be listening.

"You'll cover her next two shifts," Mark said. "I don't want her back here until she's...recovered."

I nodded.

The manager shook his head and thanked the officers for responding.

"Come on, hun. Let's get you home so you can sleep this off." One of the officers guided Morgan to the door. Her formerly wild eyes drooped, and she yawned.

Mark disappeared into the backroom. Something about writing up the incident report.

I grabbed an extra apron and put my hair up in a ponytail. When I pulled up the mats to sweep up the mess, I found a stained and torn label with a symbol that looked like a cauldron. *Well, that's why she's got witches on her mind, but where did she get it?* I tucked it into my jacket pocket with Morgan's bottle while Brian reset the coffee and opened the doors. A breeze ruffled the flyers on the community board.

7

Sipping my free spicy chai after Morgan's shift, I mumbled a prayer, hoping the cinnamon sprinkled on top would bring me luck and healing like it did when my mom added it to her brew. There was too much at stake, and I didn't want to face any of it with a hangover. I still hadn't figured out what I was going to say to Adam. Choosing a new phone seemed like a good way to stall, even if I knew I was going to have to take the cheapest one they offered.

The wind caught the door of the phone shop when I went next door. I almost spilled my chai pulling it closed but rescued it by putting my lips over the hole in the lid. Going back to Brian for a refill would probably be pressing my luck. *Not enough cinnamon in the world.*

A calendar invite pinged my new phone almost as soon as I turned it on.

Notification: Advisory Meeting @ 2pm
Location: MUND 1213C
Organizer: Dr. Nora Jennings
Guests: Hecate Corey
Please arrive on time.

How does she even know I'm back? I'd planned to go over after class the next day, but this was better. She'd known more than she had any right to before I left, and it was time she explained herself. I made it with three minutes to spare, but the professor acted like I'd kept her waiting.

"Sit, sit, sit," Nora said, skipping the welcome back speech. For once, the chair in front of her desk wasn't buried beneath stacks of papers and fashion books. The professor twisted her curly hair into a messy knot on top of her head, securing it with a couple of pencils and a binder clip, and paced the only uncluttered path on the floor.

"What's going on?" *And how much of it is my fault?* I shifted in the chair and tucked my backpack underneath so she wouldn't trip over it.

After a couple of turns, she stopped in front of me and shook out her hands. She handed me a wrinkled sheet of paper, a flyer like the one I'd seen at the café. The one posted by the freshman Death of the Endless wannabe.

I chewed my lip. "Where'd you get this? I just saw this girl putting them up."

Nora waited in front of me when I looked up. She took a deep breath, closing her eyes. When she opened them, her expression was stern. "I know you think you did what was best. But you've put us all in grave danger."

If it had been anybody else, I might have laughed at her doom-filled eyes and horror-trailer tone. What did she know about danger? She'd been here, teaching at the university for years. There was no way she could understand what was going on back home. Unless I was too late.

Then logic and denial joined forces to protect me from dissolving into a puddle of panic. Despite Nyla's story about Madi and Morgan, despite Morgan's outburst at the café, none of it meant mundanes were really practicing magic. More likely YouTube-inspired pranks and ill-advised medical experimentation. Goth culture thrived on college campuses for decades before I was even born. Sorority girls never took anything seriously. Who cared about a bunch of girls getting together to watch *Practical Magic?*

There were real witches out there who needed to be warned—people whose Craft didn't come from a movie. They were the ones I'd come back to find.

I crumbled the flyer. "From this? They're going to dance around in a circle and drink midnight margaritas. Maybe try *Light as a Feather, Stiff as Board.* It's not real."

Mundane covens weren't exactly new. Most of these kids had never seen true magic, but that didn't stop them from retelling the old stories. Fairy tales and myths from before the Trials sent actual witches into hiding never went away. I'd checked out some clubs that claimed to practice witchcraft when I'd first started at school, but they turned out to be mostly pagan study groups and nature-based religions. I imagined a few of them must occasionally harness something, just from the strength of their intentions and the power of their combined energy, but they weren't really witches. The girl had managed something in the street, but a localized light breeze was hardly cause for panic.

"It wasn't real," Nora said. "But things are different now." She twisted the beaded chain from her glasses around a finger.

"What do you mean?"

"You let it out. The magical energy you released from Queen's Creek is spreading. And the others are watching."

My stomach clenched. *How fast did the energy flow? I thought I had more time. How many witches lived outside Queen's Creek anyway?* I hadn't even stopped to figure out how to find them. *Wait, maybe they already knew? Who did she think was watching?* "The others?"

"The other magical communities. You didn't think Queen's

Creek was the only one, did you? Others formed alongside the colonies, all up and down the East Coast and more in the West. And you've endangered them all."

My heart raced. *Other communities like ours?* There'd been rumors, but how could any of us have known for sure? The covenant of secrecy prevented anyone from talking about magic or Queen's Creek while we were out on our Wakenings, and communication from inside the boundary had been almost impossible.

Except for the letters. The partnerships the elders somehow managed to maintain with universities and guides for young witches on their Wakenings. They had to know.

More secrets.

I was so naive.

We'd been so caught up in stopping the magical apocalypse in Queen's Creek that we hadn't thought about how it would affect the rest of the world. The Gate had to come down. And not just because the energy built up inside would destroy it. No one should have to make the choice the elders required of us when we left for our Wakenings—exile or prison. How could they expect us to decide, at twenty-one, where we would spend the rest of our lives? Abandon your family forever, or stay behind the Gate and pretend there wasn't a wide world to explore outside. I didn't regret what I'd done.

But our freedom had a cost.

It couldn't be as bad as she thought. The magic would dissipate, wouldn't it? Spread out and fade as the energy was used up. The wisps carried it with them, and it strengthened them, but it wouldn't last. We just needed to be cautious for a little while. Avoid drawing attention. "Aren't you being a little dramatic? Magic is drawn to witches, and most of our witches stayed behind."

"The energy is drawn to power. And even the weakest

witches have enough to call it to them. You've given everyone a boost." She stopped for a moment and smiled. "Thanks for that, by the way."

She snapped her fingers and three big pillar candles on top of her bookshelves lit up. I gripped the arms of the chair, thinking about all the paper piled around the room. The flames turned blue, then green. They went out with three quick pops. Trails of smoke twisted above them to form a pentacle. It sparked once, lighting up the dim room, and faded away.

Any doubt I might have had that my advisor was a powerful witch vanished with the pentacle. But it didn't explain how she knew so much about witches she'd never met. How could she possibly know what was happening in those other places? At our last meeting, she'd said something about her contacts in Queen's Creek, but the phone I'd left with Adam was probably the only one in town. And it wasn't like the elders were using the internet in a community that had been off the grid for centuries.

"So, everybody out here got a power-up like that? That's amazing. What's the danger?" I asked, defiantly ignoring the obvious, horrible answer as if that could make it less true. *No such luck.*

"The witches aren't the only ones who've noticed."

My skin went cold. "You mean the hunters."

She nodded. "All these sudden bursts of energy will not go unnoticed. Especially when some of our younger sisters and brothers lack the foresight to practice restraint."

I imagined the excitement of young witches, out on their Wakenings, unaware of what had happened, suddenly experiencing an unexplained power-up. Maybe they noticed an increase in wild fireflies or glimpsed a shadow where there should be none. Coincidences came more frequently, or their intuition was on point. If their scrying bowls gave back crystal clear images and their pendulums swung with unusual accuracy, it might tempt them to push things further, performing more complex spells, taking risks they knew they shouldn't.

Risks like opening a channel across the country to spy on people who've proven trustworthy every time their loyalty was tested.

I'm sure he had a reason…

Shit. What have I done?

"But it's only been a few days. Have there been signs?" *As if I haven't seen a few for myself. Denial is powerful magic.*

Nora frowned. "I don't need signs to spot a hunter. They're mundane, and their movements are not subtle. They are coming."

"How soon?" *Did it matter? What would I do differently in a few weeks?*

"That, I can't be sure of. There is a pair nearby who could arrive by the end of the week. Everything depends on what we do now. We may still change their course." She tapped her lips thoughtfully.

"What can we do? A spell for misdirection? A glamour to hide us?"

She shook her head. "It's too late for that. These hunters are not like the ones who drove our ancestors to ground on the basis of wild accusations and questionable evidence. They've had years to develop their skills, improve their tools. Energy monitors and electromagnetic field detectors come with apps for phones now. They will recognize the change in the flow of energy. Any magic we do now will only bring them faster."

"So, what? We just let them come?" I rubbed my aching head. The hunters followed the energy, and it would lead them right to us. Well, right to anyone practicing magic. If we stopped now, the trail would disappear. "You want to go dark. Hide in plain sight."

"No magic," she said. Her intense gaze made me wonder if she somehow sensed what I'd done last night.

What if it's already too late?

I crossed my arms, refusing to take the blame for another apocalypse. *She wants to stop now. I can stop now.* The flyer crinkled in my hand. *But I'm not the only student practicing magic on campus.*

"That's easy enough for me to promise, but what about the others? Are you meeting with all the witches on campus?" How many of them were there? For years, I'd thought I was the only one. Growing up in a secret community didn't exactly encourage new friendships and midnight confessions. But Nora had revealed herself before I went home. Now, I realized how ridiculous I had been to imagine that I was unique among her mentees.

"There are only a few who would draw enough energy to be of concern, even with the recent boost." She leaned back against her desk.

I relaxed a little. Maybe she had been overreacting after all.

"I need you to talk to Tori Walsh."

I blinked. "Who?"

She gestured to the flyer.

So, Nora thinks she's for real. The breeze wasn't just a breeze. Still. I tried to imagine showing up at a coven meeting and telling the giant spiky freshman to lay off the spells. "You don't think…Wouldn't it be better coming from you?"

"She has…difficulty with authority. I haven't been able to get through to her," she said.

"She doesn't know you're a witch." *Goddess-blessed code of secrecy.*

"When, how, and if I share personal information with my advisee will be between my student and me. Just as our conversations have always been privileged," Nora said, standing and straightening her skirt.

What was I supposed to say to this girl? "But you want me to—"

"She might be more open to a peer."

"Nora—"

She squeezed her eyes shut and pinched the bridge of her nose. Her glasses skewed sideways. "Don't you think you bear some responsibility for this?"

"Me? But I've never even talked to her."

My advisor held up a hand. "Before you left, she was confining her craft to occasional tarot readings. Now she's started a coven."

She plucked the flyer from my hand and held it up with a flourish.

"You're saying that's real?" How many Gifted students had outed themselves in the last few days? How many meetings had they had?

"I don't think any of the other members have the Gift, but hers has grown strong enough to support their Craft. They believe in her, and they believe in what they can do."

Magic is energy plus intention. Was it possible? Could enough energy make a witch out of a mundane? What about the children of witches who'd chosen exile? They might not even know they had the potential. What would it take for them to raise magical energy? They might attract the hunters without even knowing what they were doing.

Breathe.

Nora wanted me to talk to Tori. I could do that. How dangerous could she be? She was still putting up flyers, so she hadn't finished gathering coven members. She'd need at least thirteen. A quorum of thirteen could master the elements and perform powerful magic.

"How many members does she have?"

"Twelve."

8

With Tori's flyer in my back pocket and my new quest pushed temporarily to the back of my mind, I spent most of the bike ride back to the dorm planning out a conversation with Adam. He couldn't have seen me. Scrying wasn't a window. It wasn't like my big stupid head had appeared in the clouds. He looked up after I made a noise. Not because of it. It was a coincidence. Which was definitely something I believed in. Unlike curses.

Because if I believed in curses I would have to start considering the possibility that all of my bad luck was happening for a reason.

He answered on the first ring. "I was hoping you'd call."

"You were?" *Butterflies.*

"I was worried about you."

Like, in general, because I'd moved so far away, or specifically because he'd sensed my stupid, anxious presence last night? "You don't need to be."

"Tell me you're safe." His tone took on more of the Guardian than my absent boyfriend.

"Is everything alright?" What if last night's spell had

45

drawn attention to more than my magic? Had I put a target on Queen's Creek?

"I think we made a mistake." His words gripped my heart. *We* made a mistake? Was this about the girl he'd met last night?

"What are you talking about?" *What mistake?* I didn't have a lot of experience, but that kiss felt pretty right to me.

He paused, and it almost killed me.

Then he said, "Letting the magic out. We didn't think of the consequences."

Exhale. Here I'd been thinking about our feelings, and he was second-guessing our hero moment. The one decision I'd ever made that didn't haunt me. Hadn't anyway, until Nora laid on the guilt trip about attracting danger. I pulled out the flyer and flattened it on my desk. It looked so…mundane, streaked with printer ink, torn at the top where somebody had ripped it off a bulletin board. Nora had to be overreacting.

But twelve.

I pushed it away. We'd done what we had to do. We could face whatever was coming.

"What consequences? You mean, like, not destroying our community? Not letting an out-of-date protection spell put some kind of hole in time? The Gate was going to come down anyway. What were we supposed to do?"

"We saved Queen's Creek, but for what? For how long?" It was like he couldn't even hear me.

"I don't know. You're the Guardian. What's out there that you can't handle?"

"You haven't seen anything strange?"

A Goth girl posting public messages about coven meetings. A crazed barista under the influence of some kind of potion. The Guardian meeting someone outside the Gate. "You're going to have to be more specific."

"Have you met with your advisor yet? What did she say?" he asked.

I hesitated. *It's bad, but I can handle it. Don't worry.* "She thinks the magic is drawing too much attention. She's paranoid about baby witches getting some kind of power boost and blowing stuff up."

"What makes you think it's just paranoia?" His voice had an edge as if I'd accused him of unwarranted suspicions instead of Nora.

How to explain Tori's breathy apology and the way she'd shrunk into herself after she tripped? "I saw the girl she's worried about. She's Gifted, but she's not dangerous. She's trying to start a witch club."

"You can't let her do that," he said with the voice of the Guardian.

I didn't intend to, but his urgency felt extreme. Mundanes playing with magic was never a good idea, and the looming threat of witch hunters made their activities risky. But I couldn't imagine them raising enough energy to draw attention, even with twelve. Why would hunters care about a little college magic?

When I didn't respond, Adam let out a long breath. "We never got a chance to talk about my Wakening. There's something you should know."

Did I want to know? There had to be a reason he didn't come back with Caleb. He'd never have abandoned my brother and Duncan. I'd let the rumors get to me back then, accepting the influence of Thomas's Gift when he told me to forget him. I should have waited. I should have listened. "Tell me."

"When I left, I wanted to find a safe place for us to live. You were never going to be safe in Queen's Creek. But we'd heard all those stories about the hunters."

"They were just stories." Things our elders told us to keep

us from doing something stupid on our Wakenings. Imagine what would happen if a few teenage witches turned up in some mundane town every year and started using magic in the open. The mundanes would panic and then burn them at the stake like their ancestors did. Or make them kings and queens. Gods. Who knew? Why risk it?

"They're not just stories," Adam said. "Listen. I thought if we lived as mundanes, among mundanes, we'd never draw their attention. Williamsburg was too close. If we got caught, they'd find Queen's Creek. Besides, how many witches had already gone through that town? So, I kept going. I hitchhiked a little, did odd jobs, slept in a tent."

"Now who's living dangerously? How can you tell me to be careful when you were getting into cars with potential psychopaths?" I said.

"I knew who to trust." He said it simply with no trace of defensiveness or arrogance.

Of course. Adam's Gift. He'd always seen the truth of things, known what was buried underneath. "Go on."

"I went into the city. I figured there were so many people no one would ever notice us. But that was stupid. It's not like I was the first witch to have that idea. And the energy drew us together. The magic seeks out its match." He waited for me to process what he'd said.

My stupid, jealous brain pictured the girl in my vision last night. "What do you mean?"

"I didn't notice at first. It just seemed like a bunch of tiny coincidences. I thought I was lucky. Things started to work out. I found a job. I was able to rent a small place by the park. You would have loved it there. It was perfect for painting."

I smiled, but my stomach tightened, waiting for the bad news. "What happened?"

"My neighbor was a witch. And the neighbor on the other side of her had been raised in a community like ours.

Somehow, without trying, I moved into a building full of magic users."

I wanted to jump ahead to where that was a bad thing. What wasn't he telling me?

As if sensing my anxiety, Adam interrupted my thoughts. "Wait. Just. I want you to understand."

"I'm here." *I wish I was there.*

"Everything was great. You remember Shelley? She was a year ahead of Caleb."

Queen's Creek was small, but I didn't know everybody there. I closed my eyes and could almost picture a lanky girl with big teeth. She didn't match the girl from last night's vision.

"No," I said. "But she was in Richmond? She didn't come back when she turned twenty-one?"

The boundary spell had made a decision like that permanent. Anyone who left for their Wakening had to be back inside the Gate before their twenty-first birthday if they intended to come back at all. I'd always been told it wasn't safe to stay outside, that most people returned. But I was starting to question a lot of the things I'd been told about the world outside Queen's Creek.

"Shelley's Gift was prophecy, but it wasn't strong. It was mostly intuition," he said. "She was using it to do tarot readings. It helped cover her bills. She didn't even need the magic most of the time. People just want to hear that their dreams are going to come true."

"Sounds like a solid business plan." *Sounds like fraud.* How was he okay with that? So, the anti-Adam.

"It would have been, except that one of her clients didn't like the reading."

"I'm sure that happens…" *When you lie to people.*

"No, she really didn't like it. Shelley said she didn't know why she did it, but for some reason, she told the woman the truth. Warned her about her husband. She saw darkness in him. Violence."

The jealous part of my brain pulled back. "He was abusive?"

"Must have been going on for a while. Shelley told her to leave him, but the woman was afraid. And then the husband found out."

"Oh, no." My stomach soured.

"Yeah. But it gets worse. He wasn't just some mundane. He was a believer, a scion."

"Shit." According to our elders, not many mundanes believed in witchcraft. Few recognized any kind of magic that didn't come down the chimney in December. But we'd always been told that the scions, the descendants of the accusers in Salem, believed. They believed, and they feared, and they hated. Most of all, they trained. They organized against us, ensuring that witches outside of Queen's Creek had shorter lifespans. They sent the hunters.

Adam sounded so far away. "We set wards around her apartment, but it wasn't enough. None of us had the right Gifts, and there wasn't enough ambient magic to pull from. Most of the energy was still locked away behind Gates. You're not supposed to need magic in the mundane world."

"What happened?" I pulled my knees up, bracing them between the desk and my chest.

"He killed them. Shelley and her neighbor, too. He came in broad daylight while I was at work and set the whole building on fire. They blamed it on faulty wiring, but it was him." Adam's voice shook.

"How can you be sure? You said you weren't there." It wasn't that I didn't believe him this time, so much as I didn't want to. An electrical fire wouldn't hunt down your friends and family after it destroyed your home.

"He left a sign. A warning. There were sigils drawn in the

grime on the windows. The mundanes didn't notice, but it was there," he said. His next words came so softly I almost couldn't hear them. "I should have seen it sooner. I could have saved them."

I am an asshole. I am an idiot, and I am unworthy of someone so good. "What could you have done?"

"I could have done something. I should have gone after him. Kept him from ever hurting anyone again."

"Adam, it wasn't your fault."

"But I just left. I came home. I was going to tell you not to leave. But you were already gone."

My parents hadn't thought it was too dangerous for me to leave. The Gatekeeper had encouraged me to take my Wakening and explore the world outside Queen's Creek. "And I was fine. I came home from my Wakening because Queen's Creek needed me, not because it was too dangerous to live outside."

"I thought releasing the magic would protect us, but it's just put a target on our backs. The energy will find you, and the hunters will follow."

"That was three years ago." *If Shelley was dead, who was he talking to last night?*

"I need you to hear me because you're in danger," Adam said.

Always trying to save someone. "How exactly?"

"The hunters are real. They're dangerous. And they're coming for all of us."

9

After sleepwalking through my classes the next day with a near-permanent knot in my neck from looking over my shoulder, I couldn't take it anymore. Back at the dorm, I tossed my backpack on my bed, checked that all the low-energy wards I'd installed that morning were still in place, and sealed the door behind me.

Breathe. The hunters are coming. They're not here now.

Nora said they could track magical energy, but how much did they know? So much of the Craft revolved around mixing herbs, applying natural remedies, and completing simple daily rituals. It had more in common with science than the magic Gifted witches performed. How would the hunters ever notice that?

For all my panic and the near flooding of my laptop two nights ago, Adam hadn't even noticed I'd been scrying on him. And he usually caught any signs of deception.

Was that unexpected luck on my part or dangerous levels of distraction on Adam's? Probably the luck thing. I didn't want him to worry, no matter what came of the private meeting I'd witnessed. And there might not be anything for him to worry about here anyway. No way were the hunters more observant than the Guardian.

His story about what happened to Shelley horrified me, but it was three years ago.

Maybe they're overreacting. I crossed my fingers and hoped not to die.

Nora wants to hide. Let's hide. Grabbing a piece of chalk from the pocket altar in my desk drawer, I scribbled two protection sigils into the edge of the doorframe, low enough that my roommate would probably never notice them. Nyla should be able to cross the ward with her key. But anyone else would start to feel more uncomfortable the longer they stayed. It was barely magic. More like a booby trap. A necessary risk. It wasn't like I could put mundane bolts on the door to keep hunters out. The college would never approve of that kind of *improvement* to campus housing. *You asked for an unmagical life. Go get it.*

First, I needed to put in some time in the scene shop since the Theater department required service hours for my major. *Hunters or no hunters, the show must go on.*

I rode my bike across campus and locked it near the theater building's back door so I could cut through the stage instead of walking the labyrinthian hallways from the front entrance. Soon, I found myself backstage, in the dark. *It's the perfect place for a witch, really.* A space entirely defined by its potential power. Even without the audience, I felt the energy of dreams manifested. A Gifted witch could make much of it. Hundreds of years of theatrical superstitions had to come from somewhere. *Shakespeare. They mostly came from Shakespeare.*

The blackness folded around me the farther I stepped from the door. The crew had forgotten to leave on the ghost light. While the possibility that superstitions might be based in fact had crossed my mind, I was more concerned about what I might trip over than any spiritual visitations that could occur as I crossed from the backstage entrance to the scene shop.

I reached for my back pocket, but my phone was on a charger in the dorm. My brand-new phone's battery hadn't had enough time to charge this morning, and I'd already worn it out. I needed a flashlight or something. My mother knew so many ways to call in the light.

You're not a Gifted witch. Anymore. Again. Probably. Besides, you promised Nora. No magic. We're laying low.

Didn't I owe it to myself to try though? How could I know if the magical energy had risen as much as Nora thought if I didn't try it for myself? A little experiment that should completely fail, and then I could know for certain that Nora and Adam's fears were misplaced.

What would it feel like to have magic come when I called? Even in the Gatehouse, when I'd been linked to the ancestors, I hadn't owned it. I'd been more of a conduit for the Gifts of those who came before. If the magic was that strong…if it attracted mundane hunters…what could I do with it?

The darkness was a serious safety concern.

Just something small. A test. If the magic came to me, I'd stop immediately. It probably wouldn't work anyway, but I had to know if that energy boost I'd given everybody else could help me. I wouldn't be pricking my thumbs or calling upon anything wicked. All I wanted was slightly better eyesight. *I'm not asking for 20/20 vision. I'm happy with my glasses.* For now, it would be enough for me to see a bit more clearly. *So, I'll work a tiny, insignificant little test of a spell.* Nothing that would attract any attention. Wouldn't even draw a wisp if there were any in the city.

I stopped in the middle of the stage right wing and closed my eyes against the dark. Counting to twenty, I repeated the chant three times. "In darkest night, I shine a light, grant me now the gift of sight."

When I opened my eyes, the black velvet curtains had

more dimension. A faint glow from the shop spread across the stage, although several curtains still masked the entrance. I smiled. It might have been next to nothing, but it felt huge. I affected my environment. *Maybe.* I affected my own experience of my environment anyway. A tiny vibration tickled the back of my neck, energy dissipating. *Interesting.*

Maybe my Gift wasn't gone after all. My fingers twitched. If that worked…what else could I do? I shivered. The potential energy of the space called to me, reminding me of my own long-delayed potential.

I wanted to do more.

A dull ache replaced the tickle at the base of my skull. Using my Gift had never been free, even back home.

Back home, where people were depending on me to protect them from hunters, not to attract our enemies chasing magical highs.

I balled my fists against the temptation to call back the energy. *The test is complete. Be satisfied before you go too far.*

My shoulders tightened, the tension from my headache invading the rest of my body. If even I could access magic, Nora and Adam were right. What kind of spells were other witches doing right now? The ones who weren't expecting extra energy to respond to their castings? Even without the threat of the hunters, they might be in danger from overpowering their spells.

The hunters. Shit. What if?

I shook out my hands. *No. It was a tiny little test. That spell mostly gave my pupils time to open up. Definitely, not enough energy to bring anyone after me. Breathe.*

The air expanded my lungs, loosening my muscles. I rolled my head, releasing my neck. The headache retreated.

Eyes and attitude adjusted, I headed for the shop. I made it three steps before slamming into something I didn't see.

"Ouch!" Make that *someone* I didn't see.

"Sorry!" I said, fumbling to find my balance.

The other person scuffled likewise. "Sorry, ow, oops. Hey, are you okay?"

I recognized the voice before the shape resolved into anything familiar.

"Brian?" I shouldn't have been surprised to find another theater student backstage. *Still, why is he lurking in the shadows?*

"Cate? Sorry, you're just...standing on my..." he grabbed my arms and physically moved me one step to the side. Something pulled out from under my feet, and fabric flew past my face. "Cape," Brian finished, pinning it back around his neck.

"Why do you have a cape?" I asked, trying not to laugh. Tech crew didn't usually need costumes.

"Because I'm a deeply mysterious figure of Gothic romance?" He bowed with a flourish that I could just make out in the dim light.

"I didn't know we had a Phantom at this university."

"Oh, Cate, there are mysteries in this world that you will never know!" Brian said, using his radio voice.

I smirked. If he'd come through a few seconds earlier, he'd be quoting *Macbeth* instead of paraphrasing *Hamlet*. But I'd keep my mysteries.

"Also, I forgot my blacks, and the director wants 'a real dress rehearsal,' so...this was faster than going back to change," he said.

"He knows we won't be ready to hang the show drop until tomorrow, right?" The student director didn't come to the shop often, but according to Nyla, we were on schedule for show night, and I didn't love the idea of explaining to a grad student why he literally had to wait for paint to dry.

Brian shrugged, realized the futility of the gesture, turned on his flashlight, and pointed it at himself, lighting up his deep brown complexion. Then he shrugged again.

"Did you have that the whole time?" I asked, more amused than frustrated.

He pointed it at his face, closed his eyes, and nodded. Smiled. "I'm checking for light bleeds in the masking. Can't see them when the flashlight's on. The real question is, where's yours? I don't think I've ever seen you without your phone."

"Dead," I said, shaking my head. "Too many progress pics for my *Theatrical Makeup* practicum this morning. Point it that way for a minute, would you? Just so I can avoid stepping on any other mysterious haunts?" I pointed toward the hidden far wall, where there was a large open garage door between the stage and the scene shop.

He swung the light, and I headed through the maze of masking curtains. "Thanks!"

"See you at work later," he called after me.

I waved. After spending hours at the theater getting ready for the show, the closing shift at the café would be rough.

When I rounded the corner into the open shop, Nyla and Angel were already there. We'd gotten into a pretty good rhythm over the past few semesters. Between the three of us, we did most of the finishing work on the sets for the school's plays. Students from the current stagecraft class came in during the day to do the grunt work. Then we came in for night shifts after we got home from our classes, volunteer work, and paying jobs. It was a pretty good arrangement because it meant most of the stuff that needed power tools got done before I came in. My *Intro to Stagecraft* grade hadn't been pretty, but there were no serious injuries, and that was where I met Brian, Nyla, and Angel, so it wasn't a total loss.

As a more experienced member of the department, I concentrated on faux finishes, appliqués, and setting things up. Before we came in, the workshop was full of blank canvases, wooden boxes, and scratched-up wagons. By the time we were done, the pieces were in full color, ready for the stage. The audience would believe this flat canvas drop was a wall paneled with elaborate molding. It took a lot longer to use mundane methods than it would for almost anyone back home to create the same effect, but if I had a Gift like that, I wouldn't have enrolled here.

Besides, art was a kind of magic.

10

Hey, Cate," called Nyla. She sat about fourteen feet above me on a tower ladder, one long leg hooked through the rungs for balance. A couple of thin red box braids came loose from her bandana, and she absently pushed them out of her face with the back of her wrist. *How does she do that with a paintbrush in her hand? I'd have streaks across my forehead for sure. Must be her dance training.*

Nyla leaned out over the title drop for *Taming of the Shrew*. The massive canvas was mounted on a pulley system that allowed it to be lowered through the floor, but we were on a deadline (tighter because of my absence), so Angel had been working on the lower parts while she climbed up the ladder. Another brush and an open can of black paint lay abandoned at the other end of the frame, but I didn't see Angel.

"Hey," I said. "Where are we?"

"Angel's on high. This is almost done, but the wagon needs some attention."

I glanced up at our crow's nest and caught a glimpse of the bottoms of Angel's sneakers. Electronics obscured the rest of him. Years ago, someone built a high platform into one corner of the shop, out of the way. It held an ancient stereo routed through the sound system that was supposed to be used to communicate between backstage and the tech control booth during shows. I had no idea who made the original patch, but they would always be a hero to the construction and paint crews, even though it was a pain to get up there. The nest was just big enough for one person to climb up and change the music, but the CD changer could hold six discs, so we usually only had to do it once.

Last year, someone had taken a laptop up there in an attempt to stream an infinite playlist, but when it refused to connect to the network, the theater kids created a vast mythology of ghostly conspiracy and decided it was better to stick to the original set-up. I was pretty sure the kid who built it was now living his best life as a mid-level executive somewhere, not haunting his college scene shop in an attempt to bring back New Wave, but try telling them that.

I was in no rush to climb up there myself. My luck, I'd knock the whole thing off balance and crash down in a broken pile of vintage electronics. Our Angel of Music had seniority and the strongest opinions, so he usually got up there first. *Pretty sure he can't function in silence.* I shook my head as a familiar Police album started to play. There weren't a lot of options among the donated discs up there, but he might have genuinely liked that one. He played it enough. *He has such weird taste.*

"What happened?" I asked Nyla. The wagon looked fine from here. We didn't have a lot of time left to finish the set pieces, and I'd considered that one done when I left.

"Guess," Nyla said, tracing the lines of the title on the show drop with metallic gold paint.

I walked over to a large, low platform on wheels, set for an interior scene. It had a rug, a few chairs, and a back wall with two doors. It took me most of a week to finish painting the wallpaper design and add in the finishings, like the sconces and the *antique* door knob. Which was now on the floor.

"Did Madi pull the doorknob off again?" That girl. She was lucky our friendship predated her breakout into acting. She'd been enjoying playing lead roles now that she was a senior, but the diva didn't seem to know her own strength, and it'd been a while since she last stepped foot in the shop. The show was set to open this weekend, so they would have been rehearsing with the set changes any chance they could get, even if the pieces weren't completely ready.

"Got it in one." Nyla tapped her brush on the metal tube of the ladder, making it ring like a gong.

I knelt at the door and inspected the damage. It wasn't too bad, no broken pieces, and I found a few loose screws behind the chair. "Maybe I should glue it in there this time," I said, pulling a screwdriver from the toolbar.

"It's your baby," Nyla said.

"Who's having a baby?" Angel's muffled accent floated down from his perch by the ceiling.

"Your mother," Nyla deadpanned.

I chuckled and rolled my eyes.

While I poured wood glue from a gallon jug into a styrofoam cup, Angel descended, kicked off his sneakers, and walked across the second drop spread out on the shop floor. He grabbed the black paint, affixed his brush to a long stick of bamboo, and free-handed some outlines on the backdrop. It was pretty impressive. When he reached the edge of the drop, he lifted the brush off the line. Twirling the bamboo like a baton, he dropped one end to the floor, singing into the paintbrush like a mic on a stand. He ran a hand through his short, dark hair and swung his hips in a move that owed more to Enrique Iglesias than Sting.

I laughed.

Nyla smirked.

Angel sang louder.

"This song is so creepy," complained Nyla. "Are you listening to what you're saying?"

"Every breath you taaaaaaaake...." crooned Angel, waggling his thick eyebrows at her.

"They're all creepy," I said, pressing the doorknob base into the glue and tightening the screws. "Don't Stand So Close to Me? Wrapped Around Your Finger? This guy has serious issues with boundaries." The more I thought about the words to the songs, the more they reminded me of the hunters. How did they keep finding witches? Were they watching right now? Morgan's panic about the security cameras in the café felt less and less paranoid, even though I still wasn't sure who *she* thought was coming for her.

And what about Queen's Creek? Was the Guardian at the Gate enough of a deterrent now that *our* boundary was down? *I should call Adam.*

I tested the doorknob from both sides, wiped the excess glue on my work jeans, and hopped off the platform. *That doorknob couldn't be more secure if it had a binding spell cast on it by the High Priestess herself. Such is the power of wood glue.*

"Done?" asked Nyla.

"Done," I said.

"Nice!" said Nyla. "I dare Madi to wreck that door now."

Angel dropped his mic. The bamboo clattered on the floor.

"You knock on wood!" he shouted at her. "What are you trying to do? Curse the whole show? Que mala suerte... You knock on wood right now!"

For a minute, I considered a snarky defense of her compliment, but when I raised an eyebrow at Nyla, she pursed her lips and shook her head.

"Ummm, wow. Okay, okay, here, happy?" I backed up and knocked on the wagon I'd been fixing. "Angel? Okay?"

I know he's superstitious, but I've never seen him this upset.

"Aye, Cate. She has to do it. She's the one who said it." His hands were shaking. "You both should know better."

He spun on his heel and stalked out of the shop, pulling a mangled pack of cigarettes out of his back pocket as he went.

I looked at Nyla. She came down from her ladder to push it a few feet farther along the drop. The counterweights on the bottom made it hard to get started. I tried to help, but Nyla waved me off.

"He's right," she said. "I should know better. I might as well have named the Scottish play while standing on that stage."

"It is not the same," I said. "You barely—"

"A curse is a curse," said Nyla. She shrugged and spun in a circle, landing with a stomp and snapping her fingers. Then she tilted her head back and yelled to the rafters, "Forgive me, Thespis!"

The playful god of Theater gave no response.

It seemed like overkill. Especially since curses only worked if you believed in them, and I didn't think she did. She did it for Angel, and he hadn't even seen it.

"Come on," I said. "It's not really…"

Nyla climbed back up the ladder and gestured for the paint pan she'd been using. "We don't need to be taking chances with centuries of theatrical tradition. And anyway, he believes it," she said. "Doesn't matter if it's real to anybody else. It's real to him, and we look out for family in this theater."

I raised an eyebrow and adjusted my glasses.

She shrugged and looked down the empty hallway. "He's maybe like a second cousin, thrice removed…on my father's side…by marriage, but, you know, still family. Now, hand me my paint, cuz."

I lifted the pan up to her. As she reached down for it, she overbalanced. She hadn't hooked her ankle through the rungs yet, and she completely inverted by the time she caught herself. I dropped the pan, splattering paint across us and splashing the drop she'd been working on. I caught her shoulders before her head could swing into the ladder. Her braids tick-tocked against my arms.

She laughed. "Shit! Girl, don't take this the wrong way, but I think I'm falling for you."

I blushed, even though I knew I wasn't her type. Nyla had a thing for waify blondes. I gave her a push, and she righted herself, locking her legs and surveying the damage from a more stable position. She straightened her bandana back over her hair, then shook her fist mockingly to the ceiling, cursing the god she'd just begged for forgiveness.

This time, he answered. The heavy tower ladder rolled forward, one wheel dropping over the edge of the floor where it was cut away to allow the drop to be lowered on its frame. Nyla screamed, and I grabbed the back of the ladder as it tilted into the canvas.

"Lean back!" I yelled. There was no chance of her falling through the narrow hole in the floor, but the ladder would almost certainly rip the painted fabric if it crashed through the frame.

She threw herself backward. The ladder hovered a few inches from where the drop hung. I pulled as hard as I could, the skin of my palms pinching against the metal. Nyla untangled her legs, working against the out-of-balance tower. I couldn't hold it much longer.

"Can you get down?" I asked, straining.

In answer, Nyla jumped to the floor, turned on a toe, and grabbed a bar on the other side. Grunting, we pushed and pulled the weighted tower ladder until it rolled back over the lip and onto the shop floor. As soon as it was free, I bent at my waist to catch my breath. Nyla paced, one hand rubbing her collarbone. Neither of us said anything for a few minutes.

When I caught my breath, I started to clean up the paint, but she gently took the work rag from my hand, shaking her head.

"Oh, honey, I think we better find Angel first," she said when I protested. "Don't you?"

Outside, Angel stubbed out his cigarette, visibly calmer, until I told him what happened. He rubbed his face. When he was ready to look at us again, he calmly prescribed three turns, a lap around the building, and three knocks on a wooden door. We didn't argue, even though finding a wooden door in a building from the 1970s proved difficult. Most of the functional doors were made of aluminum. We ended up back in the shop, walking on tiptoes and loudly thanking Thespis for his contributions to the arts as we approached the door I'd just repaired.

Three knocks for each of us, and we breathed a little easier, but my hands still shook as we cleaned up the mess.

Nyla didn't believe in magic. She laughed about the curse Morgan put on her sister. Curses weren't supposed to work if you didn't believe in them.

But I'd never seen Nyla so much as trip on a sidewalk, much less fall off a ladder and send it into the show drop. The stage weights stacked at the bottom of that ladder should have kept it from moving. And I would have sworn the gap in the floor was too narrow for the wheel.

Maybe my tiny spell had been too small a test. I'd still been close to the door, and I hadn't really expected anything to happen. If there was enough magic in the theater to bring Angel's superstitions to life, what could Tori's coven do?

11

T he QR code on the flyer Nora gave me brought up a map of the campus with a pentacle marking a spot near the lake. A series of numbers and symbols gave the time and date. Some kind of code to weed out the tourists. A black half-circle with five rays sticking out of it punctuated the digits of the year, month, and day, written in reverse order. *Stealthy*.

Tonight. Sunset. *Of course*.

Later, I felt a little like a cat burglar zipping my black hoodie over a black cami and dark jeans, but my show blacks were the closest I had to something that vaguely matched Tori's goth aesthetic. Docs are not ideal for biking, but I laced up my boots anyway.

The quad was empty. Despite the implications of returning from Spring Break, the weather in Chicago was solidly adhering to the groundhog's forecast this year. Soggy and cold. Freezing rain that would have been snow if it had been a few degrees colder bounced off my helmet. I bypassed the bike rack out front, noting the emergency blue light just in case.

By the time I got to the breezeway between the church and

the commons, I could hear voices from the beach. I propped my bike against one of the arches and shoved my numb fingers into my pockets, weighing the relative security of locking the bike up against the potential need for a quick exit. I shivered. *Should have worn a coat.*

I peered into the darkness. From where I stood, the sidewalk ended a few feet in front of me, where a cement breaker blocked my view of the beach. The voices were coming from somewhere to my right, below street level. I stepped out from the cover of the breezeway until I could see where the sidewalk turned sharply to follow the lake in either direction. The breaker bordered the path along the lake until it turned in again on the other side of the building.

Some of the voices were not as far away as I thought. Three girls walked a little ahead of me, trying to catch up with a fourth, who'd already scrambled over the breaker and was making her way over the boulders that kept the beach from eroding. They'd worn dark colors for the occasion too, though their style was more fairycore than goth. Dark floral printed corsets and ruffled peasant skirts clung to their legs in the rain. One girl was barefoot, dangling her sandals by two fingers. She kicked the water from a puddle at one of her friends, who squealed.

The church bells chimed the quarter.

The girls whooped and picked up their skirts, climbing over the breaker after their friend, who'd already disappeared from view.

Someone screamed.

I ran to the edge of the cement barrier and looked over, half-expecting to see a body tangled in the rocks. My eyes squeezed shut against the sharp rain blowing off the lake. Maybe it was my mind protecting me from the gory scene that already filled my imagination. Silence. I counted to five. The wind drove the waves ashore, and the splash exploded droplets of lake water.

The girls giggled.

I pulled my hand across my face, wiping away the water and probably smearing the black wings I'd drawn so carefully at the corners of my eyes. Twelve girls stood in a loose circle on a narrow stretch of sand. Only Tori stood with her back to the water. She smiled at me, and I heard her soft voice in my head. *I'm glad you could make it. You're just in time. Join us.*

My expression must have shown the shock I felt at her silent projection. Although my brother, Caleb, often used his Gift to initiate silent conversations, telepathy wasn't exactly common practice, even back home. It felt wholly unnatural coming from a girl I'd only met once. Goosebumps rose on my arms and a slick chill ran down my neck. *What else can she do? Could she hear my thoughts like Caleb?*

As a test, I tried to make eye contact, thinking calmly, *"Thanks for the invitation."* If she heard the thought, Tori ignored it. She was laughing, spinning in the sand, her arms outstretched.

"Join us!" she yelled out loud this time. She stepped up to a stack of scrap wood half sunken into a hole in the sand. Glancing up at me one more time, she snapped her fingers. Flames leapt to the sky, a bonfire rising much higher than the wood that fueled it. Tori disappeared for a minute, obscured by the blaze. Before I could react, she raised her arms, singing as she spun around the bonfire. Her words twisted in the wind, incomprehensible.

Nora was right. If this doesn't bring the hunters, it will draw campus security at the very least. I glanced back at my bike, glad I'd skipped the lock.

The girls started to dance, some swinging their skirts and swaying, others spinning like Tori. A girl with red-blonde curls cuffed her jeans and hopped in and out of the foamy surf at the waterline. Another girl bounced in place as she adjusted the scarf wound tightly around her hair. She grinned, giving it one last pat before linking arms with a young woman in cutoffs and swinging her around like a champion line dancer. The fairy princesses I'd seen clambering over the barrier linked hands with another girl and skipped in a circle. Their giggles and shrieks echoed down the beach.

Anyone walking by might have thought the secluded stretch of sand an odd choice of bonfire location, particularly on a rainy night. But otherwise, the scene looked like something out of the college recruitment bulletins. Twelve girls, diverse in style and skin tone, frolicking in the firelight. The kind of thing that made would-be freshmen doubt the school's reputation for being academically challenging and socially draining.

But I felt the energy of the ritual. My skin vibrated in response to the rising magic. I'd come to find out if Tori was the danger Nora thought she was.

She was worse.

This wasn't just selling herbal remedies and labeling them as magic potions. She'd called down the quarters, engaged the elements, and linked the life forces of these young women. The power thrilled through all of them, whether they recognized it or not. It felt like the spell that had linked me to the Gatekeepers, energizing and terrifying at once.

It called to me.

I should have resisted.

But magic and logic don't mix any better than magic and technology. Even though part of me knew I was making a much bigger mistake than drunk-scrying my boyfriend, I climbed over the barrier, finding divots in the stone on the other side. The closer I got, the warmer I felt, heated from the inside, better than Nyla's vodka. Half-sliding over the wet rocks, I scrambled down to the beach. The glow illuminating the girls didn't just come from the fire. Each reflected the light back, glistening in the misty rain that hovered around them instead of drenching their skin. A halo brightened the blonde hair of the girl closest to me. It was hard to make out her face, backlit by the bonfire. Another girl appeared beside her, slightly shorter, her dark gold waves ruffling in the breeze off the lake. A shadow twin.

They reached out to me, and I let them take my hands, pulling me into the circle. The rain stopped as if someone had turned off the faucet. *A circle of thirteen commands the elements.* But these girls weren't witches. At least eleven of them weren't. They bowed their heads.

Tori bent and traced a large sigil into the sand. She raised her arms to the sky. "I call to the Guardians of the Watchtowers of the East! Hear me! I call to the Guardians of the Watchtowers of the South! Hear me!" Her tiny voice cracked, and she chuckled softly. A few of the girls snickered, too. *Did they recognize the words from that 90s movie?* Clearing her voice, she continued, "I call to the Guardians of the Watchtowers of the West! Hear me! I call to the Guardians of the Watchtowers of the North! Hear me!"

Thunder rolled. The waves from the Lake grew louder, closer. *Great, we're going to get caught in an electrical storm because this girl's got a vintage movie obsession. Couldn't have had her coven meeting in one of the library study rooms with central heating and a roof over our heads.* A streak of green lightning lit the distant sky. Then another, just above our circle. Tori whooped, and the girls cheered. The hairs on my arms stood, prickling against the sleeves of my hoodie. I stripped it and let it fall to the sand. The sudden chill made me shiver, and I inhaled sharply.

The cold air snagged a hole in the effects of Tori's spell, and my mind cleared for a moment. *This is bad. This is very,*

very bad. It's too much energy. The hunters—

"Guardians, I feel your presence. Lend me your power. Give me your strength." Tori clasped hands with the girls on either side of her, starting a chain reaction around the circle. As each connection was made, I felt a sharp snap, like static. My head ached, and I couldn't hold on to a coherent thought.

"Guardians, we are one. Show us the power of our wills combined! Manifest it through me, and let them see!" She flung her head back and lifted her arms, still clasping the hands of the girls beside her. The rest of the coven did the same, raising their arms above their heads. A few of them gasped, and I couldn't blame them.

My heart raced, the headrush making my cheeks flush. I didn't remember stepping closer to the fire, but my skin warmed, radiating the heat of it. I exhaled slowly. My energy had never risen so suddenly. The girl on my right clutched my hand. I couldn't have dropped it if I'd wanted to. A light raced around the circle, sparking at each connection until it reached Tori. She glowed, absorbing the energy she pulled from the rest of us.

I couldn't catch my breath. My legs wobbled. It took everything I had to stay on my feet.

No. She's taking everything I have.

This can't be happening.

The blood pounded in my ears, and spots danced in front of my eyes like the errant wisps back home. My skin buzzed.

I sing the body electric.

It's too much.

I clawed my way out, pushing back against her spell, even as it tightened around me. Something gave, and I pressed harder.

Enough!

Time contracted around me, leaving me dizzy and nauseous. Everything froze.

12

I looked into the still faces of the girls who'd first pulled me into the circle, recognizing them for the first time. Madi and Morgan. Our diva of the broken doorknob and her sister, the deranged barista. Yesterday, Morgan casting a curse on her big sister had seemed unthinkable, but if she'd had access to energy like this… *Why was Tori powering up mundanes?*

The coven leader's energy surged, and I felt her eyes on me. *Release them.* Her girlish voice took on a deeper tone, thundering through my mind.

Release who? What? It wasn't possible, but I'd seen this before. Before the Gatehouse and the boundary spell, in the childhood memories that were still fuzzy after years of being bound. My mother's attempts to protect me from my fate as the Gatekeeper, from my own dangerous Gift.

The girls around me stood frozen, like a game of statues, but without the excited, heaving breaths to give them away. Utter silence, droplets of water clinging to the tips of their hair and sparks from the bonfire hovering in the air around them.

The scene was as different from Queen's Creek as possible,

but there was something about the silent stillness that reminded me of those long-ago woods, the darkness of a panicked witch-child who yelled, "Stop!" and commanded Time itself.

But that Gift was gone. *Wasn't it?*

The air around me pricked with the charge of magic, making the hairs on my arms stand. The energy in the air was the only thing that moved. It slid around me, tickling my skin. My heart raced, and my breath quickened. I felt strong.

Tori's eyes flashed, but her body remained as still as the others. *Release us.*

The vibration on my skin burned, although the bonfire was too far away for me to feel its heat. The strange flames paused like a photograph. I forced my hands into fists, pushing the energy back. Tightening all of my muscles, I gritted my teeth and squeezed my eyes shut. The energy lifted the hair on my scalp, electric waves pinging from end to end. Static zapped between my glasses and my skin, making my nose tingle. More energy than I'd ever felt outside of the Gatehouse. It was intoxicating.

But it wasn't mine.

Tori had raised the energy, but it wasn't hers either. It came from the elements, from the lives of the girls around us. *Nothing comes from nothing, and energy can neither be created nor destroyed.* It had to go somewhere, and I couldn't keep it. It was already too much. The pressure built under my skin until I thought it would tear away.

Sucking in a shaking breath through my nose, I almost sneezed from the charge in the air. I concentrated on gathering the energy close. I had to release it with intention, direct it away from the girls. I wasn't strong enough to give it back to them. This much energy at once. It was dangerous. Explosive, unpredictable, and violent. Scarier than the hunters, who were probably already on their way. *Chaos magic.*

Opening my eyes, I raised my hands in front of me, watching the energy arc from one to the other.

Tori's eyes widened on the other side of the bonfire.

On my next breath, I forced the energy from my body, letting go of the tension from the back of my neck, down my arms. Drawing it from my chest and my stomach. Pulling it free of my legs. My feet dug into the sand. *I release you.*

The magical energy exploded from my fingertips, a ball of power engulfing the bonfire's flames, making it shoot higher. All at once, movement and noise surrounded me. The girls shrieked again, freed from the time bubble and apparently unaware of the pause in their festivities or the source of the renewed fire.

I staggered, cold and unsteady. Madi and Morgan linked their arms through mine and pulled me into their dance. I lost sight of Tori as the world spun.

I raised my head to the sky. Something heavy lifted, and the sudden shift in gravity made me lightheaded. Madi and Morgan laughed. I took a breath and lost it again. My laughter came from someplace far away—fear, relief, and exhaustion competing for control of my consciousness.

And then lightning struck the bonfire. The flames flashed higher. I lost my balance, sitting down hard on the sand. Madi and Morgan fell on either side of me. When the light faded, I lay back on the beach. The stars winked through gauzy clouds that had already started to dissipate. The other girls quieted, their shrieks and giggles gone with the lightning. It was warm by the bonfire, but my skin still prickled when the air moved across the raindrops. My heavy limbs sank into the sand, and my eyelids drooped. The damp air cycled through me, drawn in through my nose, down into my lungs, and released in a little puff of vapor from my lips.

I am one with the elements. I am like the bonfire, giving heat to the air. I am like the sand, grounding the energy of the Storm. I am the rain soaking through my skin. I accept its energy. I give it mine.

Energy plus intention is magic.

What did I intend? The universe asked for direction.

Where should I direct my will?

A coven of thirteen.

I completed the quorum.

The buzz in the back of my mind had something to say about that, but I was all spirit, and the universe flooded my senses.

Madi coughed. The sound was too human. It dragged me from Divine contemplation. Shattered the connection between my spirit and the elements. The energy dissipated.

The edges came back. The lines that divided me from everything. The sand stuck to my arm as I pulled it from the beach. I sat up, wiping my face, clearing my eyes of the rain and the vision of a swirling universe of power. The buzz became insistent. *What about thirteen?*

Morgan blinked, rubbing her eyes beside me.

Madi was still coughing. She covered her mouth with her hands, her shoulders shaking with effort. I got to my knees and rubbed her back. Morgan stood, shakey on newborn fawn legs. Madi's eyes watered and the tears traced her fingers where they clasped over her nose and mouth. The drops that fell to the sand between her feet were red and sticky. As she drew her next breath, I pulled her hands away from her face. They were splattered with blood. Her lips shone, a thin trail of watery drool staining a pink line from the corner to her chin.

What have I done?

"You ruined it!" Tori stood over me, her little-girl voice shrieking. *What would she have done with that energy if I hadn't stopped her? Why didn't I stop her sooner?*

I shivered, my skin contracting with the loss of all that energy. I missed it already.

I shouldn't have come.

Panic gripped me, and I couldn't breathe. I should have found her before the meeting. I should have taken Nora's concerns more seriously. The bonfire raged behind Tori, a beacon of magic and flame.

We have to get out of here.

I looked into Madi's glazed eyes. "Are you okay?"

She didn't answer, just stared blankly at her blood-stained fingers.

Morgan leaned over my shoulder. "What? What's wrong with Madi?"

"You broke the circle!" Tori yelled. "Look what you've done! All of that energy wasted!"

The other girls drifted closer, lethargic and dazed.

"What I've done?" I said. "Look at them! Look at Madi!"

The coven leader's eyes flickered. "She'll be fine. She would have been fine if you hadn't interfered."

"Madi?" Morgan kneeled beside her sister, taking Madi's hands from mine. "I'm sorry, okay? I didn't mean for you to get hurt. Madi? Talk to me."

I stood, but Tori towered over me, still wearing those spiked platforms, though most of her followers were barefoot. "What exactly do you think is happening here?" I said.

"I was uniting the coven, joining us all so that our shared energy could strengthen all of us. We are more powerful together." She looked around at the girls, half of them collapsing on the beach. "But you took it from us. You broke the circle. Released the energy. We all felt it. This—" she pointed at Madi, "is on you."

Morgan draped an arm around her sister, rubbing her back. Madi had stopped coughing, but blood still dripped from her nose, spattering the sand.

"Does anybody have a tissue?" I called out to the other girls, but most just blinked back at me.

Tori glared.

We can't stay here. I don't understand what happened, but I've never felt so much magic at once. Who else will sense it if we stay?

So far, none of the girls seemed aware that they'd experienced much more than an illegal bonfire and some kind of vaguely pagan dance ritual. Was it too much to hope that we might get them out of here without dragging the real witches of the world out of hiding?

I mustered my best impression of my elder brother, Gabriel, the teacher. The one with the you-must-hold-yourself-accountable-or-I-will voice. "Look, you gathered these girls. You posted those flyers. If anything happens to any of them, what do you think they will tell the nurse at the health center? Who do you think campus security will want to talk to?"

She bit her lip, white teeth digging into the black lipstick. All the air seemed to go out of her.

Big raindrops fell from dark clouds overhead, splashing the upturned faces of her coven. The girls shook themselves, waking up. A few of them squealed as the rain came down harder. The bonfire sizzled. The girls gathered their shoes and scrambled back up over the rocks, running for the shelter of the church's breezeway. Two of them stopped to help Madi and Morgan, one girl miraculously pulling an umbrella out of her bag while the other dug some tissues out of a coat pocket.

Rain pounded my head, dripping down my neck and soaking me through. I shivered. The storm put the fire out, leaving faint wisps of smoke fighting for air. Tori's makeup ran down her face, black tears against her pale skin. Without the light from the bonfire, the color drained out of the beach.

We stood like shadows on the sand while the waves crashed behind the coven leader, closer every time.

"We should get out of here, too," I said.

"I thought you would understand." She tilted her head, squinting like she could almost see through me. Or maybe she just wanted to see me through the rain.

"Can we talk about it somewhere else? Maybe someplace with a roof? And coffee? You like coffee, right?" I gestured behind me and took a step back from the encroaching lake. The waves rolled up almost to the fire pit.

"You're not like them." Her feet sank into the sand as the next wave licked the chunky soles of her shoes. "You're like me."

13

Not like them, the mundane girls who came to dance around a bonfire in the dark. The ones who watched fantasy movies and wanted to wear the costumes of powerful characters.

Like her, a practitioner of the Craft, a magic user, a witch.

But I'd never used power like that. I'd never called the energy from human lives and felt it flow through my veins. *Except that one time, at the Gatehouse...* Even then. The energy came from other witches, freely given by my friends, family, and ancestors for the good of all.

And then we'd released magic into the world. I'd wanted to stop our elders from trapping young witches in Queen's Creek, and I had. But the magic followed us. And Tori found it. Tapped into it. *How powerful had she been before?*

I tugged at the dripping hem of my black hoodie. "Umm, yeah. You're right. I think we have a lot in common. Nora Jennings is your advisor, right? Are you a theater major?"

"Don't do that," she said, her little girl voice soft again.

"What?" I was never very good at playing dumb.

"Don't pretend this is some kind of project. We're more than that. Didn't you see what we did?" She raised her arms and tilted her head back, grinning into the rain.

"I saw what it was doing to those girls," I said.

She crossed her arms with a huff. "They would have been fine."

Madi's bloody nose was not fine. All of those girls stumbling over their own feet were not fine. I shook my head, pushing back the strands of purple hair caught in my mouth. *Real talk time.* "You're right. They're not like us. The energy was too much for them."

"The sigil should have worked. It should have been enough to guide her back to me," Tori mumbled. Looking up, she spoke more clearly. "They came because they wanted something. To feel powerful, to see something special, to be part of something. And they were. My coven. I gave them that."

"What about what they gave you? Did you have their consent? Did they know you were going to use their energy? Did you warn them about the danger? You saw what it did to Madi."

"She wanted to help. They all did. They wouldn't have come otherwise."

"Help with what? Your flyer didn't have a whole lot of information on it. What are you trying to do?"

"I just needed a little more energy. And then you came. My thirteenth witch. We could have done anything. We could still. Why won't you help me?" Her big eyes shone in the moonlight.

"I want to help you," I said, and it wasn't a lie. There was something really wrong with this girl, and if someone didn't get her the help she needed, bad things were going to happen. I didn't need a witch's intuition to see it coming. She practically had *Danger to Myself and Others* tattooed on her forehead. Maybe Nora could guide her. Maybe we should send her home, wherever that was.

As long as we got off this beach before she did something I couldn't undo. Like getting us arrested by mundane police or captured by hunters. Or completing the spell she'd come here to do. *Which was scarier?* "I just don't understand what you're trying to do. You can't go around burning through mundanes like batteries."

She laughed, and I swear, the whole beach lit up. The clouds parted, the rain stopped, all of it.

Cool. Cool, cool, cool. I took another step back.

"You're funny," she said. "Like batteries. But they are though. Such useful little energy packs."

"They're people," I said. "You can't—"

"Stop telling me what I can't do! Maybe I couldn't before, but things are different now. Haven't you noticed?" She snapped her fingers, and the bonfire ignited. The wet logs burned just as brightly as they had when I'd arrived. She looked at me expectantly.

I blinked in the unexpected light. "Wow. I mean it. I've never even lit a candle."

We stared into the flames. It was pretty amazing. For her to have all of that energy at her fingertips, to summon it and direct it so quickly, she wasn't new to the Craft. *Can a person be jealous and terrified at the same time?*

I held out my hands, taking a few steps closer to the flames. The air was still cold, and the rain had soaked through to my skin. My fingers tingled as the heat came back to them.

"But if you can do this... What do you need them for?"

"I needed all four elements. Some of them must have affinities."

"But they aren't like us. You said so yourself. They don't have the Gift." I couldn't say I had no Gift after what I'd just done. I hadn't left all of my magic at the Gate after all. *Could I do it again?*

"No, but they have energy and intention. Just because they can't direct it, doesn't mean they can't be useful."

A log cracked and rolled down into the fire pit, sending up sparks. They reminded me of the wisps back home. Crazy little things that thrived on magical energy. Bright lights in the dark woods leading travelers astray. They were dangerous, not to be trusted. But I'd needed their help to bring down the boundary around Queen's Creek and safely release the energy it had contained.

What Tori was doing was dangerous. But she was so strong. If the hunters were really coming, she could be a powerful ally. She had to understand the risks she was taking. The people she could hurt.

How do you say, "You're acting like a cartoon villain," without offending her? "Do they understand what you're doing? The way that you're using them?"

She scoffed. "They're mundanes. What else are they good for? Do you think for one second they wouldn't use us, or worse if they really understood?"

She spat the word *mundanes* like its flavor made her nauseous.

We really ought to come up with a better word for people outside magical communities. The word reinforced old stereotypes. Even Thomas said it with disdain. If he could feel that way about people who lived without magic after growing up with a twin sister who had no Gift, what hope did we have for stopping the hunters?

"Do you really believe that?" I said. "After the way those girls followed you out here? They stood in the dark and the rain because they saw something in you. They believed you when you told them they would share the magic."

She rolled her eyes, the whites flashing in the firelight. "They didn't believe in it. Maybe they wanted to. Most of them came out of curiosity. Out of boredom. But they'll believe in it now. And their intentions will be stronger next time."

She smiled.

"Next time?" There'd only been one date on the flyer. It wasn't like she'd offered a bunch of meeting options for newbies to try out her club. Was she expecting these same girls to find her again? *She can't think this went well.*

But she did. "Tomorrow night. They'll come back. We'll try again. With you here—"

"They won't come back. They were terrified. Madi was bleeding." But the other girls were laughing. The way they'd all woken up dazed when Tori was through with them, they might have already forgotten their fear. Or found a way to justify it. Mundanes were always doing that—finding excuses for miracles.

"They loved it. It was exciting. You'll see. They'll tell their friends. We'll be turning girls away." Maybe she was right. Even the ones who'd screamed the loudest when the lightning hit might return for more. *What did the campus safety video say about students taking stupid risks? Adrenaline junkies? The innocent immortality of youth?* I could almost hear the cheesy theme music. *"Na-na-nah-naaaah… Stay Safe!"*

"We can't."

"Well, we'll have to. You were right. Some of them were too weak," she continued, clearly envisioning some kind of exclusive gathering, maybe even bouncers at the door. "But we can send the weak ones away. Tell them they need to meditate or something. We'll only keep the ones whose energy is strong."

I turned my back to the fire to face her. "No, that's not what I meant. We can't. You can't do this again. Any of it. Bringing the girls out here. Calling the quarters. Raising energy out here in the open. It's not safe."

The fire flared behind me. When it dropped back down

again, the heat remained. I'd missed the moment when the rain stopped. All at once, the beach felt quiet and empty, the riotous waves sighing softly instead of threatening to douse the bonfire.

Tori stood completely still, and when she spoke, I didn't see her lips move. "Who's going to stop us?"

"There are hunters…"

She laughed, her mouth wide enough to show teeth. "You think I don't know that? That's why we have to be strong now."

Caleb, Adam, and Duncan were strong before their Wakenings. All three of them Gifted witches, less dependent on ambient magical energy. It hadn't been enough to stop the hunters. Nora was maybe the strongest witch I'd met outside of Queen's Creek, but she still feared them. "It's too dangerous. You're hurting mundanes, and you're drawing attention. They'll come for us."

"Let them come." She pulled her boots free of the sand and stomped past me toward the stones. She clambered onto the cement breaker and turned back.

"What?"

"I said, 'Let them come.' Let them see who we are and what we're capable of. Witches aren't the only ones who've been living their lives in secret. Can you imagine what the other mundanes would think if they knew there was a secret cabal tracking and destroying young women? The hunters have as much to fear as we do if their secret comes out."

"You want them to find you," I realized. "It's a trap."

"We'll raise the energy, and they'll come. Like moths. They'll come, and we'll show them the meaning of power." She clapped her hands and the fire went out.

"They'll kill you," I said into the darkness.

"They'll try."

14

Tori had barely finished her ominous declaration when a tiny light flashed between us, and my brother appeared on the stone in front of me. He wobbled a little, unsure of his balance. A step above him, Tori frowned. Although she'd flinched at his sudden appearance, she seemed more annoyed by the interruption than impressed by his magical arrival. She made no effort to help him.

When is he going to learn not to blink into unknown spaces? How did he even know I was here?

He windmilled his arms for a second, paused, and straightened. A smile twitched the corner of his mouth, clearly proud of avoiding another crash landing. Then he seemed to remember why he'd come. His voice was almost panicky. "Goddess, Cate. There you are. I've been looking all over for you. Why didn't you pick up your phone?"

I patted my back pocket. The phone was there, but I'd put it on silent before I left the dorm on my covert coven reconnaissance mission. "Thomas? What are you doing here?"

Behind him, Tori cleared her throat.

Thomas twisted to look over his shoulder. "Oh, hey, who's your friend? Wait, is this—?"

He slipped on the wet stone and disappeared before he could fall.

"Thomas!"

He popped back into view on the flat sand in front of me and grabbed my arm, pulling me back toward the stones and the sidewalk above. "We should take this party on the road, huh?"

Tori watched our approach with wide, black-rimmed eyes. Possibly, the second teleportation overcame her practiced indifference.

As we passed her, Thomas held out a hand. "Let's go, Wednesday, you're coming, too."

"Where? Who are you? What do you want?" Tori crossed her arms and widened her stance.

My brother pulled out something that looked like an antique compass. He tapped a button on the side, and the cover snapped open. Inside, a dial spun wildly before settling on a direction. The whole face flashed red. "See that? That's hunters. They're close. Can we go now?"

"Shit," I said. "Come on, I'll explain on the way."

Tori's eyebrow shot up.

"He'll explain," I corrected since I had no more idea about what Thomas was doing there than she did. "Right, Thomas?"

Thomas ran both hands through his blond hair. "Not here. But yes, okay? There will be so much explaining you'll have a new thesis written. But we have to go. Now."

The compass in Thomas's hand started shaking, making the gears inside rattle. He gritted his teeth and snapped it shut, stowing it in his pocket, where all trace of it disappeared. Mary Poppins wasn't the only one who could make things bigger on the inside.

Thomas led us down the sidewalk, around the corner, and off campus. My heart jumped at every shadow. How many hunters were there? What did they look like? Would I know one if I saw him?

Five blocks later, Thomas was out of breath, but he didn't stop. We turned down a narrow street, and I cringed. Not enough exits and too many places to hide. A painted barrier holding up the elevated train tracks lined one side. Something moved in the gloomy overpass. I gripped Thomas's arm, and we kept moving.

Tori stopped.

I felt energy building again. *No.*

She faced the overpass, where a mural of a giant butterfly with blue eyes in its wings stared back at her. Sparks flew between her fingers. Another shadow appeared above her.

How many more? What kind of weapons did they have?

"Tori!" I yelled.

She ignored me until I pulled her back.

"Let's go, ladies," Thomas said, his voice terse, his eyes above the butterfly.

Tori resisted, the energy still building. Static shocks zapped between us when I touched her.

"I told you they'd come," she said.

"We'll get them," I promised her. "But not now. It isn't safe. We have to get out of here. We're sitting ducks."

She looked up and down the street, assessing the danger. With a huff, she dropped her arms and let me turn her away.

The sidewalk on the opposite side of the street led past a series of small storefronts, some of them almost hidden by evenly spaced trees the city had planted to improve curb appeal and help clean the air. The overgrown branches stretched over the shadowy sidewalk, blocking us from the sight of whoever stood on the overpass.

So, I didn't catch the sign on the shop until Thomas stuck

his key in the lock. The hand-painted store name, *Holloway's Charms*, faded above a glass door papered over with posters and cards advertising New Age events, psychic readings, and chakra healing.

Inside, he locked the door behind us and pulled down a paper curtain. We took a moment to catch our breath.

"Thomas, what…?" I didn't know where to start.

He held up a hand. "Not yet. This way. Hey, don't touch that."

Tori put down the large crystal she'd picked up from a display counter. She eyed my brother with suspicion. "I knew I'd seen you somewhere before."

Of course, she'd been in the only occult supply shop in the area before. These places attracted mundanes who wanted to believe in magic almost as much as they repelled those who feared it. A newly powered witch might think she needed showy materials to work her spells, but I could pick up most of the same supplies at the dollar store without the tourists' price hike. What was Thomas doing here?

"I promise I can explain," he said. "Just come with me a little farther. We're almost there."

She looked past him at the beaded curtain that covered the doorway to the back room. If she was hesitant to follow a stranger to a second location, it was probably too late.

"He's my brother," I told her. "You can trust him."

She scoffed. "Cause you've been such a great ally so far."

What did she want from me? Did she honestly think her life-draining ritual on the beach impressed me so much that I'd immediately jump on board with whatever insane plan she had to lure witch hunters? And then what?

Thomas held back the curtain and gestured for us to go through. He didn't have to use his Gift to influence my choice.

I ducked my head and went in.

Tori followed.

A narrow staircase twisted three times before opening to a studio apartment on the second floor. As soon as we were inside, Thomas cast a ward on the entrance. He exhaled slowly, and I could almost see his energy draining. He kicked off his shoes and collapsed on a futon, throwing his feet up on a stack of crates that served as a coffee table.

"Welcome to my humble abode," he said, stretching out his arms to either side.

"Is it safe?" I asked.

"Safe as the Creek before the boundary went down," he said.

The ward on the entrance shimmered almost imperceptibly.

Tori frowned, leafing through a stack of marketing flyers for the magic shop she found stacked on a short bookcase by the door. "Isn't this the first place witch hunters will look?"

Thomas shrugged. "Nah, there's no actual magical energy downstairs. It's all just stuff. Stuff with magical potential, sure. But none of that has any power on its own. The only real magic comes from in here." He rubbed his chest. "And I just directed it to those wards, so we're good. Any energy inside the wards stays inside the wards, tighter than Vegas. And much better at keeping secrets."

I hope he's right. Adam said he used wards during his Wakening. They didn't protect Shelley.

But things are different now. Maybe we're stronger.

Thomas pushed himself back up and picked up a little golden cat statue. "Besides, look how kitschy it is. This stuff is for mundanes who vacation in Salem and call themselves Lilith or Damien. Hunters'll probably walk right by. It's perfect."

Tori pursed her lips. She dropped the flyers back on the bookcase, letting one fall to the floor as she went to the kitchen.

He replaced the flyer, raising an eyebrow at her back.

"How long have you been here?" I asked him, pacing the room and noticing some of his things from home mixed in with the random curios and books from the magic shop.

"Umm. So, you know that day when I drove you to the airport?"

Yeah, I remembered that day. It was probably going to be our most memorable birthday ever.

"I thought you were going to stay in Williamsburg. Spend more time with Duncan," I said. He'd been flirting with my best friend's brother all morning and practically shoved me out of the car to get back.

"Oh, I did. I do. I mean…we only walked here just now because you…you know. But I can blink back whenever I want." Of course he could. With all the magical energy we released, it probably didn't even phase him to use some of it for instant travel. He'd been blinking from the kitchen to his bedroom for years growing up. Still, cross-country? *I will not be jealous of my brother's skills.*

My brother's stupid, reckless skills. I almost called him out on using witchcraft when we were supposed to be hiding from witch hunters. He'd blinked to the beach to warn us, for goddess-sake.

"You can what?" Tori asked.

"Umm…" he hesitated. Six or seven different responses crossed his face. *How much could he tell her? What did she already know?*

I wondered the same thing, but after what I'd seen on the beach, it would be safer for all of us to drop any misguided attempts at confidentiality. Another part of life that would have to change because of what we'd done. "Just tell her. The Gate's down. Magic's out. I think we're past the code of secrecy. They're going to have to amend the covenant anyway."

He tilted his head, considering. Tori clomped across the scarred hardwood floors to stand in front of him, an imposing figure in her spiky platforms. Thomas leaned back into the futon, not nearly as impressed as she'd have liked him to be.

"So, I'm a witch." He waited for her to be shocked.

I rolled my eyes. Even if he hadn't seen what she did on that beach, he'd blinked in and out in front of her more than once.

She wasn't. "Yeah? So am I."

Thomas looked at me.

I shrugged.

Thomas put his feet down and leaned forward. "No, like. For real."

She raised an arched eyebrow and crossed her arms. Everything about her screamed *show me*.

"Okay, watch." He got up and brought a candle to the crate where his feet had been, setting it just in front of her. Waving his hand with a completely unnecessary flourish, he narrowed his eyes as if what he was about to do would take great concentration. He snapped his fingers and the candle lit. He threw jazz hands. "Tah dah!"

Tori nodded. "Cool. My turn?"

"What? No, did you see what I just did? Should I do it again?" He shot me a look and blew it out.

Before he could snap his fingers a second time, she put her hand over his. "Let me."

She held his eyes and snapped her fingers. The candle lit. So did the burners on the stove, an oil lamp on the mantle, and the cheap fire log in the fireplace, still in its paper wrapping.

Thomas sat back down, staring at each of the flames in turn.

I pulled out a bar stool and sat with my back to the high

countertop that separated his kitchen space from the rest of the apartment.

Thomas pointed at Tori. "Okay, so she's... Did you know? She's not...you're not from the Creek though. Right? No. She couldn't. Where did she come from?"

"Salem, actually," Tori said before I could admit I didn't know.

15

It made so much sense. Nora had told me there were other communities. Of course there were. But we'd never met anyone from one of them before.

Thomas leaned forward.

Tori held her ground.

"This is news. Hold up. I feel like this is going to be a Tale. Lemme make some tea. Then you can spill it," he said, pushing himself to his feet and coming around the counter.

I sighed. *Why is he so cheesy?*

Thomas smirked. "You know what? I heard it, and I don't care. I stand by it."

I rolled my eyes.

My brother pulled a kettle and three cups from the cabinet. He set the kettle in the sink and turned on the water. "So, wait, like THE Salem? From the Trials? I thought it was just a front. Real witches wouldn't… You couldn't."

Tori sat on the futon, her knees falling together as her feet splayed out to either side. She leaned her elbows on her knees. "I did."

"But you left," Thomas said.

"Obviously."

"When do you have to go back?" I asked.

She shrugged.

Could she have left home without a looming return deadline?

That she had done it was obvious. How wasn't so clear. "You can just do that?"

"Who's going to stop me?" It wasn't a taunt. She genuinely didn't think anyone would prevent her from leaving home.

"Y'all don't have a boundary or anything?" Thomas asked, lifting the full kettle to his stovetop. "Like...what keeps the magic in?"

"What do you mean?" she asked.

"How do you keep the magic from spreading?" I said, gesturing to the ward on Thomas's door. "Keep hunters from finding you?"

"Oh," she said.

"Oh?" Thomas echoed.

She looked down, picking at her fingernails. "We don't."

"You don't," I said, trying to imagine a magical community that didn't fear the hunters. That didn't have multiple ancestral safeguards to monitor the use of magic and prevent it from giving them away.

She smoothed her hands down and crossed her arms over her stomach. "Yeah. I mean. I don't know what it's like where you come from, but everyone's a witch in Salem. Even the mundanes."

I'd seen pictures online. Shops with witchy themes, historical landmarks with plaques describing the victims of the Trials, a statue of Elizabeth Montgomery. The city embraced witchcraft and the tourism dollars it brought. You'd think all of the real witches would have fled, but maybe that was the wrong way to look at it.

"Hiding in plain sight," I said.

Tori shrugged. "I guess."

Thomas pulled a jar of tea leaves from a shelf. "And you

can just leave whenever you want?"

"Yeah?" she said.

It sounded too good to be true. Thomas spooned tea into the filter of a glass teapot while he waited for the water to boil. I couldn't tell what he thought about Tori's explanation.

"How is that safe?" I asked.

Tori gripped the cushions beside her. "What do you mean? Nothing is safe. Nowhere is safe if you're a witch. That's why we have to combine our energy. It's so much stronger now. Don't you feel it? This is our chance."

The kettle whistled, making us all jump. Tori whistled back.

Thomas poured the water over the leaves and put the lid on the pot to steep.

"Our chance for what?" Thomas asked.

Tori sat up straighter. "To take out the hunters. Once and for all."

Thomas laughed. "Oh, she's funny. You're funny. Take them out. Sure. Okay. Let's just wipe out a secret organization of mercenaries who've been hunting our kind for four hundred years. Sure. Let's do it."

"We're not strong enough," I said. *Surely, she knows that.*

"Maybe you're not," she said.

"Look, what you did out there on the beach was impressive. I'm not going to lie. But look at the cost. You had to pull energy from twelve other people to do it. You're lucky none of them ended up in the hospital. And for what? A light show?" I said.

She sniffed. "In Salem, being a witch is celebrated. We're honored. It's an ancestral heritage that marks us as chosen for something special."

"You know something about being Chosen, don't you, Cate?" Thomas said.

I'd have smacked him if he hadn't been on the other side of

the counter

"But out here, it's different," Tori said.

"They're afraid of us," I said.

"Shouldn't they be?" Tori stood. She took a breath, focused on a spot next to Thomas and blinked. She disappeared for a second before popping into the kitchen with the teapot in her hands.

"Quick learner." Thomas handed her a mug and let her pour.

When the cup was full, she put down the pot and gestured at what she'd done. "Look at us! Look what we can do. They're right to fear us." She pushed a mug of tea across the counter to me.

"Their fear makes them dangerous," I said. The tea was stronger than it should have been. *Had Thomas given it a little help, or had Tori?*

"We can't keep making sacrifices for their comfort, hiding and running away. It's their turn to run. My sister would still be alive if she hadn't hidden who she was. They have to pay for what they did. To my sister and all the witches who came before her. I was prepared to do this alone, but I shouldn't have to. I don't want to. And now you're here."

"I'm not your sister." But she had a point. How many witches had died while the rest of us locked ourselves away in our sanctuaries? How much longer could we live in fear? Especially now that the Gate was down. The witches of Salem might be used to protecting themselves, but the people we'd left in Queen's Creek...

She scowled. "Yeah. I know. She's dead."

Thomas sipped his tea. "I think what my sister meant to say was, we're sorry for your loss. We know what it's like to lose someone."

My tea suddenly became extremely interesting. Little ripples crossed the surface, crashing and dissolving against the sides. I'd never read tea leaves, but it felt like a message. Too much like the water in my cup when I scried for Adam, like the water of the Creek that surrounded my home, like the boundary spell before it broke, trapping my father in the time stream. Yes, I knew what it felt like to lose someone. And I carried the guilt of my failure every day. What I'd done was unforgivable, even if I could stop the hunters from finding Queen's Creek. My eyes burned, but I squeezed them shut until the feeling passed.

"I'm sorry," I said.

Tori flattened her hands on the counter. "I don't need your sorrow. I need your help."

"Help with what exactly?" *What did she think we could do?*

"Getting justice."

The candles flickered. I almost expected a clash of thunder, but none came. It was probably just a draft.

Thomas glanced past me, pursing his lips. I didn't have to turn to know the flame in the fireplace had grown. The burners on the stovetop clicked. Energy was rising again.

My brother reached for Tori's cup and blew across it, a calming influence that affected not only the tea but the one who drank it. He pushed it gently back to her. "So, I'm not saying we're not here for you and whatever wild quest you've got planned, but maybe we take a step back first and let the energy settle before we set the world on fire."

Tori accepted the cup, watching him over the brim as she sipped. She stared into his eyes, her breath slowing with each passing second. Her lashes fluttered.

Thank the goddess in all her glory for Thomas's Gift. The influence of a muse is so much more subtle than any of the ways I might have tried to de-escalate her.

Thomas smiled as the flames all returned to a perfectly mundane height.

Tori shook her head. "I'm sorry. But they're so close. Can't you feel them? I've never had a shot like this before."

"That's why I came to get you," Thomas said, turning from Tori to me. "Adam said—" He shook his head. "You know what? He can explain it better. Call him back. He'll be worried."

16

*S*even *missed calls. Holy Hera, Thomas.* Adam was panicking, and my brother had us getting to know each other over tea. *I should have called him the second we got here.*

Once again, Adam answered on the first ring. When he saw me, his face shifted from frustration to concern. "Are you okay? Why haven't you been answering your phone? Tell me you're somewhere safe. Where's Thomas?"

"Hey, hey. It's okay. We're at Thomas's place, see?" I reversed the camera so my brother could wave.

When I turned it back, Adam visibly relaxed. "Good. That's good. You disappeared for a second, and I thought—but you're there, so that's…"

"Good?" I said, smiling.

"Yeah," he said.

Thomas sighed. "Alright, love birds. Now that we've established that everybody's alive and well, do you think we could talk about why that might not last?"

"What do you know about the hunters?" Tori asked, leaning over my shoulder.

"Who's that?" Adam frowned at the pale face hovering

behind me on the screen.

"This is Tori," I said. "She's from Salem."

Adam's eyebrows jumped. He nodded, recovering quickly. "That might explain the spike."

"What spike?" I asked.

"You're going to have to start at the beginning, man. I didn't get a chance to explain. This trip has been…eventful," Thomas said, pouring himself more tea.

According to Adam, after the boundary had come down, my brothers Matthew and Gabriel went through my father's research again. They'd wanted to track the energy we released to learn more about how magic worked when it wasn't contained. Some members of our community, probably guided by the former speaker, Mrs. Kirk, feared the energy would disperse entirely, leaving them essentially mundane with no magic to command.

They'd discovered the same thing Thomas and I had when we first unpacked Dad's notes. Magic could never abandon the witches. It was created by them. Witches, even those without the Gift, were the Source of magic. Honestly, after what I'd seen, mundanes probably created some magical energy as well, even if they didn't understand how to direct it. That was how the girls on the beach could fuel Tori's spell.

To pacify the witches of Queen's Creek, Matthew and Gabriel developed a system to identify large sources of magical energy on a map and to track changes in its flow. They were pretty sure they'd discovered at least six other communities like ours. Places where large groups of witches gathered. It was possible there were more. Some of them could still be hiding behind boundaries like ours, which prevented the energy from escaping.

"We have to find them and warn them," I said. If their boundaries were like ours, they faced the same danger we had. A magical apocalypse when the energy exceeded the capacity of the boundary spell. Even if the hunters couldn't see them yet, their own protective circle might destroy them.

"Maybe their boundaries are different," Thomas said. "Maybe they found a way to vent it so it doesn't build up so much."

Adam nodded in the video chat, but he didn't smile. "It's possible. None of these communities are as old as Queen's Creek. They may have learned something our ancestors didn't know before they put up their boundaries. But your brothers' map doesn't seem to think so."

He moved the camera to show a large map spread out on a table. Little lights flashed over it, but some shone more brightly, and the largest ones were red. A few spots on the map showed faint circles where magical energy seemed gathered around something invisible. You might miss the pattern if you weren't looking for it. But we weren't the only ones looking.

"Red for danger, huh?" Thomas said. "Creative."

Adam sighed. "Some traditions work for a reason. I didn't even have to explain it to you."

"Fair enough." Thomas tilted my phone as if he could change the angle on the map.

I took it back. "Can you show us Salem?"

The screen scanned north from Virginia and a soft yellow light glowed in Massachusetts.

Tori scrunched up her face. "So...they're kind of safe? It's like a traffic light, right? Yellow means caution?"

"Hold on," Adam's voice came from outside the frame. "Shoo, you. Get out of there."

His hand swiped over the page. The yellow light flickered, dodged his fingers, and floated off the map. A will-o'-the-wisp. "Annoying little things. They won't stay down by the Creek now that the boundary is down. They follow the energy, and the energy's dispersed."

"Are you guys using wisps to track magic?" Those things could not be a reliable source of information. Their whole purpose in existence was to lead people astray.

Adam's face reappeared on the screen. He pushed a red curl back from his forehead. "The wisp population is one of several metrics that show a strong correlation to increases in magical energy."

Thomas laughed. "You sound like Gabe. Is that what he told you to say?"

Adam shrugged. "You're not the first to question your brother's methods. But look at the map. Does this look wrong to you?"

He reversed the camera again, swinging it over the map. Southern Virginia glowed with hundreds of tiny white and yellow specks of light. Most of them gathered near the coast, but there was a bright spot in Richmond and a few in the mountains. A bigger one hovered over a town in the Shenandoah Valley.

"Seems about right," Thomas said. "I'm sorry for doubting you."

"Right, so, anyway," Adam said. He held the phone back from the map so we could see more of it. "The brighter the light, the more energy can be found there. Once the energy hits a certain level, the light changes color. Yellow, then orange, then red. The Danger Threshold, Matthew calls it."

He pointed to Salem again. "This is where your friend's from? Looks like a pretty high concentration of magic users, but nothing that's affecting the area around it. Seems pretty stable for now."

Tori's shoulders relaxed a little. Then she frowned. "What do you mean *for now*?"

Adam flicked the camera back to his face. "We're putting it on a watch list. Honestly, in a place with a history like Salem, I'd have thought it would either be fire engine red or totally blank. You're telling me witches still live there after what happened? And they haven't put up massive wards or anything to keep out mundanes?"

"Why would we want to keep them out? They pay the bills. Who do you think is eating in witch-themed restaurants and touring historical homes?" Tori said.

"She has a point. Maybe we've been looking at our relationship with mundanes all wrong," said Thomas.

Adam rubbed his face. "I can bring it up when I give my report to the Speaker, but I wouldn't plan on sending out any ambassadors to the mundanes right now. The covens in Queen's Creek are pretty on edge about the hunters since the boundary came down. And between what we're seeing here and Duncan's news..."

"What news?" I looked at Thomas, but he deferred to Adam.

"Okay, so you know he went back undercover? He's running that real estate office in town to keep guiding lost witchlings on their Wakenings. Although, since the boundary came down, it's not just witchlings any more. I mean, there hasn't been a mass exodus or anything, but a few families wanted to know what they've been missing. And I think some people might have been second-guessing the choice they made at twenty-one. The quorum is trying to get people to at least report their intentions before they leave so we can update the census and keep an eye on the population. But it's a fine line, you know? Nobody wants to feel like their every movement is being tracked, but the coven leaders have been watching out for everyone for so long, they don't know how to protect them if they leave."

"How much protection do they need? Can't their magic handle the hunters?" Tori asked.

"I don't know what it's like in Salem, but the witches in Queen's Creek have never needed to learn defensive spells.

And the hunters are finding them too quickly for them to set wards like the boundary spell," Adam said.

"How quickly? How are they finding them?" Tori asked.

"So, we still don't know for sure how they find witches out there, but they must have something like this," he said, flipping the camera back to the map. "Because they keep turning up wherever there's an energy spike."

"How do you know that?" I asked.

"Well, for one thing, after they show up, the energy spike drops. No more bright red on that part of the map. Something is dispersing the energy there. See this one? That was practically a glowing coal two days ago, and now…" The yellow light over a spot in Tennessee pulsed almost imperceptibly.

"You're saying, what? This guy Duncan's sitting around watching the map all day, making guesses about what happens when the lights go out?" Tori said.

"No. I mean, we do have people watching it in shifts. But Duncan's news comes the old-fashioned way. Word of mouth. He used his Gift to get people talking, and next thing you know, he's got a network of allies all up and down the coast. And he's expanding it west all the time. I think he's sending some of those lost witchlings on reconnaissance missions."

It sounded risky, but Duncan's Gift gave him so much charisma that most people trusted him immediately. And Adam's Gift allowed him to sense when anyone stretched the truth. The two of them could probably vet any possible spies well enough to verify the news they brought.

"What did they tell him?" I said.

"The hunters are nervous. We don't think there are as many of them as there used to be because they aren't hitting all the targets at once. They're mostly ignoring anything that isn't red. But they've been more active than they have in years. More organized. They move quickly and discreetly, following the flow of energy. And as soon as they arrive, the energy spike disappears from the map. Duncan's sources say witches have disappeared from all of those places. Suddenly have to move away without telling anyone. Quit their jobs with no notice. Some of them have terrible accidents, and nobody sees them again."

"They're killing them," Tori said. "Just like my sister."

17

ate, can we talk for a minute?" Adam's voice dropped, and I saw him moving through an office, closing the door.

Thomas nodded. He pointed to a door opposite the stairs.

"Thanks. I'll be right back."

Thomas's bathroom was a wreck. I shoved a pile of clothes aside and sat on the edge of the tub, crossing my legs and bringing the phone up to my face. Adam sat behind a desk with a familiar wall of shelves behind him.

"Are you in the Speaker's office?" I asked, remembering the last time we'd been there together—the night they declared my father dead instead of just missing. We'd found a curiously labeled census in Mrs. Kirk's desk. That desk.

"Yeah, Dad's in a meeting with the coven leaders. Hearing their concerns or something. He won't be back for a while."

I guess it's Giles's desk now.

When I left, our community's Speaker, Mrs. Kirk, retired in disgrace after almost killing me and most of my family in her attempt to maintain the boundary that kept magical energy (and the witches who wielded it) trapped in Queen's Creek.

People mumbled about her best interests, unintentional casualties, and justifiable sacrifices. But ultimately the community demanded a leader who would promise more transparency in their attempts to protect them. I didn't stick around for the election, but I'd assumed it would be Giles Parker.

The Watch Commander knew everyone in town, and his friendship with my dad (the most likely candidate before he disappeared) would have made him a logical proxy.

"So when you said you're going to give your report to the Speaker, you meant..." *Just for my own confirmation.*

Adam smiled. "Dad. We try to keep Watch business in the Tower. I mean, obviously, he's given me some tips since I took over as Commander, but I still have to give him a formal report when we find something that might affect the whole community like this."

I shouldn't be surprised Adam was promoted. Somebody had to take over his father's duties when Giles was elected. Still, Adam had taken his responsibilities as Guardian so seriously that I had trouble picturing him anywhere but the Gatehouse. *Who's guarding the Gate now?*

"Oh," I said.

Adam leaned toward the camera. "Are you safe there?"

"Why do you keep asking that? What did you see on the map? Or did Duncan say something? Are the hunters in Chicago?"

"You tell me." He unrolled the map on the desk and reversed the camera so I could see my location. We'd focused on Queen's Creek before, but the Second City glowed like a lighthouse, casting red beams in all directions.

"Wow."

"I thought it might be you," Adam said. "But it's not, is it? It's your new friend. Who is she?"

"I'm not sure," I admitted. Tori was a powerful witch.

She'd called the energy of the storm and drawn more from the girls. Her strength was intoxicating, but I still didn't know how she intended to use it.

I thought it might be you. Had he been proud when he thought I'd caused the map to light up? Worried? What would he say if I told him I might be partially responsible? I hadn't called the energy, but I'd directed it. And it had felt amazing.

I couldn't outright lie to Adam. Not even if he didn't have that Gift. But I wasn't supposed to be working magic, and I'd already done it three times. Scrying. My little backstage light test. Harnessing the energy on the beach. *If I tell him, I'll have to promise not to do it again. I shouldn't do it again...* It wasn't fair. I might finally be coming into my Gift, but using it would put us all in exactly the danger our ancestors feared when they founded Queen's Creek.

Adam frowned. He knew I was holding back. "What are you doing with her? She's practically a beacon."

"My advisor told me to check on her." An easy truth. I explained what Nora had told me about her concerns, both mundane and magical. When he remembered that my college professor was a witch, he actually relaxed.

"At least there's someone there to look out for you. You'll listen to her, won't you? It sounds like she agrees with me about the danger. The hunters are on their way out there. They have to be. There's no hiding something like this. That's why Thomas came to get you."

The memory of the shadows under the overpass made me sick to my stomach. "I think they're already here."

Adam rubbed his face, resting his elbows on the desk to prop himself up. "You can't stay there, Cate."

He only wanted to protect me, but I'd had enough protection, and I wasn't ready to give up my freedom for safety. Besides, I couldn't abandon Tori. There was no telling what she might do, who she might hurt, trying to resolve her vendetta against the hunters.

"What do you want me to do? Nora told me to get her to stop using magic, but you heard her. They killed her sister. There's no way she's going to back down now. And if the energy spike is as bright as all that, it's got to be too late to hide anyway."

"Maybe you should come home."

"Maybe you should come out here."

"You know I can't. People are scared, and it's our fault. We did this. The Watch managed to put the glamour back around the Creek, but the boundary is down. Nothing is keeping the hunters from walking right through it if they find us. I can't leave our people unprotected."

"What about Giles?"

"He's not the Commander anymore. He doesn't have time to organize shifts and track the weak points in our security. Mrs. Kirk may have retired, but she's still here, and she's loud. She's telling anyone who will listen what a huge mistake we made. We promised these people that we would save them, and we did. But most of them never actually saw the cracks in the boundary spell. The way magic glitched was annoying, but they never understood what it meant. And now the Gate is down, and the energy isn't trapped, and they're free to come and go as they please, but a lot of them don't want to go anywhere. They've lived their whole lives in hiding. And maybe they were right to do it. It isn't safe out there."

"It sounds like you're the one who's scared." I couldn't keep the bitterness out of my voice. After what he'd told me about his Wakening and what I'd learned about Tori, I couldn't believe his solution was to go to ground like frightened rabbits. How long could we let other people determine our lives?

"I am." He took a breath. "And you should be, too."

"I'm too mad to be scared." *I shouldn't have said that.*

"You want to talk about it?" Adam propped the phone on something on the desk and crossed his arms in front of it, leaning toward me even though we weren't in the same room. "What's Thomas done this time?"

"It isn't him. It's just…everything. Two weeks ago, I thought I would never see magic again. And I was happy with that choice. Now I'm the Chosen One who freed magic but still can't manage it herself. We stopped the apocalypse, but magic is still the reason our lives are in danger. The hunters have only gotten stronger. And Dad's still missing."

"We're going to find him."

"I know." But I didn't. How did you find someone who might not even exist in the same timeline?

"He wouldn't want you to beat yourself up over this. He went into the time stream on his own. It wasn't your fault." He'd said it before. Mom said the same. It still didn't feel true.

"But I should have been able to get him out. We were so close. And then I lost him again. And Elspeth—" My friend had gone into the time stream to have a very important conversation with one of our ancestors. I promised to get her out safely, but when I found her, she'd aged decades. Even with the mantle of the Gatekeeper and all that came with it, I couldn't control time, only pass through it. There was no way to change her back.

Adam picked up the phone again, holding me closer. "Look, you don't want to hear this, but it could have been worse. We all knew the risks. Even Elspeth."

He was right. I didn't want to hear it. Everything can always be worse. Even though we knew what we were doing was dangerous, we hadn't really known the risks. How could we? No one had ever done what we were doing before.

"How is she?" I asked.

"She's keeping busy," he said. "Helping your mom in the healer's cottage. Actually, I think your mom is her assistant now. She says Elspeth's got more years of experience than she does."

That must be so weird for them. Mom had trained Elspeth from her eleventh birthday, preparing her to take over when Mom retired. *Who's going to take over now? Are we going to be without a healer, too?*

"I can't come home until I know how to fix this," I said. Dad's notes on energy transmission and the time stream waited for me, stuffed in a notebook with my own research and what I remembered from our ancestral grimoire.

Unfortunately, Dad was an alchemist, and a lot of the science was beyond me. I needed help, but I didn't know how to ask a mundane scientist for assistance with a magical problem. My only connection to the physics department didn't know about my secret life, but he might be my only hope. *I need to talk to Brian.*

"You're not going to fix anything if the hunters catch you," Adam said.

"You think I don't know that?" I bit my tongue before something meaner slipped out. He'd always done what he could to keep us safe. He'd seen what the hunters could do up close during his Wakening and made a plan with Duncan to protect Queen's Creek. But the plan had meant Adam running home and leaving Duncan outside the boundary to distract them. It worked, but it felt a lot like hiding.

The same as our ancestors had done for hundreds of years. And what had it bought us? We'd trapped ourselves in our own homes. I had to barricade myself behind wards in my brother's apartment and have a long-distance conversation with my boyfriend even though he could blink his eyes and appear in front of me in an instant. Every day, I saw problems Nora could fix with a snap of her fingers, but she didn't dare lift one beyond lighting a few candles. What good did it do witches to get out in the world if we couldn't use magic to make it better?

Tori was right. It was time to fight. Ultimately, I couldn't leave Chicago for the same reasons he had to stay in Queen's Creek. "I'm not the only witch out here. I can't just abandon them."

18

Thomas checked his compass six or seven times over the next hour and basically announced that he was holding us hostage until he could be sure it was safe for us to leave.

"What is that thing anyway?" I asked. "Where did you get it?"

"It's a kynigolabe," Tori said, holding out her hand. "Isn't it?"

"Uh, yeah," said Thomas. He handed it to her, visibly disappointed that she recognized it. "Duncan found it for me. They used to be more common. That's how a lot of our ancestors escaped the trials. They left their villages before the hunters found them. But you don't need to track them if you spend your whole life behind wards. So they got lost, damaged, and forgotten. Somebody's going to have to figure out how to make a lot more of them if witches want to travel freely."

I looked at the smooth metal contraption in Tori's hand. "What does it do?"

Tori popped the lid, showing me the complex gears inside. "It's like an astrolabe, but it doesn't track the stars. See? It tracks the things that are tracking you."

The dial spun, an arrow pointing toward the glass door that led to Thomas's fire escape balcony. My brother peeked through the blinds. He shrugged. "I don't see anything, but that doesn't mean they aren't there."

"How does it work?" *How do we know it does?*

Thomas sat down again. He rubbed his hands on his knees. "So, you know how Mom always says magic is just energy directed toward an intention? What do you think the hunters' intention is? And where are they directing it?"

"You're saying the witch hunters are using magic to find us?" *The hypocrisy of hunters using magic to chase us, to murder us because we used it first.*

Tori stood in the middle of the room, turning in circles, watching the arrow spin around, always landing in the same orientation. "The kynigolabe detects the flow of energy toward whoever holds it and identifies the direction of its source. So, while I'm holding it, it's looking for anybody looking for me."

"But if they're using magic…do they have those? Are they using them to find us?"

"I'm not sure," Thomas admitted. "They must have something similar. I don't see how they could be as efficient as they seem to be if they were doing it all the old-fashioned way."

"The old-fashioned way?" *I don't want to know. Don't say it. Why did I ask?*

"Spies. Interrogation. Torture." Tori snapped the metal case shut. "Their methods may have changed, but the results are the same. Witches are dying. And we're just sitting here."

"You're welcome," Thomas said. "I could have left you out there if you're in such a hurry to add to their body count."

"Thomas, that's not fair," I said. *Apparently, it's my turn to apologize for my twin's insensitivity.*

But he kept going. "It's not just about you, you know. If I take down the wards, and you guys go out there and so much as light a candle, you're going to lead them right back here. I haven't been living in this room for the past three years, pretending to do magic for mundanes, only to have a couple of dark sorority girls show up and out me to the people I've worked so hard to avoid. You might be ready to throw your life away, but I'm not."

He's been here the whole time?

"We wouldn't do that," I said, although I honestly wasn't sure what Tori was thinking.

"Better safe than dead," Thomas said, pulling a couple of extra blankets from a hall closet. "You guys take the futon. I'll sleep in the chair."

Tori looked like she might argue, but she looked down at the kynigolabe in her hand and shook her head. She set it on the kitchen counter. Turning, she caught Thomas's eye and said, "You got something I can sleep in?"

My brother dug through a drawer and tossed her a t-shirt and a pair of shorts. She caught them with more grace than I would have expected, but then, she'd changed a lot since we first met at the café. The witch who challenged me on the beach never would have recognized the cautious kid who'd tripped over my ankle in her attempts to look smaller. This version was somewhere in between, a confident young woman whose power seemed to come more from her attitude than her Gift. *Sucking the energy out of sorority girls must have that effect on a person.*

While she went into the bathroom to change, I helped Thomas move the coffee table and pull out the futon. He positioned a pillow and blanket on the ratty recliner, then threw himself on it fully clothed. "So, how's Adam?"

"He's worried." I sat on the edge of the futon, trying to figure out how to ask my brother about my boyfriend without coming across as some kind of possessive psycho. Every time I'd actually talked to Adam, he'd done nothing but ask about my safety and try to make me understand the danger I was in.

But I couldn't stop thinking about the girl I'd seen him talking to in my scrying mirror and how he smiled at her. Maybe it wasn't what it'd looked like. Who could he possibly have met outside the Gate? I'd had so much to drink that night.

"Can you blame him?" Thomas said. "It's his job to protect everyone, and the witch he cares about the most went and moved too far away for him to watch over."

Am I the witch he cares about most, though? Why couldn't I be sure? My feelings confused me. I knew that I loved him. Knew that he loved me. But sometimes, our relationship still felt like something that happened to someone else. I could blame that on Thomas, but we'd already had that fight. I'd formally forgiven him before returning to school, agreeing to assume positive intent from here on out.

Well, now I definitely can't ask about that other girl. I latched onto the other thing Thomas said. The part about it being my fault I was too far away to be babysat. "I don't need to be watched over. I don't want to be taken care of. I don't need to be protected like a child. I'm not some broken thing. Just because I grew up without a Gift—"

Thomas threw up his hands. "Whoa! Hey, this is not about that. What Mom and Dad did, binding your Gift, they were wrong, okay? I get why you're mad, and you should be. I'm not going to defend them. The elders in Queen's Creek did a bunch of stupid shit in the name of keeping us all safe. This is not that."

"Really? Cause it feels a lot like the same old paternalistic crap I've gotten from Mom and Dad, and Matthew and Gabe and Jonathan and Ben and..." All of my brothers tried to keep me safe growing up, the only witch in town with no Gift. Perks of being the youngest. Caleb was less direct about it since his Gift allowed him to hear my thoughts before I voiced them. He knew better than to push me. But Thomas was my twin, and I'd always thought he understood me best, even without telepathy.

"That's not fair. I know you can see the difference here. This is about whatever almost set that map on fire, lighting the way for every hunter within a five-mile radius. What happened on that beach? Who is that girl?" He jabbed his finger at the bathroom.

The toilet flushed, and we both waited a minute to make sure Tori wasn't about to join a conversation about her. The faucet turned on, and the water ran. *How long would it take her to wash all that makeup off?*

"What did she tell you while I was on the phone?" I said, lowering my voice. If she'd let anything more slip about her plan to avenge her sister, we should all be on the same page. She'd asked for help, but other than a kind of vague argument for justice, I wasn't sure what she had in mind.

Thomas stood, still watching the bathroom door. "She's pretty scared. I gave her a little push to see if she wanted to talk about it, but I don't think she's ready."

Scared was not the word I'd have used to describe the witch who wanted to go to war with the hunters, but Thomas had always been more empathetic than me. I rubbed my eyes. Duncan could have used his Gift to get her to trust him. Thomas's influence was a little more limited. As a muse, his push mostly encouraged someone to act on their own ideas and desires. He kept telling me he could never make anyone do something they didn't actually want to do, deep down. It was the only reason I had almost forgiven him for making me forget Adam. I believed him when he told me it wasn't intentional. He'd been trying to comfort me. And I had wanted to let Adam go at the time. We'd thought he was a traitor who'd abandoned his friends. We'd been wrong.

I couldn't afford to be wrong about Tori. Was she the threat that had Nora worried enough to call me in on a Sunday, or the damaged girl still processing grief over the loss of her sister? Both?

A T-shirt landed on my head, followed by a pair of track pants.

"It's late. Sleep now. Save the world tomorrow," said Thomas. "Again."

I rolled my eyes. I really did think we'd saved the world a few weeks ago, at least as far as the people of Queen's Creek were concerned. But what did we save them for if any time anybody did magic, it drew the hunters? Hiding behind wards in the city wasn't any better than staying behind the boundary back home.

Thomas's shirt was a little snug, but his joggers sat comfortably on my hips. "I'm going to need more tea first. Want any?"

"Yes, please." The small voice came from a figure I'd never have recognized. Tori stepped out of the bathroom in bare feet, and I would swear she'd lost eight inches of her height. With her dark hair pulled into a low ponytail and the black make-up washed away, she looked vulnerable, more like the freshman she was. I had to remind myself that she'd thrown me across the beach.

"I'm good," said Thomas. He pulled himself out of the recliner and headed for his turn in the bathroom. As he passed behind Tori, he pointed dramatically, silently mouthing, "Talk to her!"

I very maturely stuck my tongue out at him.

Tori laughed.

I dug through the drawers in Thomas's kitchen until I came across the one with tea supplies. The space was small, and he'd mostly thrown a bunch of hand-labeled brown paper packets together with boxes of store-brand tea bags. I held up a few options. "Sleepy Time Bears, or something that smells like lavender but is labeled chamomile?"

"Feel free to correct anything you want. There's a pen... somewhere in there." Thomas's voice came from the bathroom. Then he turned on the shower, and the water drowned out anything he might have said.

I sighed. How many times had I cleaned up one of Thomas's messes? Like, literally, cleaned up the messes he made back home because otherwise he'd lose something important, or someone would step on a rare talisman or something. *He can label his own tea.*

"I can do it," Tori said. "My mom has a tea shop. I've been studying herbs my whole life." She reached across the counter and dragged a few of the bags closer.

The little bottle behind the counter the day Morgan had her breakdown. The label with the cauldron. "Have you been selling potions at school?"

She sat on a stool across the counter from me. "Yeah? Nothing too fancy. Just like tinctures and stuff. Nothing too strong. Nothing illegal. There's a lot of kids with anxiety and ADHD...depression, or whatever. And they can't afford the scripts. So, I offer an alternative. All natural. Safe. And then I get to eat that week. My financial aid didn't cover the meal plan."

She said it so matter-of-factly, like it was the logical extension of the homesteading trends that had people baking their own sourdoughs and growing veggies on fire escapes instead of peddling unregulated medical treatment. It wasn't that I couldn't relate—I had the job at the café for the same reason. But it wasn't caffeine that made Morgan act crazy.

"You know you can't do that, right? For one thing, you have no idea what these kids are doing with it. Do you explain the side effects and complications? Drug interactions?"

She scoffed. "What interactions? They're buying from me because they can't get the other stuff."

"Tori, you can't—"

"Who's going to stop me?" she said so quietly her lips hardly moved. She unsealed one of the bags and sniffed. "Valerian root. Try that one for the tea. It has soothing properties."

19

In the morning, Thomas checked his compass (I refused to call it a kynigolabe), announced that the hunters had moved on, and removed the wards from the apartment entrance. I had just enough time to return to the dorm, shower, and change before class.

"No magic," Thomas cautioned. "Just because they aren't here now doesn't mean they aren't close by. You don't want to draw more attention right now."

Tori nodded.

I crossed my fingers and sent a quick prayer to the triple goddess that she'd take his warning seriously.

After class, I had a shift at the café. Morgan showed up an hour into it. She wore her usual sorority tee and shorts, but her hair hung limp instead of the customary bouncing high pony. "I need coffee."

"Are you alright?" I handed her a cup.

"Yeah. Sorry about the other day." She didn't look at me.

I smirked. "You mean when you called me a witch or when you showed up at a coven meeting?"

She winced. "Both?"

Since there was no way Mark would be okay with me

taking a break so early, I grabbed a couple of bottles of creamer and went to restock the condiment station.

"What were you even doing there? Nyla said you put a curse on Madi?" I tried to make it sound ridiculous. How much did she understand about what happened on the beach? *Maybe she won't remember. Tori pulled so much energy from those mundane girls that they should all feel pretty hungover today. Next-day regrets have a way of rewriting events.*

Morgan ripped open three packets of sweetener at once and dumped them all into her cup. "It was dumb. I don't know. I didn't think it would actually do anything. But she's been so insane lately. I think Lilli Vanessi is going to her head."

"Yeah, but a curse? When did you get into witchcraft?" *Casual. It's all just a joke.* I stuffed sugar packets into the dispenser.

Morgan shook her head. "I'm not into witchcraft. I just thought, you know how superstitious she is. Ever since we did *Macbeth* last year. It was a prank. I looked up some spells online, and it seemed pretty easy. You just need something that belonged to her, some string, a box…I put it all together and stuck it under her bed."

She's mundane. The magic wouldn't come for her.

But magic is just energy plus intention. And magical energy has been higher since the Gate came down.

She meant it as a prank, not magic. She had no intention of—

"But then, you know, she was such a bitch at rehearsal, I actually hoped it would work." She laughed. "Like that could happen."

Shit.

"How did Madi find out about it?" I poured half and half into an aluminum carafe and screwed the lid back in place.

"Oh, she saw it right away. Yeah, I suck at hiding shit from her. I was probably looking right at it when she came into the room. And then she's all, 'What is this? Why would you do this to me?' As if she didn't know." Morgan dumped a third of her coffee through the hole in the condiment station, then filled it back up with the fresh creamer.

Please tell me somebody tied off the bag in that trash can. Customers were always dumping coffee in there. Half the time, the bag leaked, or whoever had emptied it last didn't tie down the bag, and it slipped off the edges and got buried in the trash.

"So, you had a fight?" I said, wiping down the counter with a rag and trying to show my annoyance. *She should know better.*

"Oh my god, she's so dramatic. The RA had to come in and tell her to chill. And then, of course, she decided not to talk to me for a few days. Real mature." She stirred her cup with one of the wooden sticks in the condiment stand, knocking a couple of others free when she pulled it out. *No wonder Mark was so quick to give me her shift.*

I unlocked the storage space under the station to get more stirsticks. "But she's talking to you now, right? I mean, you came to that meeting together."

"Mmm-hmm." Morgan tapped the stick on her coffee, nodding. "She saw a flyer somewhere. The caf, maybe? I don't know. But she said the only way she'd forgive me was if I came with her and asked that witchy chick to take the curse off her."

"Did she?" I asked, crouching to find the right box.

"Did she what?" Morgan said, pressing the lid on her cup.

I'd been thinking about Tori removing the curse, but something about Morgan's tone made me change direction. She was worried about her sister. I sat back on my heels. "Forgive you?"

Morgan sipped her coffee, and her eyes watered. Maybe it was still too hot, but I didn't think so. "She said some things are unforgivable. I wished I'd never read *Macbeth*. And that meeting was a waste of time. Just a bunch of wasted girls dancing in the rain. We shouldn't have pre-gamed before we went over there. Ugh. My head."

"Had you met Tori before?" *She must have, right? How else did she get that vial with the St. John's wort potion?*

"Who? Oh, is that her name? No. I mean, I guess I must have seen her around, right? She's got kind of a...unique sense of style." Something behind me caught Morgan's eye, and she shifted her weight, leaning against the condiment station.

"You sure? Cause when I came in the other day—" I slammed the cabinet shut and stuffed the new stir sticks into place.

Her eyes flicked to mine and then back over my shoulder. "Yeah, about that. I said I was sorry, right? I wasn't myself. I had some kind of bad reaction to my new meds."

"Your meds?"

"Yeah, you know, I have ADHD, so..." She turned back to the condiment station, letting her hair hide her face.

Before I could ask another question, the manager's voice boomed behind me. "Oh no, absolutely not."

I turned around to see him striding across the café, his apron clutched in one hand. His shift had started twenty minutes ago, but I guess time works differently when you're on salary.

"Hey, Mark," I said, forcing a smile. "Look who's feeling better."

Morgan turned slowly, keeping her back braced against the stand. She flipped her hair out of her face, straightening with conscious effort. "I'm so sorry about last week. It was a medical emergency, but I've been cleared by my doctor to return to work."

"Oh, he's cleared you? I didn't realize your doctor worked

for this company. Well, I guess that's okay, then." Mark glared at both of us.

What did I do?

"Mark, please. I need this job," Morgan said.

Does she though? I'd always thought Madi and Morgan came from money, sorority dues, brand-name fashions, overseas vacations, and all. *I guess she really wants that car.*

"Absolutely not," Mark repeated. "In fact, you can see yourself out. We don't need another disturbance in here."

A couple of customers watched him raise his arm and point to the door, but the shop wasn't busy, and most of them were engrossed in their phones anyway.

Morgan sighed dramatically. "Fine. Okay? I'm going, Mark. You can put your arm down."

He pointed again. "Now."

"Thanks for the coffee," she said, ignoring him and hitching her bag higher on her shoulder. "I'll see you at the theater later."

Mark watched her until the door closed behind her. "She can't come back."

"She had a medical emergency," I said before I remembered the way he reacted to my family emergency.

"Everything's an emergency with you girls. Lord, protect us from college girls and their existential crises." He straightened the apron he'd been clutching and put it on.

"That's not fair," I said.

He scowled. "Life's not fair, kid. I need you on register."

A short Black girl with soft twists spiraling down her back stood at the counter.

Oh great, Jasmine's here. Thank you, universe, for proving Mark right.

I followed the manager behind the counter and signed into my register while he straightened the cups by the bar.

"Good afternoon!" he said brightly, modeling the customer

service he expected. "What can we get you this fine day?"

"I'll have an iced white chocolate mocha, please." She smiled at him.

It felt like a bad rehearsal. *Are we filming a commercial today, and no one told me?*

"Coming right up." Mark flipped the cup like a trick bartender, grinned at her appreciative giggle, and moved down the line to pull the espresso.

"Brian's on break," I told his girlfriend. "Do you want me to get him for you? I think he's sitting out back."

She swiped her credit card, the same fake smile still on her face. A silver charm bracelet jangled on her wrist. "Oh, I know. I'm on my way to meet him."

"Okay, well. Thanks for coming in."

She took the receipt but didn't leave the register. "He told me you were back."

"Yeah. You know, Spring Break's over."

"I hope everything's alright," she said, fiddling with one of her charms. "Brian was worried when you took off."

"He's been a good friend," I assured her, not wanting to get into my family drama with someone who didn't actually care.

"That's what I love about him." Her eyelashes fluttered as if the confession embarrassed her, but her tone staked a claim.

There it is. She'd been jealous of my friendship with Brian ever since Nyla introduced her to him. As if I could compete with a pretty pre-med dance captain, even if I'd wanted to. It wasn't my fault I'd known him longer.

Mark finished the drink and called it from the other end of the bar.

"Your drink's ready," I said. "Have a good day."

"Thanks. Take care of yourself." She grabbed her drink and went outside to find Brian.

She makes him happy. Jasmine had never said or done

anything overtly rude to me. Brian would never date someone like that. But there was something about her I couldn't trust. I always felt like we having two conversations at once, and I could only follow one of them.

20

Mark stuck around, mostly making noise at the end of the bar and chatting with customers as if he served alcohol instead of coffee. When the line got backed up because he took so long making drinks, he called Brian back from his break early. Jasmine walked him back to the front of the store, dropping a kiss on his cheek and waving to me on her way out.

Maybe I was the jealous one, still processing the fact that I had a long-distance boyfriend. I missed Adam, even though I barely remembered our relationship. *There's nothing wrong with her. She just doesn't like you.*

"Four minutes," Mark said as Brian washed his hands. "From the end of the line to picking up the drink. No more. Let's get this line moving."

Mark positioned himself as an expediter, standing between my register and the espresso machines. He called out to the next person in line, who had been about to place his order with me. "What are you having?"

The guy looked from me to Mark and back.

I shrugged.

"Umm. I'll have a medium latte with mocha," the guy said,

half to me and half to Mark.

"Grande mocha!" Mark shouted. He labeled a cup and slammed it down in front of Brian, calling out to the next customer before his hand was off the cup.

His system worked great until somebody ordered a drip coffee, and he had to step behind me to fill the cup from the silver server. He stepped on my foot, and I knocked the stack of cups off the counter when I hopped back. He reached to catch them, but he'd already opened the tap, so hot coffee ran over his other hand.

"For the love of...pancakes," he muttered, shaking his hand and grabbing a wet rag.

"We got this," Brian said. "If you want to put an ice pack on it."

Mark hesitated, but the line was down to the last three people, and Brian had already started their drinks. He ducked into the backroom.

The customers visibly relaxed. Even mundanes could sense the shift in energy.

It lasted about twenty minutes.

Tori's giant platforms echoed across the room. "How do you do this, Cate?"

She collapsed onto the counter, burying her face in her arms. Her necklaces clanked together.

I shoved a croissant into a bag and passed it to the waiting customer, who'd barely raised an eyebrow at the puddle of goth. The tongs hooked into a bar behind the pasty shelf.

Brian looked over, but I waved him off.

"Do what?" I asked.

Her response melted into the counter.

"Sorry, what?" Thirty minutes left on my shift, I'd taken all my breaks, and it was too early to start shutting things down. I would never keep this job if Mark thought I was some kind of magnet for trouble.

Tori sniffled. *Is she crying right now?*

I patted the top of her head. "There, there."

She lifted her face, black lines spider-webbing from the corners of her eyes.

"Geez, you want to get yourself together? You're scaring the norms." She wasn't, really. The café had mostly cleared out, and it took more than an angsty freshman to faze Brian. She was scaring me, though.

"Tell me how you do it," she sobbed.

I knelt behind the counter to get closer to her level.

"Do what?" I whispered. "I'm not doing anything."

"That. That exactly. How do you keep pretending?" Thank the goddess she matched my tone.

"I'm not pretending anything. This is who I am."

"You're not. I'm not. The world is so much bigger than this. How do you pretend it isn't? How do you go on day after day, acting like the energy isn't there? It's right there. The magic..." Tiny flashes of light winked at her fingertips. I covered her hand with mine.

"We can't talk about this here," I said.

I grabbed the bathroom key from under the counter and signaled Brian to watch the register.

"What's going on?" I asked Tori once we were safely behind the locked bathroom door.

"I haven't used magic all day, just like I promised. It's killing me. Everything is so slow. Don't you feel the energy building around you? How do you keep this up?" She pulled herself up on the counter by the sink and swung her legs.

I pulled some toilet paper from the roll and handed it to her to blow her nose. *How do I explain growing up with my Gift bound?* I'd only really started using magic over Spring Break, and it scared me. The energy made me feel strong but also connected me to everything. I felt it in the air, in the water of the creek, in the trees that grew on either side. I felt it in the people of Queen's Creek. When I released the mantle of Gatekeeper, I let it all go. But it was still there, all around me. I didn't know what would happen if I reached for it. Nothing I'd tried had gone the way I'd expected.

"How long have you been away from Salem?" I asked.

"I left last summer," she said.

"And they didn't warn you not to use magic in front of the mundanes?"

She sniffed. "No more than they do at home. *Don't do anything so big they can't ignore.* Mundanes ignore a lot."

"The hunters don't," I said.

"I know that now. Goddess knows I do. But I miss the feeling of being part of something bigger. I tried to go all day without it, like Thomas said, but I feel so empty. I'm alone." Her head dropped down and her shoulders shook.

I pulled off some more toilet paper and got it wet in the sink.

"You're not alone," I said, wiping her face.

Her dark eyes peered out from under lashes so long they had to be extensions. "Promise me?"

Someone knocked on the door.

"We're going to figure this out, okay? It's not going to be like this forever. But I'm going to get fired if I don't get back out there. Lock the door behind me. When you're ready to come out, bring the key back to the counter." I pressed the key into her hand and stepped out of the bathroom, pulling the door shut behind me.

I told the customer waiting outside that there was a problem with the toilet and the bathroom would have to be closed temporarily. She started complaining, but I handed her a free drink coupon and pointed her to our sister store down the street. I had three or four left from when I'd grabbed a pile to clear the place after Morgan's episode. *We're going to run out of those if this keeps up.*

I completed my side work and was about to close my register when a couple of guys came in. They didn't look familiar, but from their conversation, they might as well have been wearing T-shirts with our college mascot on them. The athletes ordered green tea and an almond milk cold brew. I hoped they'd take it to go, for Brian's sake. He was closing with Mark tonight and the manager would never let him start shutting the machines down early if customers were hanging out.

They headed for the door, but one stopped when he saw Tori slouching in a corner of the couch. She had her legs stretched out in front of her, crossed at the ankles. One hand scratched at a rip in her black jeans while the other twisted the chain of her pendant. The guy elbowed his friend and tilted his chin at Tori. The other guy took a draw from his iced tea and nodded. They knew her somehow, but I couldn't imagine her choosing a conversation with them.

The guys stood between Tori and the fireplace she'd been absently staring into. Green Tea Guy said something to her. She ignored him, still twisting her necklace. Almond Milk Bro tapped her foot with his shoe. She twitched but otherwise stared through them. The guys looked at each other. Green Tea Guy shrugged. His friend waved a hand in front of Tori's face. She snapped her teeth at him, and he jumped back. Green Tea Guy laughed. Almond Milk was not amused. His eyebrows lowered, and he said something to Tori that made her sit up straighter.

I braced for an explosion.

Walk away. Walk away. I didn't pull any energy behind my fervent wish for this to end better than I dared hope. I wasn't even really sure who I should direct that intention to.

Maybe she felt it anyway. Tori looked back over her shoulder, chewing her lower lip.

I tried to send her a look that asked if she needed help.

She shook her head. Reaching down, she slung her bag, a black tote with Medusa's head on it, over her shoulder. She followed the guys outside.

Brian looked up at the bell on the door and frowned. "What do you think that's about?"

"Seems sketchy, right?" I said.

Tori and the guys hadn't gone far. I could still see them standing by the bus stop shelter on the corner. The guys were significantly less intimidating now that Tori wasn't trying to disappear into the couch. She was taller than one of them in her spiky platforms and looked the other in the eye. She still looked more like the squeaky-voiced girl I'd met at the community board than the warrior-priestess I'd confronted at the beach.

The register dinged, a warning that I'd had the drawer open too long. Brian stepped up to the second register and signed in. "Go ahead and count out. I'll keep an eye on your friend."

"She's not my... Thanks." *She might not be my friend, but she's my responsibility.* Even if Nora hadn't all but charged me with managing the overpowered witchling, after hearing about her sister, I couldn't let her put herself in danger. Especially if anything she did might put the rest of us in danger, too.

21

In the back room, Mark lectured me about the risks of letting *dangerous people* into the cafe and told me to alert him if I ever saw Morgan come in again.

"She's not dangerous. She didn't even really break anything. And we cleaned it all up," I said, handing him the record of my count.

"We can't have disturbances like that in here. This is supposed to be a safe place for our customers. Corporate expects professionalism." He shoved the last bit of a lemon loaf into his mouth and balled up the cellophane, tossing it across the tiny room to the trash can.

I untied my apron and hung it on the wall. It wasn't worth the argument. Maybe Morgan could apply to the store down the street. I didn't think Mark would warn them away from hiring her. He just didn't want her here. Actually, he might help her get a job over there if he thought she'd give them trouble. He had some kind of weird rivalry with the other manager. "Okay, Mark. Have a good night."

Brian had a customer when I came back with the cash drawer. He pointed his chin toward the couch. Tori had returned. She sat there leaning forward with her elbows on her knees. Her chunky heel bounced on the floor, shaking her whole body.

"Thanks," I said, signing out of the register.

He nodded, still talking to the customer as he moved behind the bar to make her drink.

I pulled an armchair across from Tori. "You alright?"

She nodded, but it might have been from her leg bouncing.

"Who were those guys? What did they want?"

She shrugged.

"Did you know them?"

"No. Yes." She wouldn't look at me.

I reached out to still her leg.

She froze.

"Hey, what's going on?" I asked.

"You won't like it. So, I don't think I'll tell you. Yeah. This has been…fun. I guess. I don't hang out here very often. I should go." She stood, gathering up her tote.

I stood, too. "Yeah, like I'm going to let you walk out by yourself after that."

"I'm fine. You're fine. Look, ma, no hunters." She waved her hands out to either side.

Brian raised an eyebrow behind the bar. The customer he'd helped stood at the condiment station, but she definitely had an eye on us, too. *Great. I'm so fired if Mark comes out to another* incident *on the café floor*.

"Let's get out of here, okay?" I gestured to the door.

"Yeah. Okay. But I'm not going back to that magic shop so you can lock me in again." She clomped ahead of me.

"That's not what happened," I said, more for the benefit of Brian and the increasingly suspicious customer.

"Whatever you want to tell yourself," she said.

I waved to Brian and pushed her out to the sidewalk. *He's going to have questions tomorrow.* I didn't want to lie to him, but since he still didn't know I was a witch, our whole friendship was basically built on lies. *What's one more?*

"Where are you staying?" I asked.

She named a girls' dorm.

"Will your roommate be home?" I couldn't take her back to mine. Nyla was probably already at the theater, but I couldn't risk it.

She shook her head. "No."

We walked there in silence.

Tori's room was on the third floor, in the corner, next to a broken vending machine.

The beds had been unbunked, even though it made the room smaller. A black fuzzy blanket embroidered with tiny purple skulls covered the unmade bed on the left. Tori's entire wardrobe appeared to be piled on the floor around it. Black leggings and tees, skirts held together with safety pins, and at least one wide-brimmed hat cascaded into the shared space between the beds.

Everything on the roommate's nightstand sat at right angles. The bed had military corners. A smooth green bedspread lay beneath a mountain of rainbow-colored floral-print throw pillows, some of them actually shaped like flowers.

Tori dropped her bag at the foot of her bed and sat down, immediately reaching for the line of buckles on her shoes.

I stepped around the mess, cautious of invading her space. The corkboard above her desk held a collage of photos. All of them featured two smiling, nearly identical girls, one a little older than the other. It took me a moment to recognize Tori in the rosy face of the younger girl.

These photos came from her pre-goth period. The older girl's ankh pendant gave the only clue to Tori's new style. Now, Tori twisted it around her neck, the chain rasping against the bail.

Tori pulled her feet up and sat cross-legged on her bed. Her pink socks had unicorns on them. She looked up. "Just sit down. You're making me nervous."

"What happened to her?" I pulled out the chair from her desk and sat slowly.

"There was a fire." Her voice came out just above a whisper, barely a breath.

Why is it always fire? "Goddess, Tori."

"It's the truth," she said.

I didn't doubt it, but after Adam's story and Tori's vendetta against the hunters, there was no way she believed it was an accident. "What really happened?"

She pulled a worn stuffed bear wearing a white coat out from under the covers and hugged it to her chest. "I was so jealous when she went away to college. She wanted to be a doctor, you know? She was going to save the world. But she couldn't even save herself."

The bear's head lolled to the side, its big glass eyes staring at the ceiling. "I don't know how they found her. She always followed the rules when we traveled. The rest of the world's not like Salem. No magic outside the house. Don't share your Gift. She knew better than to practice her craft in public. She was like the golden child. That's why they agreed to let her go so far away."

I leaned back and looked at the empty bed behind me. "Did she come here with you?"

"No," Tori said, rubbing the bear's fuzzy ear. "Grace died three years ago. In Virginia."

Alarm bells sounded in my head. Three years ago, Adam had been on his Wakening, trying to start a life for us away from Queen's Creek. "Where did she go to school?"

"VCU. I guess they have a really good medical program? She was going into her first year. She loved it there. She had an apartment in Richmond. But they found her, and they burned the whole building down." Tori dropped her face into the bear's fur.

It couldn't be a coincidence. How many buildings in Richmond were destroyed by faulty wiring that summer?

Adam said he'd moved into a building full of magic users. The hunters killed Shelley and her neighbor. Had they known? When the scion came for Shelley, had he realized there were others in the building?

My breath caught. How close had I come to losing Adam that night? And I never would have known. I wouldn't have questioned my memories if I'd never seen him again.

Tori waited for my response, but I didn't have one. What could I say to her?

"I'm so sorry," I said, hating myself for it. But it was what people said, wasn't it? None of the neighbors who'd said it to me at the Reading had meant it as much as I did right now.

Tori flopped back on her bed.

Three years ago, she'd been fifteen. The kid in those pictures obviously idolized her big sister, and she'd kept Dr. Bear as a reminder of her. But why was she seeking revenge now? Why in Chicago if her sister died in Virginia?

"Why did you come here?" I asked.

She spoke to the ceiling without sitting up. "Well, my family owes the world a doctor, don't we? And my parents were never going to let me follow Grace after what happened to her. Plus, here, there's a witch on faculty."

Nora. She talked about other magical communities. How deep did her connections go? Was she recruiting witches? Or just guiding them like Duncan did in Williamsburg?

Was this the conversation she wanted me to have with Tori? To commiserate over our losses and convince her to give up her vendetta? Hide her magic away, even though hiding had killed her sister?

There was evidence of the Craft all over the room if you

knew what to look for. The window behind Tori's bed was lined with little paper cups. Her herb garden held twice as many plants as mine, some climbing up the glass and snagging in the window locks. Below it, a low bookcase meant for textbooks held rows of little glass vials and jars. Some of them had stickers on them with a familiar cauldron logo. A small electric crock pot sat on the floor, the cord snaking behind the bookcase.

"What did those guys want at the café?" She'd already admitted to selling potions, but her set-up indicated a slightly more productive business than I'd imagined.

"Who?" she asked, throwing an arm over her eyes.

I took a closer look at the pot. Condensation dripped inside the glass lid. I patted the side of the bed. "Hey, this is serious. What did you give them?"

"You think I don't know what serious looks like?" She sat up, glaring.

"I think you know better than I do what could happen if you accidentally poison a couple of mundanes. What's in here?" I put my hand on the lid.

"Chill. You're going to ruin it. That batch has been brewing since the last full moon. It's almost done." She swung her legs off the side of the bed, and I stepped away from the crock pot.

"We can't be doing magic right now. If you raise the energy —"

"I'm not doing magic! I swear. I charged that pot with the full moon, and I haven't touched it since. It's practically mundane cooking at this point. I haven't so much as called on the goddess all day. But those guys wanted something to keep them up at night, and I already had a couple of energy potions done." She dug into her tote and handed me a vial. The liquid inside shimmered with gold flecks.

I raised an eyebrow.

"It's mostly ginger and turmeric." She shrugged. "And

some pulverized maté for caffeine."

I shook it up and watched the gold flecks swirl. Mundanes could get all of those ingredients at Whole Foods. *Did they buy it from her because of her image, or was she adding something they couldn't get at the store?*

Her expression was defiant, but her fingers worried the frayed ends of her sleeves.

I took a guess. Tori's secret ingredient would never show up on a label. It would be almost impossible to test for in a lab. "But you raised the energy when you mixed them. Those are like little magic bombs waiting for the right intentions."

She smirked, tapping her fingertips together in front of her face. Then she flipped them out at me, mimicking an explosion, her eyes wide. "Ka-boom!"

22

Maybe I could have phrased that better. But I kept imagining those guys going back to their frat house, chugging the potions with cheap beer chasers, and proceeding to have panic attacks like Morgan at the café. Who knew what else was in their system? Even without the potential for magical side effects, Tori's entrepreneurial witchcraft was, at best, ill-advised.

By the time I convinced her to shut down her business for a while, my stomach was growling, but I didn't have time to go by the caf if I was going to get anything done at the theater tonight. *Praise Hestia for vending machines.* I gave Tori my ID so she could use my meal plan. It felt like the least I could do after cutting off her illicit income.

At the scene shop, Angel was too distracted by Morgan's presence to question mine. Anyway, I'd done the anti-curse routine last time, so his superstitions should have been appeased.

"Isn't she a little early for rehearsal?" I asked.

"Better her than la hermana," Angel said. He'd finished most of the last touch-ups and had his hands buried in bubbles, cleaning the paintbrushes. "She's crazy, but her sister? She's a real diva."

"Who's a diva?" asked Nyla, flipping her braids as she carried a couple of empty buckets to the work sink. She batted her lashes in imitation of a prima donna.

"You know." Angel plunged a brush under hot water, scrubbing the bristles with a comb.

Nyla looked back at the big garage door that opened to the stage, where Morgan stood in semi-darkness, reciting her lines to a large empty chair. "Oh right, the blonde bombshell. Where is Madi, anyway? I thought she forgave her for the whole hex thing."

She stacked the paint buckets by the sink and stretched, noticing me for the first time. "Oh, hey! Look who showed up just in time to wash buckets. Thanks, Cate."

I smirked. "Nice try, but I'm running crew tonight."

Something tipped over on the platform Nyla had been painting. Morgan had managed to trap herself between the immobile flat that formed the wall at the back of the platform and a folding screen meant to make it look like an old-fashioned dressing room. It didn't weigh much, but her position was awkward. Almost any move she made would set the rest of the props off like dominoes. "Crap! Ugh. Stupid thing. Can I get some help here?"

Without looking back, Nyla smiled serenely. "Oh, so she's your problem then. Good luck."

Angel shook out the paintbrush and dropped the handle into an empty can to dry. "You're gonna need it."

"How did you even get back there?" I asked Morgan.

"I was testing the space. I have to do a quick change back here in the second half. Clearly, there's not enough room." Her voice was muffled.

"Well, just hold still for a sec while I move this stuff. Then we can see if there's a way to set it up differently." I pulled things off the platform one at a time, setting them safely on the floor of the shop. "I'm sorry about what happened with Mark."

"It's fine. I probably wasn't going to have enough time for that job anyway. There's always *another opening, another show.*" She sang the last words to the tune of the opening number from *Kiss Me, Kate.*

I didn't even try to hide my eye-roll since she couldn't see me from back there. "Glad you're feeling better then."

"Yeah, I'll be alright. It was just a hangover. You should see Madi, though. She must have fallen or something. There was blood all over her shirt when we got home last night, and her nose was all stuffed up." Morgan scuffled around behind the screen, and it shook.

I grabbed the screen, simultaneously relieved that Morgan didn't seem to remember what happened at the beach and nervous about what that meant about the strength of Tori's spellwork. The screen didn't fall away when I pulled. One of the legs was stuck under an antique dressing table. "Just, hold still, okay? I'm almost there. I have to move the table."

"I don't want to be rude…" she said.

But you're going to be.

"But can you do this any faster? My leg is cramping up." She stomped her foot in demonstration.

"Doing the best I can," I mumbled. The table was exactly as heavy as it looked. *Not built for the stage, I guess.*

In the end, I had to get Angel to lift one side while I picked up the other, and Nyla straightened the screen.

Morgan had the good sense to appear sheepish when she escaped, endearing herself temporarily to the set builders.

"Look, the screen doesn't have to move during the scene. I can put a stage weight back here to block it from slipping again," Nyla offered.

"Thanks," said Morgan.

Angel huffed something about actors and their impossible

needs, but most of it was in Spanish, and he gave her a smile as he left.

I checked the time on my phone. "Ten minutes to your call time. You want to grab coffee?"

She clutched my arm. "I always want coffee."

Although the character Morgan played on stage had her own dressing room, the student cast shared two large rooms connected by a common green room. The green room was the only space backstage where food was allowed. We kept it stocked with paper plates and snacks, and most importantly, a single-serve coffee maker with a basket of pods.

The short couch probably hadn't seen a cleaner in decades, and the bathroom smelled like fish. The space didn't really encourage actors to hang out.

We leaned against the wall, waiting for the coffee maker to heat up.

"Is Madi going to make it to rehearsal? You said she had a bloody nose?" I asked, still trying to gauge Tori's impact.

Morgan twisted a strand of hair around her finger. "She's fine now. If she doesn't show, it's not because of her nose. It's because of me."

"It's that bad?" They seemed like they'd made up last night, but if they didn't remember it…

The coffee machine beeped, and she pressed a pod into it. "I put a curse on her, and then she had a bunch of bad luck. So, it has to be my fault, right? I don't think she's going to forgive me until she gets even."

Maybe she already did? Morgan seemed to be experiencing more than her share of bad luck lately.

I poked through the basket of coffee pods, pretending to choose a flavor while I worked out how to ask Morgan if she remembered who gave her the little bottle I'd found behind her drink. It had smelled like St. John's wort, and if she was already taking meds for ADHD, the interaction would explain her episode. And if it was one of Tori's potions, agitation and confusion might not be the only side effects we needed to watch out for.

"I'm sure she'll come around. You guys are sisters. She can't stay mad at you forever. Besides, she doesn't really believe in curses, does she?" I said.

"Girl, you are so lucky Angel isn't here right now," Morgan said. "Do you hear yourself? Are you asking for trouble?"

"Really?" I rolled my eyes and knocked on the counter three times. *That's not how this works.*

She pulled her coffee from the machine and switched places with me so I could put mine in. She dosed hers with three packs of fake sugar from a plastic drawer on the counter. The green room fridge held a half-empty bottle of creamer, a box of soy milk, and a few bottles of water. She added the soy, then pulled a familiar little bottle out of her pocket.

"What's that?" I asked.

She held up one of Tori's bottles. "It's for my anxiety. Don't worry. It's all-natural. I got it from my Big. You want some? Don't take this wrong, but you seem stressed."

"You got it from your sorority sister, not Madi?"

"Please. Like Madi cares about my anxiety. She's the cause of it." Morgan picked at the wax seal on the bottle.

"How long have you been taking it?"

"I only use it when I need to chill, you know? I can't go into rehearsal all shook from my near-death experience."

It took me a minute to realize she meant when the screen fell on the platform. Might have been a near-bruise experience.

"You took some at work the other day."

"Did I?" She thought about it. "Yeah, I guess I did. Mark was on my ass all morning. I swear if I heard 'If you've got time to lean...' one more time. I thought he was going to fire me. And he did, so clearly I was right."

The wax popped off, and she pulled out the cork.

"I don't think you should take that," I said.

"Why? It's herbal. Like nature's Prozac."

Goddess, bless me with patience. "You said you had a reaction to your meds."

"Yeah, but this isn't medicine. It's like a supplement." She dumped most of the bottle into her coffee and put the cork back in.

"Morgan," I reached for the cup, but she pulled it away, dropping the bottle back in her pocket. "Do you not remember what happened at the café?"

"You know what? You are contributing to my stress right now, and I need to focus." She sat on the sofa and held her cup in both hands.

"What if you have another reaction? That's not the drama we need right now," I said.

"It is homeopathic," she said, enunciating each word like I was some kind of idiot. "It's a calming tincture."

I crossed my arms and leaned back on the counter. "Yeah, it works great. You were so calm, Mark called the cops."

"I told you. That was my ADHD meds. The doctor switched my script. It's fine now." She stirred her coffee with her pinky.

"Did you tell the doctor about this supplement you're taking?" I asked.

"Please. It was student health. They barely asked what my name was."

"I just don't think—"

"You know what? I don't care what you think right now. Don't you have somewhere to be? Go check in with the stage manager or something. Find somebody else to help. Because I. Am. Fine." She settled back into the couch.

I bit back my response. *Tech makes people crazy. Even if they aren't already self-medicating with untested magical remedies. Who knows what's happening in her brain right now?* Nyla and Angel had written the sisters off, but we'd all been friends freshman year and—

The coffee machine beeped.

"Perfect timing," Morgan said. "You can take it to go."

Maybe our friendship had run its course.

23

R ehearsal went smoothly enough to set everyone on edge, waiting for the other shoe to drop. If a bad rehearsal means a good performance, how much were we pressing our luck if nothing went wrong in practice?

Nothing beyond Morgan's mood swings. Was she this bitchy when we were freshmen? Could have been worse, I guess. At least we were saved a replay of her weird paranoiac performance from the café.

Maybe she didn't take enough of the potion to have a reaction this time. Maybe the new meds didn't cause the same interaction. Maybe she was off her meds. *Something's off, anyway.*

Madi showed up five minutes to call time, hit every cue, and didn't even bicker with her sister.

I didn't realize I'd been gritting my teeth until I got back to the dorm and lay down. It took a conscious effort to pull my tongue down from the roof of my mouth. I rolled over and stared at the cracks in the cinder block until I fell asleep.

The next day, I got another urgent message from my advisor. I walked over at lunch, half afraid of what she might say. I did what she asked. Above and beyond, really. I practically adopted her wayward witch. Was I supposed to report back?

Wait. Maybe the manic pixie-goth did something while I was at rehearsal. Did those guys turn her in? Why would they do that? *Shit.* Did they have a reaction like Morgan? Little magic bombs exploded in puffs of glitter behind my eyes.

"Did you give this to Tori?" she asked, handing me my ID.

"Yeah, I told her she could use my meal plan," I said.

Nora sighed. "You know that's not allowed, right?"

I did know that. But it was one of those things nobody ever checked. Who really cared if your friends got some extra bottles of soda and pizza slices once in a while? We paid for the plan. I figured it was one of those things, like driving without a seatbelt. It only got checked if you were already in trouble.

Shit.

"What did she do?" I asked.

"As I understand it, she said something rude to the cashier when they questioned how many bags of chips she needed," Nora said.

"So they carded her?" *Unbelievable.*

"She's going to be expelled." Nora sat behind her desk and gestured toward the chair in front of it.

I sank into the seat. Keeping up with this girl was starting to get exhausting. "What? Why?"

"Violations of the student code of conduct. She received a formal warning and has ignored it."

If she gets kicked out, can she be somebody else's problem? I didn't say it out loud, but it must have shown on my face because Nora frowned and crossed her arms. I took a shot. "Maybe it's for the best?"

"If Tori is removed from this university, she will be completely unchecked. She may go back home to Salem, drawing the hunters' attention to one of the biggest magical communities in the country. One which has successfully evaded conflict by hiding in plain sight for centuries. Or she may continue her work with the coven from an off-campus location. There is nothing in the code to prevent students from visiting her away from the school. And then we are right back where we started." Nora folded her hands in front of her.

"Right. We definitely want to be able to talk to her more." I chewed my nail.

My advisor tilted her head. "I didn't expect you to become her new best friend, but I did hope that your recent experiences might give you some level of sympathy. She's also lost someone."

Ouch. "Nora. It's not that I don't have sympathy…"

"And a responsibility."

There it is again. Didn't I have enough guilt without Nora piling it on? Forgive me for trying to save my people. "I am not responsible for her. You know why I did what I did. I had to. There was no other way. The magic was going to come out no matter what happened. At least this way, it didn't take out the entire state when it did."

Nora pursed her lips and took a breath through her nose. "Yes, it could have been much worse, and that is to your credit. But it's not over yet. These are dangerous times, and you have a Gift. A great power has always flowed through you."

"I swear, if you say 'with great power comes great

responsibility'..." *Ha Ha. See? This is no big deal. I still have a sense of humor.*

She didn't smile.

"Do you still have the card?" She tapped a deck of tarot cards on her desk. It was incomplete.

Of course I still had it. What kind of witch abandons a magical tarot card gifted to her by a mentor on the eve of a great quest? Nora's card had guided me home and helped me make sense of the strange things I found there. I hadn't used it as much since I'd been back. I had my own deck for daily divination. But the charmed card was still in my back pocket.

I pulled it out, rubbing my thumbs over the smooth surface and along its softened edges.

I didn't want to give it up, but if I was honest, I was surprised she'd waited this long to ask for its return. Her own work must be suffering with a card missing from the deck. Or maybe not? The card she'd given me changed with each reading. Why would she need a full deck if all of them could do that?

I sighed and held it out but didn't meet her eyes.

She closed my hands back over it.

My eyes widened, and I looked up.

"This is yours now," she said. "It resonates with you, and I will not take it from you. But if you still question the strength of your Gift, you should consult it now."

She pushed back behind her desk and made a show of shifting through some papers. "Take your time. But our conversation isn't over."

I stood and turned my back, unable to concentrate on my connection to the card while I could see her, even if she wasn't looking. I held the card in both hands and grounded myself, imagining the earth beneath my feet through the hardwood floor and the foundation of the building. A few cycles of breath, and I was ready. I closed my eyes. Magic is energy plus intention, so I had to be clear in my direction. *Guide me. Reveal the truth.*

The breath flowed in through my nose and out my mouth. I could almost see the image on the card before I opened my eyes. My lashes fluttered, and I let them lift. The card shimmered, settling into a familiar shape. A beautiful woman with wild red hair bent over a lion, her curls tangled in its mane. *Strength.* I'd pulled this redhead before. It represented resilience and inner strength. She tells us we can overcome our fears and face the challenges of the world.

I cast a furtive glance at Nora. The strength of my Gift? Did she know what it would say? Maybe she'd been guiding the card all along. She kept her head down, marking papers as if nothing happened while I questioned our entire relationship. Ever the mysterious mentor.

The card warmed, drawing my attention back to it. The image shifted to a man standing behind a table, one hand raised. The Magician with all of the tools of magic in front of him. *You've always had the power, Dorothy.*

Did I, though? If my Gift was so strong, why didn't it come when I called? I couldn't even light a candle.

But I froze a bonfire. Did magic count as mine if someone else raised the energy?

Nora looked up when I turned around. "Satisfied?"

I held up the card. "I know what you think this means, but I'm still not sure. Maybe it's saying that I should be confident without any magical Gift."

She shrugged. "Your own interpretation is the only one that can guide you. Mine is of no consequence."

I gritted my teeth to keep from rolling my eyes.

She leaned back in her chair, clasping her hands in her lap. "And? How will you direct your newfound confidence?"

"They're really going to expel her for using my meal plan?" I said.

"They really are. Well, false representation, the sale of controlled substances, endangering others. There's a hearing tomorrow. I might be able to talk them down to probation if I can assure them she has ceased all disorderly conduct."

"And if she hasn't?"

Nora looked down at her hands, then raised them, still clasped. "Then I'll have to bind her."

The betrayal of my own binding still hurt. But I'd been accustomed to living an unmagical life, had been doing it for years before I knew it should have been different. It would be worse for Tori, who would remember the magic. *Her face this morning after only a few hours without performing magic.*

"You can't," I said.

She raised an eyebrow.

"I mean, you won't. Will you?"

"Is there another way to stop her? Because if she keeps drawing magical energy, she'll bring the hunters down on us. She's advertising her Gift, and they won't ignore it."

"Advertising? Really?" *She promised she'd stop.*

She pointed to the paper in front of her. There were so many student papers and theater magazines that I hadn't noticed it at first. It was just like the last one, a photocopy covered in pentacles and moons. The same backward orientation of the date.

Tomorrow night.

Not again.

"I'll talk to her."

24

Tori's flyer set the meeting for sunset on the beach again, so I had almost twenty-four hours to track her down and convince her to call it off. My phone rang as I locked my bike on the rack outside her dorm.

"Hello?"

"Come get your girl," Thomas said. In the background, someone yelled something I couldn't understand. My brother's response was muffled. He must have covered the phone with his hand. "Easy with that, Morticia! You break it, you buy it."

I twisted the bike lock and stood, processing. "What? Wait, Tori's with you? Where are you?"

Thomas scuffled with the phone, then answered. "At the magic shop. You gotta get her out of here. She's killing the vibe. I don't get a lot of customers to begin with, but nobody's buying crystals from a shop that's haunted by a leaky Goth."

A what? "What's going on?"

Thomas sighed, shifting his tone to something a little more compassionate. "I don't know. She came in here all tears and snot, saying like, 'They can't do this,' and 'I just need a little more time,' and threatening somebody with things I can't repeat on an open phone line."

I guess she got the expulsion notice. If she would just chill until after the hearing tomorrow… "I'm on my way."

I heard her before I opened the door. Inside the magic shop, Thomas followed Tori as she stomped up and down the aisles, catching candles and straightening statues before they could fall off the shelves. Black tears ran down her face. Her words spilled out of her mouth, mundane and magical curses without direction that made me shiver with their potential energy.

I locked the door behind me. Thomas hadn't been kidding. She'd scared all of his customers away.

My brother turned when he heard the latch, relief lighting his face. "Nike-be-blessed, the cavalry's arrived. Hey, look, your ride's here."

Tori ignored him, picking up a piece of black tourmaline and slamming it back on the shelf. The display shook.

Thomas performed a series of dramatic gestures to indicate how grateful he would be if I removed the dark shadow from his shop. He'd never handled emotional scenes well.

I don't know what ride he thinks I'll give her. I'm hardly going to pedal back to campus with a tearful freshman on my handlebars. Looping around to the back of the shop, I leaned against the counter and waited for her to make it up the aisle.

She sniffled and wiped her nose on the back of her hand, staining the dark purple fingerless gloves she wore. Her black hair fell around her face, and she shrank in on herself. I almost couldn't hear her when she said, "What am I supposed to do?"

"Let's go upstairs and talk about it. We'll figure something out," I said, avoiding Thomas's eyes. He wanted her out of there, not more comfortably settled into his living space, but I couldn't take her out on the street in this condition. Who knew what effect her energy would have outside the magic shop's wards?

I pulled the beaded curtain aside, and she went through without argument.

"She can't stay here," Thomas said.

I rolled my eyes. "Like she wants to hang out with you. She just didn't have anywhere else to go. They're trying to kick her out of school. Give me a minute to talk her down, or you really are going to have to be her new landlord."

"That's what she was talking about?" Thomas said. "They can't do that."

"Apparently, they can. But they won't if I can get her to play nice for a few days. There's a hearing tomorrow, and Nora thinks she can get her probation."

"You can not let them expel her. She's unstable. The balance is already out of whack since the Gate collapsed. The hunters—"

"Are coming. I know. I get it. Danger at every turn. Goddess, do I not need any more dire warnings, okay? I'm here. I'll handle it." I stomped up the stairs.

When I got to Thomas's living space, Tori sat on his futon cross-legged, her little pink-socked feet sticking out under her knees. The giant platforms she always wore lay on their sides on the floor in front of her, the laces tangled around the spikes at the ankles. Since I'd last seen her, she'd chewed most of the black lipstick off her lower lip and, by the looks of it, picked away the nail polish from all the fingers on her left hand.

Pulling a washrag from under the sink in my brother's bathroom, I wet it with cold water before I came to sit beside her. I held out the cloth so she could take it, but she sucked in a shaky breath and closed her eyes. I wiped her face gently. The trails of dark eyeliner smudged at first, but the cool cloth quieted her skin, and soon, the evidence of her tears was down to a slight puffiness under her eyes.

"You're going to be okay," I said, half asking.

"There's no such thing," she said.

I sighed. *She's not wrong.* I amended my statement. "They're not going to expel you for using my meal plan."

"It doesn't matter," she said. "Nora contacted my parents about the hearing. They're going to come out here."

"She contacted your parents?" Salem's witches really did live completely different lives than we had in Queen's Creek. When I was a freshman, even if the school had managed to reach my parents, they'd never have crossed through the Gate, no matter the accusations I faced. They couldn't have before the boundary spell came down.

"She said she had to because of the nature of the allegations against me. As if nature had anything to do with it." She wiped her nose with the back of her hand. "They're saying I distributed controlled substances."

What was in those potions? "Did you?"

Her eyes narrowed. "I'm going to pretend you didn't just say that. Because I thought you wanted to be friends."

"I do want to be friends. And as your friend, I have to remind you that Nora is going to your hearing tomorrow. And she'll try to get them to let you off with probation. But if you broke the law, I don't know if there's anything she can do. So, did you put something illegal in the stuff you sold those mundanes or not?"

"I'm not an idiot," she said.

I didn't respond. Any of the options running through my mind would have ruined my chances of winning her over.

"I gave them what they wanted. Something to help them focus. Something to take the edge off. Nothing they couldn't have grown legally in the middle of the quad." She sat back, pulling up her knees and wrapping her arms around them.

I don't think you can legally grow anything in the middle of the quad. "You've got to stop. All of it. No potions. No meetings. No spells. No magic. They think you're a danger to the other students."

"You agree with them."

"Are you going to tell me you're not? After what you did at the beach? They may not understand what you did to them, but I do. You told them you were making them stronger, but you siphoned their energy. The only one getting stronger out there was you."

"I need it more than they do. They don't even know how to direct it. Why are you protecting them? They're mundanes. Those girls might be drawn to our power, but it's their kind, their families, who destroyed ours."

"You said the hunters killed your sister. None of those girls were hunters. They're somebody else's sisters and daughters. And they don't deserve to have you draining their energy like some kind of vampire."

"Have you ever even met a vampire? I didn't take anything they won't get back as soon as they drink some Gatorade or eat a banana. Most of them probably have Pedialyte in their mini-fridges."

"Tori—"

"No. It's too late. Don't you get it? My parents are coming. You think what I did was bad? Wait until my parents find out the hunters that killed my sister are walking free. I didn't find them, and I didn't avenge her. You think I care about getting expelled? You have no idea what's coming."

"So tell me."

"The witches of Salem have been waiting for an excuse for years. Centuries. Living in a mockery of the old ways, hiding our true power under flash bangs and herbalism. It's embarrassing. It's an insult to the goddess. But now, if the hunters come out in the open, so will they. They're not going to wait around for history to repeat itself."

"What'll they do, start an open war in front of the mundanes?" I said it like a joke, but my mind reeled with images of magical battle scenes. *Please let it be a joke.*

"The mundane world is broken. Witches don't want to hide anymore. If they see a chance to remake it, to create something better, they're going to take it," Tori said.

My brother had said the same thing, but this time, it sounded less like hope and more like vengeance.

"When are they getting here?" *Why aren't they here already?*

She looked out the window, and I half-expected her to announce their arrival right then. "They're flying in tomorrow. It's a long way, and we've never done that blink-and-teleport thing your brother does. Seems like it would take a lot of energy. Besides, the mundanes in town would notice if people were popping in and out of Salem all the time."

"So we still have time then," I said. "Just don't do anything until after the hearing."

"Time to do what? As soon as they get here, they're going to find someone to blame for what happened to my sister. The hearing's not going to matter," she said.

"Just promise me you'll lay low until after the hearing. Let Nora try to help. Then we'll deal with your parents, okay?" *One emergency at a time.*

"You want me to stay here. Again." She looked at the door like she might make a run for it.

"Please?"

"Fine," she flopped back on the futon. "But you should know I won't be responsible for what might happen when my parents get here."

"Let's cross that bridge when we come to it," I said, escaping back down to the shop.

Sorry Thomas.

25

I almost got out of there without having to explain to my brother why he had a temporary new roommate.

"Just one more night," I begged. "She's got the hearing tomorrow, and you already warded upstairs. I really need her to stay under the radar until this whole thing blows over."

He quirked an eyebrow. "Is that likely to happen?"

"It's going to blow over. It has to. If she stops endangering the lives of mundane college kids with unregulated potions and unapproved bonfires, they'll have to let her off with probation. And if she's not doing magic, the hunters may pass us by. I'm so close to graduation. Won't you just give me this?" A week ago, the chance to graduate seemed all but out of reach. But my Wakening decision hadn't been as permanent as I'd thought it would be, and I intended to make the most of it. Even if I had no idea what would come next.

"Look, I know you wanted an unmagical life. And maybe I should never have brought you home in the first place. But almost three hundred years' worth of pent-up magic is out now. The mundane option is gone. They just don't know it yet."

"You want to tell them?" If Nora only knew. Tori might be the least of our problems if Thomas decided to stop keeping our secrets.

He rubbed his face, considering. "We have to be careful about this. We have a chance to remake the world so no one has to hide anymore. No one has to choose."

I closed my eyes, imagining what it would have been like to leave home, knowing I could return whenever I wanted. Knowing my family could safely leave Queen's Creek to visit me. How much less would I have had to prove if I could show them I was alright on my own? Would it have been easier to accept their help if I hadn't felt so dependent on it?

"You really think it's possible? For witches to live in the open?" I asked.

He looked past me. "How many girls followed her to the beach the other day? They weren't afraid."

"But they should have been," I said. "Before you got there... I don't think she's the one who's going to convince the mundanes we aren't a danger to them."

"Someone has to," he said.

"Don't look at me like that."

He grinned and put a hand on my shoulder, turning me back to the front door. "We're all counting on you."

I was already late for my afternoon class, which made the decision to skip it much simpler. It would be disruptive to the rest of the students to walk in now. I was doing the professor a favor, really. I could catch up later. Most of the discussion happened in an online forum anyway.

Right now, I just wanted my bed. My ugly, lumpy, extra-long mattress cave under Nyla's bunk called my name from across campus. Not that I hadn't slept well on Thomas's futon. I slept fine. But I needed just a few minutes of solitary spiraling before I jumped back into saving the witches of the world from themselves.

Ducked into the corner, I pulled my comforter up around me.

I needed help but didn't know how to ask for it.

Hey, Brian, you're majoring in physics, right? You want to teach me about quantum mechanics in your spare time? You know, just the basics of Einstein's theory of special relativity and maybe some string theory? Why? Oh, just for fun. I know I've never shown an interest in any of those sci-fi movies you like, but some stuff happened over break that I can't talk about, and now I'd really like to live a day in the life of Penny and Leonard from The Big Bang Theory. Without the awkward will-they-won't-they stuff. Cool?

I groaned and slid under the covers.

I had just over a month of classes left, one week until the play opened. If I quit my job, I couldn't make the payments on the tuition that wasn't covered by my financial aid.

And none of it mattered if I didn't stop Tori from forcing a showdown with the witch hunters who miraculously hadn't found us yet.

Maybe I should research cloning instead of time travel.

My stomach rumbled. *Did I eat today?* I dug my way out of the comforter and hung over the side of my bed, dragging out the box of snacks I stored underneath. Armed with a granola bar, I leaned back against the wall and pulled my phone from my back pocket, intent on doomscrolling away my real problems until I finished my snack.

Nora's card fell out with the phone. *Strength.*

Stupid card. Stupid universe. Stupid messages from the ancestors.

The card lay there on the bed, judging me while I scrolled cat videos and movie trailers.

Fine. Okay? Tell me what to do.

I dropped the phone on the bed and picked up the card. The redhead on the Strength card had a dreamy expression as if she couldn't imagine the danger posed by hugging a lion.

Moron.

Sighing, I climbed out of bed and sat on the floor, where I could ground myself and sit straight without hitting my head on Nyla's bunk. I put the card on the floor in front of my crossed legs and pulled myself up, stretching to either side and shaking out my hands. My eyes closed, and I let my hands fall open on my knees.

Just breathe.

The air came in through my nose, all the way back to my throat, then released through my parted lips. *Slow. Even. Loud.* The sound soothed my nerves. *Who needs a white noise machine?*

I called on Hecate, my namesake, for guidance. Too many problems fought for my attention. How could I focus my intentions when my mind was jumbled with conflicting priorities? The hunters. Tori. Nora's plan to bind her. Tori's sister. Shelley. Adam. The hunters. Tori's coven. Morgan and Madi. Morgan and the potions. The show. Angel's superstitions.

What if Nyla and Angel found out about real magic? About me? What had I done on the beach? It had felt...amazing. *Strong.* But that was just because I redirected the energy Tori pulled from the girls, wasn't it? An overload.

That I directed.

I froze time. And it wasn't the first time I'd done it.

My Gift had been MIA since I released the mantle of the Gatekeepers and separated myself from their time stream. But maybe it was still part of me, waiting to be called. I might have recognized it if I'd had training. If I hadn't been bound all those years. Who would train me now?

Maybe Adam was right. Should I go back home? Hide

behind the glamour? Close the Gate again? The Gate. Who had Adam met outside the Gatehouse? I opened the Gate. I had to. Dad's notes said. Dad. How do I get him back?

Just breathe.

I lifted the card, holding it in both hands as I waited for the next message.

Ocean waves. In and out. Concentrate on the sound. Thoughts pass through but do not stay.

And now I'm humming a Disney song… Let it go…

The card shifted. Seven of Cups. Two of Pentacles. Seven of Swords.

Too many choices. Confused priorities. Running away.

Show me something I don't know.

Queen of Wands.

Ugh. That's basically Strength again. Have confidence. You're an independent leader. Sure. Look where that's gotten me.

Three of pentacles

The card grew so hot it burned my fingers. It fluttered to the floor.

An apprentice collaborating with masters. Teamwork. Commitment. Strategy.

Time to ask for help.

It made sense. It was why I'd come back here in the first place. If I could understand the time stream, maybe I could free my father from it.

Maybe he would know what to do about the hunters.

I started the text over a dozen times.

I need your help. Too desperate.

Hey, can we talk? Red flag.

You want to watch one of those sci-fi movies you like and chill? He might get the wrong idea.

So, tell me about your physics major… What, is this a job interview?

Do you think you can introduce me to your professor? Eww.

Weirdo.

Can you meet me at the library? Maybe? I mean, we've studied together before. Brian writing out complex proofs with his earbuds in, me staring at the same old graffiti on the table until I remembered the right declension for an obscure Latin noun.

My phone buzzed.

Brian.

My breath caught, and I actually scrolled back through our previous messages to make sure I hadn't sent any of the ones I'd just typed and rejected. No. Safe. How did he know? Was his nose itching?

Hey, you on your way? SM looking for you.

On my way where? This wasn't about my unexpected desire to meet up and talk about physics.

Shit. Tech rehearsal.

Only a couple of days left before we had an audience, and I definitely had not memorized my backstage tracks. The stage manager was going to kill me. *Thespis, protect me from the wrath of an angry theater major.*

I threw on my show blacks and got ready to book it across campus. At least Brian would be there. We wouldn't be able to talk much since he'd be stuck at the soundboard. But maybe we could set something up for later.

Nora's tarot card glared up at me from the floor. If an inanimate object could say, "I told you so..."

It shifted quickly, moving from one card to the next before cycling through all of them again.

Seven of Cups. Two of Pentacles. Seven of Swords. Queen of Wands. Three of Pentacles.

I knew the keywords like I knew the recipes for lattes at the café. They flew through my mind unbidden, but I struggled to find meaning in the spread.

Illusion (like stagecraft?). Time Management. Getting

Away with Something. Social Responsibility. Collaboration.

My phone pinged another notification.

"I get it. I get it. I'm late. For so many things." It wasn't that my first interpretation had been wrong, but life and the cards were more complex than that.

I'd been overwhelmed because I was looking at all of my responsibilities separately. *I need to see the connections underneath.*

The illustration on the Seven of Cups depicted cups filled with different treasures, but they all floated in the clouds, ephemeral and fleeting. Something isn't what it seems.

The man dancing on the Two of Pentacles juggled two large coins. They formed an infinity symbol. It's all in the timing.

The Seven of Swords showed a man sneaking away with stolen goods. Who's escaping their responsibilities? Me? Or is it the theft of the swords? A betrayal?

And the Queen of Wands is also queen of the shadow self. She says not to hide the darker sides of yourself.

Is she siding with Tori? Telling me to stop hiding?

Look for patterns. Sevens are challenges that must be faced before you can move on. Pentacles are grounding. Focus on what's right in front of you.

What am I missing?

26

The upside of being late to tech rehearsal was that everybody was already too stressed out to be mad at me. The stage manager tossed me a headset and the cue sheet and tapped her mic. "She's here."

I bolted up the metal spiral staircase to the fly loft, gripping the handrails to keep from slipping. The treads creaked, and the whole thing wobbled more than I liked. At the top, I grabbed a pair of leather gloves I'd set aside and stuffed them into my back pocket. I walked out onto the fly rail, ignoring the fact that I could see all the way down to the stage through the grate under my feet.

Deep breath.

Turning my back to the lines so I could look down at the stage manager's console, I clicked on the radio and adjusted my headset. The student director, sitting at the tech table somewhere in the audience, had left his channel open.

"If you keep doing it like that, this will take all night. When I tell her to call a cue, it's because that's when I want it to happen, right? That's what warnings are for. If you're not ready, don't say *Standing* when you hear the standby cue. This is not rocket science."

I cringed for his assistant director, who ran lights for the show. *At least go off comms before you ream her out.*

The stage manager looked up when she heard my line go live. I gave her a thumbs up. She nodded. "Standby Cue 12."

"Standing," I said into the mic.

"It's about time," the student director grumbled.

It's going to be a long night.

When the stage manager called the cue, I pulled down on the rope, bringing in a new backdrop for the next scene.

"Heads!" yelled the stage manager.

I froze, listening to some commotion on the floor. *Please tell me the actors were clear.* The drops moved quickly, each carrying a weighted baton at the bottom to hold it straight. If somebody stood in the wrong place backstage…

The headset crackled. "What's happening? Let's bring it all the way in," said the director.

I locked off the rope and turned to look down, imagining some idiot freshman crushed under the descending set piece.

"Hello?" said the director. "Let's go. We've got lots of these to do tonight. Take it back out. Let's run it again."

"Safety check," I said into the mic. I didn't see any bodies on the floor, but the hanging drops blocked my view of the other side of the stage.

"All clear," said the stage manager. "We're good. Some of the cast need to learn their tracks, but we're good. Reset Cue 12."

"Everything alright back there?" asked the director, sounding more bored than concerned.

"We're good. A bit of a close call on Fred, but that's what understudies are for, right?" The stage manager said the last part loud enough for the actor to hear.

"Hey!" he yelled.

"Line 12 going out," I called before pulling the line back up and locking it down.

We ran the cue again, this time without any near-fatalities, as far as I could tell. The next fly cue wouldn't come until almost the end of the act, so I checked the locks and climbed back down. I kept my headset on.

At the bottom of the spiral staircase, I leaned on the handrail and went over my cue sheet. I had three assignments to do at floor level before I had to go back up to shift the drop again. A prop had to move from one side of the stage to the other, an actor on the far side needed help with a quick change, and then the same prop had to come back to its original station.

The headset crackled as I dropped the prop into place. Brian spoke over an electronic hum from the soundboard. "Hey, can we do a mic test on Lilli and Fred before the next sound cue? I need to check the levels."

"Yeah, okay. Let's get Lilli and Fred to the stage, please," called the director.

"I've got Fred," the stage manager said. She pulled her mic away from her mouth and stage whispered, "Can you get Madi from the dressing room? I don't think the intercom is working."

The light in the back hallway blinded me as I stepped out from backstage. Madi wasn't in the girls' dressing room. One of the girls from the chorus told me she'd said she needed coffee. "Check the green room."

The sisters' voices echoed down the hall before I opened the door.

"What is this? Don't you think you've done enough? Why are you trying to take this from me?" *That'll be our lead actress.*

"Okay, first of all, that's got nothing to do with you. God, Madi, you are so conceited. Not everything is about you." *I guess Morgan didn't make up with her sister after all.*

"You've been acting like a psycho for weeks. Is this why?" The first voice dropped, but it was a stage whisper. "Are you on drugs?"

I pushed my way into the room.

Three cast members sat, squished together on the sketchy couch, watching Madi and Morgan like a tennis match. One of them even had popcorn. The whole room smelled like burnt movie theater snacks.

Madi held the vial I'd seen Morgan using to dose her coffee. She raised it out of Morgan's reach, announcing to the assembly, "My sister is trying to poison me."

"Madi, you're wanted on stage," I said. "She'll have to try again later. Poisoning feels more like a cast party activity anyway."

The peanut gallery snicked. "I know that's right! Told her."

Madi glared, still holding the bottle over her head.

"Let's go," I said.

The kids on the couch groaned.

"It was just getting good," one of them said.

Morgan rolled her eyes. "Am I on drugs, or am I trying to poison you? If you're going to throw baseless accusations around, at least be consistent."

"How do I know what you're doing? You say you want me to forgive you, but then I find a hex bag under my bed. And some kind of weird powder in my shoes. And now you're putting something in my drink!" Madi yelled. She dumped the contents of the vial down the sink.

Morgan snatched the bottle back. "Hey! I paid for that. I said I was sorry about the hex. It was a joke. And I don't know what powder you're talking about. Was it baking soda? Because your feet reek."

"My feet? I'm sorry. When was the last time you took your hamper to the laundry? I can't even stand to be in our room anymore. You know, the smell doesn't stay on your side," Madi said.

"We're ready for Madi," the stage manager said in my

headset.

"Standby, she's on her way," I said. "Madi, we have to go."

"Boo, hiss." The kids on the couch threw popcorn at me.

"Guys, hello? We have an actual show to do? Come on, Madi." I reached for her arm, but she pulled away.

"This isn't over," she said, glaring at her sister. She marched out the door ahead of me.

"You okay?" I asked Morgan, but I didn't have time to wait for a response, and she knew it. She nodded.

Madi waited for me at the backstage door. I grabbed a flashlight with a blue gel over the bulb and guided her through the darkness to the stage.

The stage manager raised an eyebrow.

"Just a little backstage drama." I tried my best to minimize the issue, but my acting skills left something to be desired.

The stage manager wasn't fooled, but she had too many other concerns to care about Madi and Morgan beyond how they affected the show. She held the mic away from her face. "Is it over?"

I shrugged. "For now? She's pretty mad at Morgan."

The stage manager groaned. "Ugh. Again? I swear if we had understudies for them…"

"We don't?" There were so many girls in the cast.

"None that can hit that note in "So in Love." I mean, Morgan can do it, but then who'll take over as Lois? Honestly, that's the bigger problem. A lot of those girls just aren't funny. Can you imagine Petra singing "Always True to You"? Hold on."

She released the mic to respond to something the director had said. "Thank you, test complete." She looked over the show bible in her lap as she read the next few cue warnings. With the last one, she looked up at me meaningfully. I'd only have a minute or two to get back to the fly loft before my cue.

I climbed back up to the fly loft and tugged on my gloves.

When the stage manager called the cue, I pulled on the rope, dragging the heavy scenery into the air. It wasn't so bad once it got started since the carriage on the other side balanced the weight, but that initial pull required some muscle. *See? I know about physics. Objects at rest…*

Locking the line, I peeled off my gloves and pulled the cue sheet out of my pocket. It looked like I had a few pages before my next cue. I texted Brian.

"Chat on Channel 2?"

He responded with a thumbs-up emoji.

I flicked the switch on my belt pack to move from the open channel where the stage manager was calling cues to the secondary channel. I spoke softly. "Brian?"

"Here," he said.

"How much trouble do you think I'm in?" Just because no one had mentioned my tardiness didn't mean the director hadn't noted it. After Nora and Thomas, I didn't need another lecture about my personal responsibilities once rehearsal ended. *Maybe I could slip out early.*

"Meh. It wasn't that big a deal. We started late anyway. You know actors can't tell time." Buttons clicked on his keyboard.

I chuckled. "What'd I miss?"

"Umm… One of the dancers got sick in the dressing room. General Harrison Howell missed his call time because he was making out with the First Man in the back of the house. And, you know, Madi and Morgan have been going back and forth between aggressively not talking to each other and just transparently accusing each other of all kinds of high crimes and misdemeanors."

"Typical Tech Week stuff, then?" I said.

"Pretty much. Hold on a sec." He clicked back over to the main channel in time to run cues for the beginning and ending of the next song.

I sat on the edge of the loft, hanging my feet over and leaning on the safety rail.

On stage, Madi, as Lilli Vanessi, sang the opening to "So in Love" two or three times while the kid on the spotlight practiced his cue to shift colors. Then, they skipped ahead to the end of the song to practice the shift. Half of me wanted them to let her sing it all the way through, but we'd already taken over an hour to rehearse the cues for the first half of Act 1.

Brian clicked back to the side channel. "Hey, they're going to skip ahead to "We Open in Venice.""

"Thanks." I switched back over and disentangled myself from the railing.

The next shift was kind of a big one. The characters on stage had to switch over to their Shakespearean costumes, and we had to change the scene from their dressing rooms to a traditional *Taming of the Shrew* set. Madi went behind the screen that had trapped Morgan earlier, where her character would pretend to change while the stage crew rolled the whole platform into the wings. She had a minute or two to pull her Katharine gown on before joining Morgan and the two male leads on stage. Meanwhile, I'd raise the masking curtain that hid a drop painted to look like an Italian market street.

"Standby Cue 37," said the stage manager.

"Standing." I pulled on the sweaty leather gloves again and unlocked the line. The rope took off, running on its own while the heavy drop came in over the stage.

The rigging was out of balance.

27

eads!" I yelled. Completely against all safety protocols, I tried to grab the rope. It slid through my gloves.

"Clear the stage!" the stage manager called without covering her mic. Her binder hit the floor and other feet scrambled across the decking.

I reached through the rigging to try and grab the back rope before the arbor full of stage weights could crash into the ceiling. The arbor coming up meant the drop was going down, and even if no one was standing under it anymore, it could do a lot of damage if it hit the floor at this speed.

The rope ran through my fingers, making the gloves burn. But it did slow down. I felt someone else pulling from the base, maybe more than one someone. We regained control of the line, and I pulled the lock into place. Leaning over the rail, I told whoever was down there to lock that rail too. Then my legs gave out, and I fell in a heap on the landing. My heart had stopped when the drop ran away. It started back up, double timing to make up for missed beats.

In my headset, everyone was talking at once.

"What's going on back there?"

"Is everyone okay?"

"What happened?"

"Who's on the fly rail?"

The spiral stairs creaked. The stage manager's head popped into view, but she didn't come onto the landing.

"Everyone's okay," she said. "What do you need?"

I need my dad. I need to feel safe. I need to know that whatever is coming, we can handle it.

"I'm good," I lied.

The stage manager waited for me to amend my statement.

"We can't run that line again tonight," I said.

"No," she agreed. "I'm calling this rehearsal. We'll reset tomorrow when we can get some more hands."

"We're not calling it," the director said through the headset.

"It's unsafe. I'm not putting any of our cast in a position to —" the stage manager said.

"Lock it off and pull the crew out of the fly loft. We won't run any cues that use the rigging. But we have two hours left and pages of light and sound we could run without anybody up there." His tone made it clear his decision was final.

The stage manager flipped her mic off. "I could walk. He can't do it without me."

It wasn't a question, so I waited for her to decide what she wanted to do next.

She sighed. "You're good?"

I pulled my legs underneath me, but I couldn't stand up yet. "Yeah. I just need a minute."

"Take ten. Then check in with me, okay?" She waited for me to nod before climbing back down.

I closed my eyes.

Breathe.

When I no longer felt my heart beating in my throat, I opened my eyes again. A tiny light flickered beside me.

Channel two.

My headphones had fallen off but were still attached to the belt pack by their cord. I put them back on. The stage manager was quoting safety protocols to the director, who relayed them to the cast in a booming voice. The student actors must have been sitting on the apron of the stage because I couldn't see them from the loft.

I switched the channel.

"Cate? Are you there? Are you alright?" Brian sounded worried.

"I'm good. I'm good. Might have rope burn." I peered at my gloves in the darkness. Definitely cracked, maybe all the way through.

"Jesus, that was close," he said.

I panicked again. "How close? Who?"

"They hadn't cleared the platform all the way. It looked like it was going to take Madi out," Brian said.

"Shit. Maybe she really is cursed." The words came out before my brain could stop them.

Brian laughed. "Don't let her hear you say that. She'll go after Morgan all over again."

"Nyla said they had some kind of fight while I was gone? How bad was it?

"Let's just say it's a good thing they weren't in costume yet. I don't think these gowns would have survived."

Holy Hera. "Wow. Over a superstition?"

"Yeah, I don't know if theater draws the crazies or just draws the crazy out of people, but Madi is a full-on believer right now," said Brian.

I'm going to throw up. It hadn't occurred to me before, but what if Madi and Morgan were capital-B Believers? How scared did a mundane Believer have to be to report signs of magic to a hunter?

Somebody had to be helping the hunters. It didn't make

sense how they kept finding us so quickly. Even if they had a magic map like Adam's, they shouldn't be able to get from one energy surge to another as fast as they did.

It's not like they can blink in like Thomas. Using magic to chase down magic users would be pretty hypocritical, even for murdering extremists. So, either the hunters were much more widespread than we'd ever imagined, numbers that rivaled Christian missionaries, or someone was giving them a head start.

"You don't Believe in curses…do you?" *Do I want to know? Goddess, it would be so much simpler if he did. I'd wanted to tell him the truth for so long. Hexing covenant of secrecy.*

"Nah, my crazy is a whole different flavor," he said.

The lights shifted on stage, and Brian cursed.

"What was that?" I asked.

"Sorry. Missed the cue. Come down and sit with me so I can stay on the active channel. They don't need you up there anymore, do they?"

I double-checked the locks on the lines, even those I hadn't used, and climbed down, leaving the headset next to the stage manager's console. She didn't look up, her pencil gliding down the next row of cues.

Brian had set up the soundboard on a temporary tech table near the back of the audience. The director and assistant director sat much closer to the stage, script pages spread out next to the light board on a plywood table top that fit over the row of seats in front of them.

"How'd you manage to get your own table?" I asked, flopping into a seat in the row behind him. Student directors tended to be control freaks. I'd have thought he'd want the whole tech crew together.

Brian patted the soundboard affectionately, "Bessie's a sensitive machine. We can't be too close to the mics or there'll be feedback."

"Ah, yes. Actors do hate feedback," I said, leaning forward to rest my arms on the back of the chair in front of me.

Brian turned completely around to cross his arms and give me a withering look.

I smirked. "Tell me I'm wrong."

Brian looked back over his shoulder. Onstage, the actor playing Fred called something out to the director. I couldn't hear the response, but the actor frowned. He put his hands on his hips and turned back upstage, shaking his head.

"You're not wrong," Brian said. He responded to a cue on the headset and held his finger over the button for the next one.

I laid my head on my arms and watched the actors pacing the stage. "So, how close was I to killing someone?"

"I thought we decided that was the curse," Brian said, still looking at the stage.

"You don't believe in curses."

"No, but she does." He hit the button and orchestral music came through the house speakers.

"Where are my actors?" yelled the director. "That was the big entrance, guys. You're supposed to be running out here to do the opening number for *Shrew*. Where is everybody?"

Madi walked out on stage, holding her dress closed behind her. "The clasp is stuck."

"I said I would help you," Morgan called from backstage.

"No. Thanks," Madi yelled.

"Here we go," Brian said. He sat in the chair next to the one I leaned on and pulled his headphones around his neck. "It's about to get loud."

"Gee, if only we knew how to turn their mics down," I said.

Brian shook his head gravely. "All changes to sound levels must be approved by the director."

His impression of the director's condescending tone was

spot on.

I laughed.

The director leaned over and whispered something to the assistant director, who nodded and spoke into her headset. The stage manager came out on stage, shielding her eyes to look into the audience.

"Does she have a dresser for this shift?" the director called.

"Can't spare anyone," the stage manager said. "Only three of us are back here, and it takes two to push the wagon off."

The two crew members took a couple of steps on stage.

"I thought we had a four-man crew? Where's the other one?" called the director.

I hunched down farther in my seat, and Brian shifted, stretching his arm along the back of the chairs in front of me. I peeked over it.

The stage manager glared at the director. "In show conditions, she'll be at the fly rail, bringing that—" she waved at the offending drop behind her, "in safely. Right now? I hope she went home. That rigging is a hazard. She could have been seriously injured."

"SHE could have been injured? What about me? I'm the one she almost decapitated!" Madi cried.

28

"Give it a rest, Madi. You're *fine*," Morgan said, walking out on stage.

"No thanks to you," Madi huffed.

"Okay. Let's reset that shift and run it again," the director said.

The crew members went backstage and pushed the rolling platform with Lilli Vanessi's dressing room on it back out.

"I guess no one cares about my personal safety," Madi said. The lights shifted back to the cue for the previous scene, plunging Madi and the front of the stage into darkness.

The assistant director, who controlled the light board, giggled. The lights came up on the empty dressing room set.

"Thanks. Thanks for that." Madi's voice almost disappeared into the darkness as she stomped back upstage.

"Oh my god. Stop being such a drama queen," called Morgan from the wings.

Brian pushed a slider up the board and hit the go button, bringing up the outro to "So in Love."

Madi ran the last couple of steps in the dark and jumped on the platform, grabbing her prop bouquet and belting the end of the song.

The director coughed into the god mic so he could be heard over her. "Thank you, Madi, but save your voice. The music is the cue for this next one."

She put her hands on her hips, crushing the fake flowers. "I thought we were testing the lavaliers."

"Nope, not this time. You're good. Thank you." He paused, whispering something into his headset. "One more time, please. Just the outro. Let's do the scene shift."

The lights went out on the dressing room set.

"So, why am I even here? Do you need me for this at all?" Madi called from the darkness.

"I could do it!" Morgan yelled.

Madi stomped across the platform, making it creak. "You'd like that, wouldn't you? That's what you wanted this whole time. You just can't handle the fact that I got this role. You think you're better than me."

"Ladies." The director's voice boomed through the speakers.

They ignored him.

"I am better than you," Morgan said. "Everybody knows why you got this role. You think I don't know where you go when you sneak out at night? Everybody knows."

The assistant director turned sideways at the tech table. The director raised his hands, shaking his head. He pointed to the light board, and the assistant director hit a switch but didn't take her eyes off him.

A spotlight came up on the platform. Madi's face was red under her stage makeup. "You are delusional! What's wrong with you?"

Morgan stepped out of the dark onto the platform. "You know I used to idolize you? My amazing big sister. So beautiful. So talented. I wanted to be just like you. But it's all a lie, isn't it? None of it's real. You're not real!"

Madi backed away, putting a chair between them. "What

the hell are you saying? I'm not real? Are you guys hearing this?"

"It's all a show with you. *Another opening, another show.*" Morgan spun around, spreading her arms out in the spotlight.

Brian sat down. "What is happening right now?"

"So, remember when we found that vial at the café when Morgan had her...umm...episode?" I whispered.

"I thought you said it was just some herbal thing?" he said.

"Yeah, so...you're not supposed to take it if you're already on a prescription."

Brian looked up at the stage, where Morgan was advancing on her sister. "Oh, she's definitely on something."

Plus, you know, she might still be affected by what happened on the beach. Tori drained their energy. That's got to at least make them feel a little sick. And if she's been seriously trying to hex her sister? Forget the drug interactions. Morgan was probably on a magical hangover.

Something popped on stage, and the platform shifted.

"What was that?" Brian asked.

Madi and Morgan kept hurling insults at each other, oblivious to the fact that the dressing room set they stood on had started moving. The stage crew, in all black, had come up behind the set piece and released the break. They started to push the platform off.

"Yes!" laughed the director. "Thank you!"

"They're too far upstage," I said. The back wall of the dressing room wouldn't fit under the weighted pipe that held the backdrop straight. They needed to push the platform straight into the wings, but they were distracted by the actresses and weren't on their track.

Brian flicked the switch on his headset and reported what I'd said to the director and stage manager. The director stood up, leaning over the tech table to get a better look. The stage manager took a few steps onto the stage, standing by the drop and looking up at the pipe.

The platform jerked, caught on something on the stage floor. Madi fell back against the prop door. The whole frame shook. Morgan tripped but caught herself on the dressing screen she'd knocked over before. The stage weight Nyla put behind it held it in place. They lost their breath for a second but got their bearings and went right back to their argument.

This time, Madi pushed away from the door and advanced on Morgan. "You see what's happening? You put a curse on me, and now the whole show is falling apart. Because this show needs me."

"You don't even know your tracks. It's time to leave the stage, Madi. All you had to do was stand back there and ride it out. But you have to be the center of attention all the time." Morgan shoved Madi behind the screen.

The top of the dressing room wall scraped the hanging pipe on the drop. The stage crew stepped out from behind the platform and looked up. The drop rippled in the air, one side caught on the set piece. Shaking her head, the stage manager walked farther onto the stage, gesturing to the drop and pointing to the platform. The crew shrugged and disappeared behind the platform again. It shook.

We could barely hear the instructions the stage manager gave the crew over the noise of Madi and Morgan's argument behind the screen.

"I should go up there," I said.

"What are you going to do?" Brian said.

"I should be on the fly rail." *Somebody should be watching those lines.*

The drop shivered.

Brian stood, taking off his headset. "You can't hold it by yourself."

We made it to the aisle before the crew got the dressing

room wall free. Something cracked on stage, and then the drop fell.

"Stop!" I screamed, holding my hands up as if the drop were falling on me instead of the actresses and crew members on stage.

My head throbbed, and I saw spots like a migraine. A buzz in my ears intensified until I couldn't hear anything else.

Everything in front of me froze. The drop suspended in midair, the stage crew throwing themselves out of the way, the stage manager crouching with her hands over her head. Like someone had hit the pause button on a live-action performance.

I froze too. *What do I do now?*

I didn't need Adam's Gift to know I'd been lying to myself for days. My Gift didn't disappear with the boundary spell, and I'd never learn to control it if I went on pretending it didn't exist. After my little vision test backstage, I should have tried again, no matter what Nora said. The danger the hunters presented couldn't compare to the risk of my untamed Gift. Tori harnessed chaos magic on the beach, but I had been the one to direct it. My Gift had mastered her intent. She wanted mundanes to fear her, but I was the one who'd been afraid. Mine was the magic we all should fear.

My arms ached from holding them up. What would happen if I put them down?

Hecate help me. What do I do now?

She didn't answer. *Wouldn't it have been cool if she did, though? I'd love to have a goddess on call.*

My arms drooped, and I pulled them back up. What if I moved closer? Could I release the mundanes to get out of the way without letting the drop crash down on them? And then what? How was I going to explain this? The covenant of secrecy was going out the window. Maiden-mother-and-crone, I was going to burn for this. Adam's map must be flashing like a neon light right now.

Sorry, Nora, I know you sent me to stop Tori from doing magic, but it turns out I'm the one who's going to lead the hunters right to us.

At least now Nora didn't have to bind her. It was going to be way too late after this.

"Cate?"

29

ever underestimate the goddess's sense of humor.
"Cate?" Brian said again. He stood behind me, which was the only explanation I had for why he hadn't frozen like everyone else.

What do I do? What do I say? "Umm, yes?"

"What's happening?" He stepped into my peripheral vision. He didn't sound terrified. He should have been terrified, right? *Maybe he was in shock.*

"The drop was falling," I said, keeping my eyes on the murderous piece of scenery. My head throbbed.

"Yeah." *Almost definitely shock. Now what?*

"I had to stop it," I said. *Otherwise, it would have killed my most annoying friends.*

"Right." Brian moved a little farther away from me. Or maybe he was nodding. It was hard to tell without turning my head.

"It's stopped now," I said. *One thing to be sure of, even if I have no idea how or why. I mean, I know…how. How is magic. How is my Gift, which I never understood and hardly ever practiced and certainly never trained to wield.*

"It's…yeah. It stopped…" Brian stopped, too. His voice

trailed off.

"Are you okay?" *I broke my best friend here.* My eyes welled up, and I tried not to blink, but between the sweat beading at my hairline and the new tears rising in the corners of my eyes, it wouldn't last. *What happens if I close my eyes? Ugh, my head.*

Brian exhaled slowly. "Am I? Cate, are you holding that up?"

I probably should have said something like, "No. What? That's impossible. I'm just as confused as you are."

Instead, I said, "Yes?"

"Is it heavy?" he asked quietly.

I had to think about it. My arms were tired from holding them out in front of me, and my head felt like it would implode. This enormous pressure made me want to squeeze my eyes shut, but what would happen if I gave in to it? Could I focus the magic without looking at it?

"Kind of," I said.

Brian stepped toward the stage, and half of me panicked that he would be caught in whatever time bubble I'd created around the stage. He must have had that thought too, because he paused before he passed my fingertips.

He cleared his throat. When he spoke, his voice had returned to something like normal. "So this thing you're doing…is it like zone defense, or are you going more man-to-man?"

"What?" It wasn't that I didn't understand the sports metaphor, so much as I had never heard him use one before. *Hidden depths, this guy.*

Also, why is he taking this so well?

Brian gestured toward the stage. "This spell, is it cast on the whole area, or are you grabbing everybody individually?"

"It's not a spell," I said. A spell would have taken more forethought. This was something else, a reflex. I hadn't intended to do it. *Okay, maybe I sent an intention into the universe, and the energy reacted to that intention, but it wasn't the same thing. What was it?*

"Agree to disagree," Brian said. "This is magic, and you're doing it, and maybe I'm wrong, but it doesn't look like you can do it indefinitely."

Sweat dripped down my forehead and caught in my eyebrow. *This is Big Magic. How long until someone notices? The hunters from the beach could be anywhere. Goddess, what if they attack now? I've got to get out of here.* "You're not wrong."

"So, what are we going to do now?" Brian asked.

Aye, there's the rub. No. *That is the question, isn't it? Wrong play, Cate.* My breath shortened, and my heart raced. *Time may wait for no man, but it waited for me. For how long, though? If my parents hadn't bound my Gift when I was a child, I might have learned to control it.*

I wish Thomas were here. No. If he blinks in, and I've attracted the hunters…

"Cate?" Brian said. "I don't want to rush you, but there are actors in the green room who are going to notice if they never get called out to the stage."

Why does he have to be right all the time? Hunters may be coming, but a few dozen mundane witnesses are already here. What do I do? I took a cautious step toward the stage. "Okay. So. Umm. Okay."

"Do you think they can see us?" Brian asked.

"What?" *Trying to figure out if I can move without dropping the energy here.*

"Are they conscious? Do you think they're aware of what's happening to them?" He didn't sound worried, as much as curious. I'd mostly only known the creative, singing-behind-the-counter, working-in-theater side of Brian, but he was a physics major after all.

Enter the scientist.

"No, they're frozen in Time," I said. *Goddess, let them be frozen in Time.* I had no memories of the time I'd missed when I skipped myself ahead at the Reading last week. Just one minute, everything felt normal, then a headache, and then *whoosh.* Time passed. Maybe they were in the *whoosh* part now? Lots of white noise and snow.

My vision started to blur from the effort. The pounding in my head sounded loud in my ears. Familiar, but no less confusing. When I used my Gift at the Reading in Queen's Creek, I'd felt the same way. But not on the beach. The energy Tori collected had made me feel strong, more like being connected to the Gatekeepers.

Don't blink. Whatever we're doing here, we need to do it soon.

"So, would they stop aging if you left them there? The rest of the world just keeps turning around them, but they're frozen in carbonite?" Brian's head tilted. I could practically hear the gears turning.

Is it possible to be grateful for someone's calm presence and also want to kill them for it? He was so observant. Did he not see what this was doing to me?

"We're not going to wait to find out." I took a step forward, then another. Nothing changed in front of me. I rolled my shoulders and kept moving, testing how close I could get without losing anyone from my line of sight. I had to stop at the front row.

Brian followed.

"Okay, so I think what needs to happen is someone needs to pull them out of the way of the drop. And then I can release it without killing anybody." *Fingers crossed.*

No way could Brian and I lift the off-balance drop on our own, even if it were possible to get to the lines without breaking my concentration on the time bubble.

That thing was going to fall. The best we could do was keep everyone safe when it did.

Why does this feel familiar?

"So, it's man-to-man then." Brian clapped his hands together and rubbed them against each other, leaning forward.

I flinched. "No sudden moves."

"Right. Sorry. Say when." He moved to a runner's start position.

"Just be careful, okay?" *What if it is zone defense? What if he gets up there and freezes, too? What if he pulls someone out of the way, and they unfreeze before I drop the energy?*

It was one thing to come out of the broom closet to Brian. It would be completely different to awaken the entire Theater Department to the existence of witches. *Angel would never let me back in here.*

Brian climbed the steps at the side of the stage, testing each one like it might collapse beneath him. When he reached the top, he turned and gave me a cheesy grin and a thumbs-up.

"Do you think you can push the platform downstage? It's not stuck on the pipe anymore." That would get Madi and Morgan out of the way at once. Assuming they didn't fall off it when it started moving again.

Brian jogged across the stage to the set piece. "I think so. But I'm going to try and pull these guys back first. They're right under it."

He stepped behind one of the crew members and wrapped his arms around the guy's chest. "Don't take this the wrong way, man, but maybe lay off the Axe body spray."

"I really hope he can't hear you," I said, gritting my teeth against the pain in my head. Brian's forced humor might be the only thing saving me from a full-blown panic attack, but knowing that didn't make his nonchalant attitude in the face of imminent doom easier to take.

Brian dragged the guy into the shadowy space by the back wall. "I thought you said they're frozen in time?"

"They are," I said, shaking my head a little to shift the sweat from my brow.

Brian came back for the other crew member and dragged them to safety without further comment. Then he walked behind the mobile dressing room set and out of my vision. *Shit. What if he gets stuck back there?* "Brian?"

His head popped around the corner of the prop door. "Hey. I'm good. You just keep doing what you're doing."

I wish I knew what I was doing. My fingers tingled, and I couldn't tell if it was from the magical energy or the blood draining from my hands after holding them up for so long. "Hurry."

The platform creaked on its wheels. Behind the dressing room screen, Madi and Morgan remained frozen mid-argument, their shadows barely visible now that they were out of the spotlight.

If he could just get it moving. *Objects in motion…*

The platform rolled toward me. Slowly at first, but then smoothly. Brian pushed the set piece ten feet forward before jogging around it to stop it from the other side. Madi and Morgan swayed at the shift in momentum but stayed safely planted behind the screen. "This shift is definitely a two-man job. I don't know how they get it going as fast as they do."

He turned to salute the two crew members he'd left in the dark.

"Is that everybody?" I was concentrating so hard on the drop my vision closed in, a pinhole in the black.

"Yeah, I think…whoa, whoa! Hold up! One more!" Brian ran across the stage, sliding to a stop in front of the stage manager. He pulled her closer to the front edge of the stage, took a minute to steady her, and then hopped off it, coming back to stand beside me.

"We're good?" I asked. My arms shook. "Everybody safe?"

Brian paused, and I almost panicked. *Did we miss anyone?*

"Everyone's out of the way. Let it go, Elsa. Let it gooooooooo," he sang.

I took a deep breath and dropped my arms, releasing the energy with the air. My legs gave out, and I probably would have hit the floor if Brian hadn't guided me into one of the front-row seats. He plopped down next to me as the drop crashed magnificently to the stage, probably wrecking the rigging and permanently scarring the boards but hopefully avoiding any human casualties.

Brian applauded. "That was amazing. I feel like the Flash."

Someone screamed.

30

I'm going to throw up.

My head dropped between my legs, and I put my hands over my ears to drown out the shrieks. Someone ran past me. On stage, people called out for each other, swearing and groaning as the metal pipes clattered to the floor. Something swung in the rigging, clanging every time it collided with another batten. People tripped over each other, trying to assess the situation and sort out the damage.

Brian touched my shoulder. "You okay?"

His voice got lost in the noise of shifting debris and panicked actors. I didn't look, but the whole cast had to be out on the stage now. The director clapped his hands from the middle of it.

"Everybody freeze! I'm not sure what happened yet, but we need to make sure everybody's okay, and then we need to see how bad it is," he said.

"What happened was some idiot forgot to balance the weight on that drop, and it slipped the lock," the stage manager said. "Who was in charge of load-in?"

"Can we do a roll call before we get into laying blame? I'd like to make sure we know everyone's safe," the director said.

It was the right call, but somehow, he still sounded pompous when he said it.

The stage manager fumed off the stage but returned with her binder open. Facing the scattered actors, many of whom were inspecting the fallen drop and pointing into the rigging, she called, "A simple *here* when I call your name, okay?"

She ran through the cast first, then called the names of the crew members, including the assistant director, Brian, and me.

"Here," I mumbled into my knees.

"She's here," Brian clarified. "Mark us all safe from the Show-pocalypse."

"I thought she went home," the stage manager said.

"She was on her way out," he said.

If I had left when she told me to, Madi and Morgan would be dead. The stage crew would probably be maimed, at the very least. Maybe the show really was cursed.

It wasn't my fault. Whatever Angel thought, you couldn't jinx a production by acknowledging how well it was going. That kind of superstition directly contradicted the way real magic worked. The energy followed your intention. How could a recognition of positive experiences cause something bad to happen?

But I wasn't the only one raising energy on this campus, and I wasn't the only one in this building who practiced the Craft. Mundanes shouldn't mess with magic. What had Morgan done?

No wonder Adam's map had lit up so brightly. Between Tori's coven meeting, Thomas blinking in and out, whatever curse Morgan laid on her sister, and the energy I'd just expended, the college must be a lighthouse now.

But what was I supposed to do? Let them die?

My stomach twisted in on itself when part of me answered, *Maybe?*

Would that be better than whatever the hunters will do when they find us?

Brian pulled me out of it before I could have a full-blown panic attack. "Okay, Glinda, time to go home."

Right. Because he knows I'm a witch now. So, not only have I destroyed the stage (not my fault) and drawn more energy than Tori's little bonfire (not my fault) after explicitly promising my advisor I'd get her to stop, but I outed myself to my mundane friend (accidentally), who I've been lying to every time I've ever talked about home or my family.

Okay, the lies were on purpose, but I was bound by the laws of my community and the covenant of secrecy. So, honestly, what was I supposed to do?

Time to take responsibility for my actions. I can fix this. I hope.

The rules of the covenant are clear.

To break the covenant was to risk binding and exile. With the adrenaline of what I just did flooding my veins, I couldn't imagine letting the energy go, never feeling the power of my Gift again when I'd just gotten it back.

Brian can't know.

But he does.

Do I have any memory spells in my journal?

How much of a hypocrite would I be if I messed with Brian's memories on purpose, for the safety and sake of everyone back home, after the problems I was still facing because Thomas had done the same thing to me unintentionally?

What if I screwed it up and scrambled his brain?

I can't do that to him.

The hunters were coming. I was sure of it. What would they do to him if they knew what he knew? That he'd allied himself with a witch?

Maybe he'd be safer not knowing…

I squashed the tiny bit of relief that came with the

realization that Brian knew my secret, and I didn't even have to tell him. How selfish of me to want to share this part of my life with him when it put him in danger. What kind of friend was I?

What do I do?

I let Brian lead me out of the theater and down the path to my dorm. I'd have to pick up my bike later. My hands were shaking too hard to ride back.

The room was empty when we got there. Nyla had been going out after her paint call and coming in late the last few nights. Maybe her girlfriend came back from Cancun with an apology. More likely, she got back together with Emi. That friendship seemed to have benefits with no expiration date.

"You should probably sit," Brian said, eyeing my university desk chair and the cave of my bottom bunk. He grabbed the pillow and comforter off my bed and made a nest on the tile floor while I leaned against a wall and waited for it to stop spinning.

I managed not to trip getting to the floor and leaned back against my dresser. Brian moved my trashcan next to me and sat on the floor on the other side of it, armed with two bottles of water from my fridge.

He hadn't said anything the entire walk over, and now that we were seated, he'd apparently said all that he'd intended to. Plugging his phone into the HDMI cord I used to connect my laptop to a bigger monitor, he pulled up his streaming service. Brian started to hand me the phone, but I shook my head.

A mistake that had me grabbing the trash can and hanging over it. I sucked in my breath and willed my stomach to stay put. *Don't give me anything else I'm going to have to erase from his memory.* In through my nose, out through my mouth. My stomach stilled, but my head buzzed.

These magical hangovers were killer.

I looked up just as the monitor flashed. Bright white, blue, and yellow spun in a portal on the screen.

Brian turned the sound down on an electronic intro theme. "Sorry."

"No, it's fine. You don't have to stay." *Please don't leave before I figure out what to do.*

He smirked and turned back to the screen. "Yeah, 'cause I have more important things to do than hanging out with Wanda Maximoff."

Who? About that… What do I say? What do I do? He hadn't asked any questions. It was just like when I told him I had to go home because of a family emergency. He'd never asked for details, never pressured me to tell him more. He just showed up with boxes and helped me pack.

I can't use the Craft against him. He's a good person. What if I do something wrong, and he forgets we're friends?

He'd probably be better off. I don't deserve him.

I don't have the energy. Goddess, if I pull energy again now after what I just did?

What have I done?

Any second, the hunters will slam open my door and drag me away. Will they burn me immediately? Or will they torture me until I name all the witches I know?

What if they find Tori first? She won't go down easily. She'll fight them for what they did to her sister. Her poor parents.

I sniffed. On the screen, four people ran into a vortex and disappeared. *Why do people always run into wormholes on these shows? They never know what's on the other side, and they inevitably stumble and fall as soon as they come out.*

"We can watch something else," Brian said, his eyes glued to the screen, where, yes, all four characters stumbled and rolled after exiting the vortex.

"What is this?" I asked.

Brian side-eyed me but covered by handing me one of the

water bottles. "Sliders? It's a classic sci-fi show from the 90s. They traveled the multiverse before the MCU."

"It's cute how you think I should know that," I said, pulling my knees up to my chest and wrapping my arms around them. Brian knew I'd grown up in a home without a TV, but he didn't really understand how sheltered that experience had been. *Besides, a sci-fi show from the 90s? That isn't really my brand.* It fit with his, though.

"So, that's Quinn. He's a student of Professor Arturo. That guy," He pointed to a tall, middle-aged man in a three-piece suit with a close-cropped beard.

"He looks familiar," I said. "Wasn't he in that movie about the archaeologist that fights Nazis?"

Brian pursed his lips. "Yes. He was in *Indiana Jones.*"

Score one for movie night at the student center. "So, they're what? Jumping in wormholes and exploring different universes?"

"Basically. Quinn invented this machine that creates an Einstein-Rosen bridge. It warps gravity, and that tears a hole in the universe."

"It warps gravity? Is that a thing?"

"Sure. I mean, it's a theory. The Einstein-Rosen bridge wasn't made up for the show. If something has a big enough gravitational field, it bends space-time. You see it with clocks and things that go up in spacecraft. Time passes faster for them."

"Time passes faster in space?"

"Incrementally. It's not like they're noticeably traveling through time. Astronauts aren't opening wormholes like this. Nobody's ever done it in real life because the only thing with enough gravity to create a bridge like that is a black hole. You'd be crushed."

A bridge, or a Bridge? Dad's notes said to take down the Gate, we needed to build a bridge. I'd thought he meant something practical, to let us come and go across the Creek.

What if he'd meant the Time Stream? It wasn't bound to the Gate anymore. The Creek was just water now. But for centuries, the spell that hid the town had linked the Creek to the Time Stream, effectively placing Queen's Creek in an alternate dimension of time, separate from everything around it.

Time passed differently inside the Creek. I'd met my ancestors in their own versions of the Gatehouse. We'd lost Elspeth in one of them long enough for her to age decades. My father was still in there, somewhere. Some when.

Was it possible to build a Bridge that linked us to all those other times?

"So, on the show, how did he manage it?" One of my Lit professors had gone on about how the best innovations came from scientists and inventors who'd been inspired by fiction. Didn't we have Star Trek to thank for flip phones and tablets? I'd never seen the show, except for the clip the professor played to back up his point, but maybe he'd been right.

Brian raised an eyebrow. "Umm, there's a lot of talk about special relativity and gravity wells, and then he does a bunch of pseudo-math on a big board. And then his double from another universe shows up and finishes it for him."

"Special relativity?" I asked.

He nodded and took a swig of his water. "Time is relative. It moves differently the faster you travel."

"Eighty-eight miles per hour?" It was only partly a joke. I wasn't completely sure how much real science was in mundane media.

He almost choked on his water, laughing. "Oh sure, you don't know *Indiana Jones*, but *Back to the Future* you've seen."

I shrugged. I'd never actually seen the movie, but Marty and the Doc turned up in the Modern Musical unit of Theater History last month. "Is there a musical version of *Indiana*

Jones?"

He considered it. "I don't think so."

"There you go then." I sipped my water, feeling my heart rate slow down. No more panicking. Everything is normal.

Brian rolled his eyes. "Okay, so no. You'd have to go a lot faster than eighty-eight miles per hour. The speed of light."

The storm. The lightning. The wisps.

My heart rate jumped back up, leaving burning tire tracks through my chest.

31

What if it had all come together? The Equinox ritual, the chaotic energy trying to escape the boundary, the trapped Time Stream, the electric lightning flashes. All feeding the will-o'-the-wisps, who thrived on magical energy. Energy that traveled faster than light. Lightning that moved slower than it should because of the warped time on the Gatehouse bridge. I'd frozen time there to stop Mrs. Kirk, to save her. The wind had funneled around us. More than the wind. I'd opened passages to the past.

Were they wormholes?

I tried to work out the science out loud. "But you're saying time can move differently depending on where you are…if you're moving…"

Did blinking count as moving? Had my father blinked across the Creek when he disappeared?

Brian abandoned the show entirely and turned to face me. "I'm saying you'd perceive it differently. If you're standing still, and someone else is moving fast, your perception of them… Wait, is that what you did? You changed how they experienced time on stage? Cause I figured it was telekinesis."

The water splashed as I set the bottle down. I'd let myself be distracted by the long-awaited science conversation. But I couldn't ignore the fact that Brian had seen me do magic. Hel's-nine-worlds, half the production company of *Kiss Me Kate* had seen it. He deserved an explanation.

We're doing this now.

"It wasn't telekinesis," I said.

"Yeah, that idea didn't really make sense when they all started moving again, and none of them seemed to have noticed they were on pause for like…ten minutes. Nobody reacted to the fact that I'd dragged them across the stage. They didn't experience that." Brian rubbed his face.

"It's like you said. Their perception of how time passed was different from ours." I'd never done anything like that before, but it sounded true.

Brian tilted his head, resting it in his hand while he studied me. "I called you Wanda before, but it's not a joke, is it? You really are a witch. What else can you do?"

"Isn't that enough?" *Goddess, why does everyone expect so much from me?* He didn't even know magic existed half an hour ago, and now he's wondering what other tricks I have up my sleeve.

Brian didn't move. "It would be if it were true."

"What are you saying?" I almost accused him of calling me a liar but managed to avoid that bit of hypocrisy. *How dare you suggest that I haven't been telling you the truth when I've been outright lying to you for years?*

He twisted the cap on his water bottle, fidgeting it on and off. "Look, I mind my business, right? I think we both know there are things you haven't said over the last few years."

"I'm not—" *I'm not what? Not a witch? Not hiding the most essential part of myself? How did that sentence end?*

He shook his head. "No, it's fine. We all have stuff. And

normally I'd say tell me when you're ready. But after what I just saw… You can trust me, alright? But what you did in there… Nobody should be able to do that. I have to know how you did it."

I'd imagined so many ways this conversation could go, but this response matched up with exactly none of them. Mundanes usually reacted to undeniable evidence of real magic in one of three ways: terror, anger, or awe. The first two led to witch trials, and hunters, and burning stakes. The last one explained the sudden rise to fame of more than a few unexpected celebrities. Hiding in plain sight taken to the extreme.

But Brian's eyes didn't glow with a worshipful light. And his hands didn't shake in fear as he absently played with the water bottle. He studied my face with an academic interest.

It was almost worse. Visions of men in white hazmat suits examining me behind transparent plastic walls flashed so clearly through my mind I heard the keys jangling in their pockets.

Please, I just want to go home.

Maybe I should wipe his memory after all.

"I'm not a science experiment." *Why isn't he afraid? Even a little?* I finally used my Gift, affecting at least six other people and freezing a literal ton of scenery in place. And all I get is a little scholarly curiosity?

I don't want him to be afraid of me. But it's a little offensive that he isn't. I mean, did he see what I just did? Behold my incredible power! Look on my Works, ye Mighty, and despair!

He put the water bottle down and held up three fingers. "On my honor, I promise not to drag you to the lab and run crazy experiments on you."

"As if you could." I tried to straighten, but it was hard to look impressive while clutching the trash can. I shoved it away. My eyes burned, and my head still ached.

Brian smiled. "Absolutely not. But I wouldn't dare try."

"Just so we're clear on that," I grumbled.

"Crystal." He released the salute. "So, how long have you had these powers? Did you discover some kind of book with instructions, or get splashed with radioactive materials, or get bitten by a spider, or what?"

I raised an eyebrow. "I'm not a superhero."

The page flipped behind his eyes, and I sensed him mentally checking off his notes. "Right, no. So, you were born on another planet or some kind of alternate universe where time works differently."

His eyes drifted to the show, where the heroes had closed their wormhole and wandered down a dystopian street.

"That's still science fiction," I said.

"It had to come from somewhere," he said. "Nothing comes from nothing."

"It came from me. I have a Gift." *What am I doing?*

Brian tapped his phone, and the video froze.

"Everyone in my family does. It's who we are." *Shut up. Shut up.*

"You're all witches," he said.

"Yes." *This is bad. This is so bad. What am I doing? May as well set the covenant of secrecy on fire.*

He nodded, rubbing his chin. "Okay. But how does it work?"

"What do you mean, 'How does it work?' It's magic. It works by magic." *Seriously, not even a little awe? I'm over here spilling secrets, breaking the covenant, risking the eternal wrath of the covens back home, and Brian wants to talk about the engineering of our mystical powers?*

Mrs. Kirk would have me exiled, bind my Gift again, and publicly chastise me for betraying our sacred oaths. Actually, maybe not. She wasn't in charge anymore. With the Gate open, was exile even an option? If our people came and went at will, releasing magical energy on both sides of the boundary, did any of the old rules still stand?

Brian kept talking, more to himself than to me. "Something connected you to the people on stage. For you to affect them from a distance, there has to be some kind of force exerted, maybe a wave. Is it like gravity? Or electricity? Oh man, are midichlorians a thing?"

"What?"

"Do you think you could do it again? If we went to the lab, I mean? If I could measure—"

"No crazy experiments. You promised."

"Right. Sorry. But maybe. What about just a couple of completely sane measurements? Energy readings? Don't you want to know where it comes from?"

"I know where it comes from," I said. The Source of magic is the people. My people. My family and friends back in Queen's Creek, who I'd left unprotected when I took down the Gate. I'd never forgive myself if I led the hunters there. I couldn't be firing off spells in the physics lab after I'd promised Nora to stop Tori.

What if it's already too late?

How bright was Chicago on Adam's map after what I just did? I'll call him as soon as Brian leaves. Just because I outed myself as a witch, didn't mean I was ready to trust him with the safety of everyone I knew and loved.

My phone lit up. Adam. *Or, we could talk now.*

Brian was still looking at me expectantly.

"I'm sorry, I have to—"

The door slammed open. If I'd had time to think about it, I might have wondered if my roommate knew any other way to enter the room. As it was, the shock of her entrance knocked the wind out of me before I could register her appearance. I dropped the phone.

"There you are!" Nyla dropped her bag at the door and

enveloped me in a suffocating hug.

Brian scrambled out of the way.

"Are you okay? They're saying the fly system is thrashed, and Madi almost died?" She mumbled further concerns into my hair, but I couldn't catch my breath, much less her tumbling words.

I patted her back, gasping for air.

"We couldn't find you. Somebody said they saw an ambulance..." She shifted her hands to my shoulders and pulled back to get a better look at me.

The air flooded back into my lungs, making me cough.

Nyla's eyes widened. "Oh no! Do you need to go back to the hospital? Should I call 911?"

Before she could get her phone out of her back pocket, Brian started laughing.

Nyla noticed him for the first time. "Oh, hey. What are you doing here? Did you hear about the accident at the theater? Did she see a doctor? Is she okay?"

Brian's eyebrow twitched. "Yeah, I didn't have to hear about it. I was there. And she's fine. I'm fine, too. Thanks for asking."

"You were? Oh, right. Techie stuff. Sorry. I'm glad you're okay, but you should hear what people are saying! Angel and I were heading out when we heard it. It sounded like the roof was caving in." Nyla rocked back on her heels, taking in the room.

Brian's show played on the monitor. The trashcan lay on its side, knocked over by Nyla's enthusiastic entrance. My fallen water bottle soaked the corner of my blanket nest and spilled across the tile.

"Wait...am I interrupting something? Here I was worried you finally succumbed to that curse Angel's been warning us about, and you've been...what? Chilling with Netflix?" She stood, crossing her arms and tilting her head at me, the mirror of my eldest brother when I decided to attend college out of state: *You'll probably be fine, but why risk it?*

"What? No." I tried to stand, but my legs tangled in the blanket, and I fell back down. Leave it to Nyla to start more drama. *That's all I need. Social consequences on top of magical ones.* Brian's girlfriend already had trust issues. Let's definitely get that rumor going.

"It's not like that," Brian said, leaning against the end of our bunk bed, apparently unconcerned.

I wish I were that confident in my relationship with Adam.

"What is it like?" Nyla said, shifting her attention to Brian.

He caught my eye over her shoulder, and I shook my head. *I'm not ready to explain the truth to her.* Revealing my secret to Brian had come of necessity, and even though it seemed to have worked out well so far, I didn't know how Nyla would take it.

"Like you said, it was a scary situation. Cate had a panic attack. I brought her back here to recover," Brian said.

It definitely felt like a panic attack. Maybe someday I would access my Gift without the accompanying chest pain, nausea, and shivers. I didn't love the tunnel vision or losing my breath either.

Nyla considered his answer before turning back to me. She tapped my foot with hers. "Another panic attack? Jesus, girl. Maybe you are cursed after all."

32

When I woke up the next morning with only a dull ache where the mind-shattering pain in my head had been, I counted myself lucky. After all, I survived the night, and no one burned down my dorm, killing hundreds of innocent mundanes to wipe out the threat of witchcraft. The hunters hadn't found me yet.

That last word seized me by the throat. *Yet.* How much time did I have?

I should call Thomas and ask to borrow his compass.

I should call Adam and see what the map says.

I should call Nora, apologize profusely and beg for advice.

I should have put the trash can closer to my bed last night.

My stomach heaved as my breath shortened. I pulled myself to the bathroom and released everything I'd eaten the day before, and any energy I'd recovered in my sleep, into the toilet. I sank to the floor, letting the cool tile soothe my skin.

Down the hall, doors opened and shut. Students called out to each other on their way to class. Somebody dropped something. Somebody laughed. The unmagical life I'd almost had seemed out of reach despite the thin cinderblock walls separating me from my mundane hall mates.

The energy I felt at the theater, so all-encompassing at the time, abandoned me in the cool morning light. *What had I done?*

What would I do to feel it again?

Even with the hangover, the memory of the rush thrilled through my veins, almost as strong as when I controlled the energy on the beach. There had to be some kind of balance between living without magic and letting it control me. I dragged myself off the floor and washed my face, promising my reflection to do better.

Be better. Whatever that means. I can't be the reason my friends get hurt.

Nyla had already left for class. A detailed illustration of a four-leaf clover with *Good Luck* written in cheerful calligraphy graced a post-it on my laptop, her contribution to protecting me from the curse she only half-believed I was under. The joke fell too close to the truth. *If she only knew...*

Brian left shortly after she came home last night without any further requests for lab time. How would I have explained that to Nyla? *Yeah, I haven't taken any science classes since I finished my Gen. Ed. requirements, but Brian needs my help...*

My phone pinged. The time told me more than the notification. I didn't have to check Nora's message to remember where I needed to go.

The school might think Tori was a danger to herself and others, but if the hunters found me, I wanted her by my side. Not to mention, Nora had promised to attend the hearing. Three witches in one place, our own tribute to the triple goddess.

Tori groaned. "I said it was *like* Adderall. I didn't say it *was* Adderall."

"No, no. She said, 'It's, like, Adderall in a bottle.'" The guy mimed studying his nails and flipping his hair. "My prescription was out of refills, and the doc couldn't see me until after exams. As if that would do any good. She said this would work the same. Help me focus so I can study."

Tori leaned over the table, giving the guy a pitying look. "Oh, for the love of—that is not how I talk. And even if it were…what? You thought it was Adderall, and taking it with a side of antidepressants seemed like a good idea? I'm only a first-year pre-med, but I don't think you're supposed to mix those."

Nora put a hand over Tori's, and the young witch sat back, still glaring at the guy.

"You try studying organic chemistry. It'll give anyone anxiety," he mumbled.

The conduct administrator had started Tori's hearing by asking her accuser to read his report and describe how he felt she'd violated community standards. Almond Milk Bro from the café sat at one end of a long table with his advisor while Tori and Nora sat at the other. The conduct administrator and two other school employees I didn't recognize sat in the middle. They'd agreed to let me sit in *for moral support* as long as I stayed in my chair against the wall and didn't interrupt the proceedings. Almond Milk's friend sat next to me, occasionally mumbling supportive comments that were mostly ignored by the administrator.

Apparently, when Almond Milk took Tori's potion, he'd already been self-medicating with Prozac or something, and the combo had led to a visit to the emergency room to get his stomach pumped. He claimed Tori had spiked an otherwise harmless dose of herbal stimulants with a controlled substance. He turned the bottle over to local police, but their lab couldn't guarantee results any time soon. Nauseous college students weren't exactly a priority.

Honestly, after Morgan's reaction, Tori was lucky that there was only one disgruntled client at the table. Hopefully this would end her career in pharmaceutical sales.

"Miss Walsh, you'll get your turn to share your account. I must ask you again to hold your comments until the complainant has finished," the administrator said. He sighed and gave Almond Milk a withering look. "Please continue your account. You thought you were purchasing Adderall from Miss Walsh?"

Almond Milk turned pale, suddenly realizing that he might incriminate himself in his effort to take out his anger on Tori. Getting your stomach pumped might be embarrassing, but getting arrested for possession might stall those pre-med plans. His advisor whispered something in his ear. "Umm, wait. I'm covered by the Good Samaritan policy, right? Like, I can't be charged because I'm just trying to help somebody here, right? I just don't want anybody else to go through what I did."

His friend leaned forward as if his own fate depended on the response.

"Very noble," said the administrator. "Unfortunately, the Good Samaritan policy is in place to protect students who call for help when another student is facing a drug or alcohol-related medical issue. It does not protect you from issues you inflict upon yourself."

"So, I'm good then," mumbled the guy next to me, relaxing in his chair. When he saw me raise an eyebrow, he whispered, "I'm the one who called 911 when he started seizing."

The guy had a seizure? Goddess, what were these bros doing?

Almond Milk backtracked as fast as he could. "Umm, I guess I didn't think it was Adderall, exactly. But it must have been, or why did I end up in the hospital?"

The administrator's face was blank. "You're saying you bought a vial of unknown contents from another student with the expectation that it would provide results similar to those you get from an amphetamine?"

How did this guy get into this school? I thought this was a good college, but I guess if they let in witchlings with no real previous academic records, their standards couldn't be that high.

Almond Milk looked at his advisor, who shrugged. "Umm. Yes?"

The administrator exchanged glances with the other staff members at the table. When they nodded, he turned back to Almond Milk. "Thank you for bringing this matter to our attention. You may go."

"Wait, that's it?" Almond Milk said as his advisor stood and motioned for his friend to come with them.

"Was there anything further you wished to share?" the administrator asked.

Before the guy could answer, his advisor put his hand on his shoulder. "I think he's done all that duty requires today. Thank you."

The guys shuffled out of the conference room, closing the door behind them.

The administrator turned to Tori. "Miss Walsh, we have several violations to discuss today, but before we move on to the next one, would you like to give your own account of the incident involving that young man?"

She checked in with Nora, who nodded. Tori sat up straighter, reciting a practiced response. "I'm a gardener, sir. And an amateur herbalist. I started a small business selling tinctures, teas, and extracts from various plants that I cultivate. They are all-natural, and none of them are illegal. I warn all of my buyers to check with their doctors before ingesting anything. How am I to know what other prescriptions they're already taking? I'm sorry for whatever happened to him, but I didn't cause it."

Nora patted her hand and looked at the administrator expectantly.

He rubbed his jaw, checking his notes before he continued. Folding his hands over the papers, he turned to the other staff members. "Do you have any questions for her?"

They shook their heads. Most of them seemed distracted by their phones, their own notes, and a fly that kept hitting the window. The administrator eyed the clock on the wall above my head.

"Let's take a short break," he said. "We can discuss the other charges when we resume."

The staff filed out, finally regaining their energy as they chatted about lunch plans.

"How do you think it's going?" I asked Nora when the three of us were alone.

"I think she's going to be cleared of the drug charge. As long as the lab doesn't find anything?" she said, looking at Tori for confirmation.

"There's nothing to find. I swear on the bounty of Mother Gaia, there's nothing in that potion that didn't come from her," Tori said. "It was safe."

"Natural doesn't always mean safe," I said.

"Anything he suffered, he did it by his own hands. Not mine," she insisted.

"Be that as it may," Nora said, "we are in agreement that your business is closed for now, are we not? I don't intend to come back here to argue with health inspectors or members of the DEA."

Someone laughed outside the conference room.

Blinds covered the window separating the room from the reception area, but the slats were open. A tall couple had just stepped off the elevator, conservatively dressed in tailored suits. The woman's laugh sounded forced, too loud to have come from someone so refined.

"My parents are here," Tori said, slinking down in her seat.

Nora stood, repositioning a pen in her hair. "Then it's best we go out and greet them, don't you think?"

Tori rolled her head on her shoulders, stretching her neck like a fighter preparing for a match. When she stood, a faint glow emanated from her cross-body bag, a reddish light bleeding through the knit.

33

hat's that?" I asked.

"It's bad. Look." Tori opened her bag on the table, revealing a mass of comfort objects: make-up, tissues, and Dr. Bear. Reaching deeper than seemed possible, she pulled out the source of the strange red light—Thomas's compass.

That's one call I don't have to make.

The compass vibrated against the table, and when she touched the latch, it popped open. The red arrow inside flashed in the direction of the reception area, brighter than the flashlight on my phone.

"Hunters? Here?" I mean, of course, hunters were here. We'd practically painted a line down the road to lead them here between Tori's coven meeting, my superhero moment, and probably a thousand other tiny workings in between. But witch hunters in an academic administration building? It felt anachronistic and just...wrong.

Tori peered between the blinds. "Maiden-Mother-and-Crone, not now. Oh, Hel's bells. What are we going to do?" Her hand shook, and the blind snapped back against the glass.

"Who's out there? Aren't those your parents?" She'd warned me they could be dangerous, but I didn't think she'd meant to us.

Tori turned away from the window, grabbing the chain that controlled the blinds and pulling them closed. "They are. But someone else is coming. Can't you feel that?"

"What?" The temperature in the room dropped at least ten degrees, making the hair on my arms stand up. The administrative building had never felt warm or lively, but the air seemed to lose its vitality as if the space held its breath.

The elevator dinged. Two familiar voices drew me to the window. Tori and I peeked around the side of the blinds, trying not to bend them down like some kind of TV detective. Madi and Morgan stepped out of the elevator, already arguing.

"Ugh. What are they doing here?" I grumbled.

A man stepped out after the girls. The ground seemed to drop away under me, and I staggered.

What in the name of Holy Hecate?

Tori clutched my arm, her black nails digging into my skin.

"It's him," she whispered. Her eyes widened, and she shook against me.

The man who'd come in with Madi and Morgan stood several inches shorter than Tori's parents. He had broad shoulders and slightly bowed legs, dark, shaggy hair with long sideburns, and the beginning of a beard. His jeans ended in cowboy boots, and he wore a green army jacket. He did not seem amused by Madi and Morgan's behavior.

I bit my lip to hold back a nervous laugh. No one in that room fit the image of a man who'd made it his life's mission to protect mundanes from magic more than that guy. Maybe no one on this campus. No one in this state. *This is where hysteria comes from.* I'd never been so scared. A cold wave washed over me, pricking the hairs on my neck, and I wasn't sure if I would faint or throw up. My legs trembled. I swallowed the laughter and nearly choked on it.

Nora calmly stepped beside us, pulling a piece of chalk from her bag. Ignoring the covered window, she drew a series of sigils on the doorframe beside it, murmuring words of power over them until they disappeared into the metal. She turned to Tori. "You recognize that man?"

She gulped, nodding. Not just a hunter. *The* hunter.

"He's the one… ?" But I knew. His entire aura was darkness, a cold emptiness repelling the energy around him. The absence of light, and life, and magic. That man killed her sister. He burned an apartment building in Richmond with two women in it and would have murdered Adam if he'd tried to stop him.

Tori's face gave her answer.

I pulled the blind a little farther from the window, looking for anything that would confirm what we all felt. "Do your parents know him? Do they know what he—"

"He came to Salem once. He was alone then, too. But his energy was so dark. Can't you feel it? It's like a black hole. There's nothing there but anger and hate." Tori's face went cold next to mine as if she were absorbing some of that darkness.

She couldn't. Could she? Pull his energy like she had with the girls on the beach? Without so much as a ritual or meditation to prepare?

I put my hand over hers and pulled her away from the window. "Hey, hey, stop it. Just, stop for a second. Breathe."

Tori gasped, choking on her inhale. She shook her head, and her fingers finally loosened on my arm. Red crescents dotted the places her fingers had been. "I'm sorry."

Nora tapped the doorframe, eliciting a tiny spark.

I guess there's no point in hiding our magic anymore.

"What do we do?" I asked.

"For the moment, nothing," Nora said, although she didn't sound as confident as she had before. "He won't attack in front of civilians. They might not approve of his methods."

"So, we're just going to leave him out there with my parents?" Tori said.

"They are two of the strongest witches of their generation. They'll be fine." Nora turned from the window and snapped Thomas's compass shut. "As will we since I'm in the company of two of the strongest witches in yours."

"What is he doing here?" I asked. As much as I'd expected hunters to appear around every corner, I couldn't rationalize seeing one under fluorescent lighting.

Tori sat on the table, kicking her feet back and forth. The table creaked. "He's here to kill us. Obviously."

"He's not going to kill us in the middle of a college campus." I hope. He'd have to be insane, right? *Was he insane?*

"Won't he though? You think nobody's ever died at this school?" Tori practically sneered.

I crossed my arms. "Nobody's been murdered in broad daylight, in front of the entire administrative staff, no. I think I would have caught that news story."

"They control the news. How do you think they covered up the fire that killed my sister?" Tori's breathy voice raised a few notes.

Her paranoia sounded less farfetched with the hunter right outside. But I wasn't ready to give in to the panic. "What is he going to do? Set off a bomb and call it a gas leak?"

"Maybe." Her legs stilled, and she gripped the table on either side.

"You're crazy." *Because the alternative is we're all dead.*

Nora coughed. "Ladies, as much as I'd like to let you work out this fun logic problem, I find myself in a teachable moment. Notice the energy around you."

Shit. The hairs on my arms stood out. My fingers tingled. Tori's usually lank black hair had more body than it had when we'd arrived. We were raising the energy in the room.

Strong emotions are a powerful conduit.

"Take deep breaths," Nora said.

I relaxed my arms and focused on a spot on the floor. Tori and I inhaled in unison, held for a count of three, and released. The tension and the energy dispersed.

"Good. Now, take your seats and try to compose yourselves. The administrator will be returning shortly to continue the hearing. We can hardly prove you aren't a danger to others if you set fire to the evidence and launch an unprovoked attack on whomever your friends have brought with them," Nora said. She pulled out her chair and waited for us to join her.

"Unprovoked? He killed my sister. He's here to kill us." Tori's face flushed.

Nora sat and tucked her skirt under the table. "If hunters killed every witch they ever met on sight, they'd be arrested for mass murder. And then who would save the world from our evil ways?"

She tented her fingers on the table to demonstrate.

Tori wrinkled her nose but settled into her chair beside Nora.

"Okay, but if he's not here to kill us, why is he here?" I asked, holding my place by the window.

"I believe he'll tell us himself. Shortly."

The compass started shaking in Tori's hand. Maybe it was Tori. Nora closed her hands over Tori's, and the shaking stopped.

"I don't think we'll be needing that anymore today. Why don't you put it away now?"

The hunter's shadow loomed outside the window, an unusual trick of the light since he wasn't the tallest person out there.

I stepped back. "Those wards will keep him out though, right?"

"Wards?" Nora watched Tori wrap the compass in a black silk scarf and stuff it back into her bag. The fabric muffled the glow, but it was still there if you looked for it.

"The sigils you drew. You warded the door to protect us," I said.

Nora looked up. "What would be the point of that? The administrator would want to know why we blocked the door. No. No, keeping him out would just cause more problems."

"More problems than our imminent deaths?" I said.

"He's not going to kill us here. Weren't you the one making that argument?"

How is she so calm?

"Are you sure?" Tori asked, barely above a whisper.

"If you weren't warding the door, what was that? The chalk and the disappearing sigils. What was the point if not to protect us?"

"Oh, it will protect us. It will protect them, too. And hopefully, it will keep things civil for the rest of your hearing. No matter who they bring in as their next witness," Nora said.

Tori's parents spoke with the administrator. He nodded gravely, gesturing toward the conference room.

"What time is it?" Tori asked, ignoring the clock on the wall.

Nora produced an old-fashioned pocket watch from her skirt. I suspected it told more than time. "Our break is just about over."

The administrator greeted the hunter and the sisters, then checked in with his cohorts. There was a lot of nodding and inaudible discussion, filled with furtive glances in our direction. He nodded, holding out his hands to guide them all back to the room.

I backed away from the door. "So, they're going to come in here, and we're..."

"Going to listen to what they have to say. This is still a disciplinary hearing. I'd like you to emerge without too much of a stain on your record."

Tori pushed out of her seat again. "Are you joking? Who cares about my record? My sister's murderer is standing out there with my parents, and—"

"And they haven't killed him yet. You could learn something from their restraint. You want justice, and you will get it. But there are ways to approach this that still allow us to live in the world afterward. First, we defeat the legal threat. Then the vigilante. Justice will come."

34

Tori smacked the table. "When? When will Grace get justice, Nora?"

Our advisor held up a hand, but Tori ignored it.

Her eyes filled with tears. "It's been three years. I didn't—"

Nora shook her head, avoiding Tori's eye contact. "I know that you've waited, and you will not have to wait much longer. But we can't wage a magical war in the middle of a mundane campus, and we don't have time to plan your revenge right now."

I took a breath. *Now or never. I should have told her already. Stop making excuses.* "Actually..."

Nora turned in her chair as if she just remembered my presence.

"There's something I should tell you," I said.

She looked at the clock on the wall over my head. "Can you tell me in the next two minutes before they reach the door, or can it wait until after the hearing?"

I stepped closer to the table, dropping my voice. "That's what I'm trying to say. We have time. I have time."

"What do you mean?" Tori asked.

Nora frowned, and I swear I saw complicated math equations shifting behind her eyes.

My stomach tightened. But the wolf was literally at the door. He found us. *No point in hiding anymore. I should have been practicing, exercising my Gift all this time. What have we gained by playing it safe?*

I had to show Nora we could protect ourselves.

I can do this. Just because I've never done it on purpose before…

I lifted a pen from the table, where the administrator left it behind, and tossed it into the air.

Stop.

I reached out with my Gift, focusing my intentions on the pen. It hung in the air. The noise from the air conditioner stopped. So did the ticking from the wall clock. Outside the conference room, everyone held their position like a strange game of freeze tag.

It worked! I did that! I don't even care if Nora says, "I told you so" now. I have a Gift, and I can control it. I grinned.

Nora did not say, *I told you so.*

Nora and Tori didn't move.

Right. So. Time to level up. Take one more step.

At the theater, I'd frozen everyone in front of me, but I had left Brian out of the time bubble. I hadn't done it on purpose, but that still proved it could be done, right?

I split my focus. The tiny voice in the back of my mind repeated, "Stay, stay, stay." I let that part maintain my intention to freeze time in the conference room and the reception space outside.

Nobody move.

I let it play like a song that gets stuck in your mind.

Then I shifted my attention, my active mind, to Nora and Tori. A new intention formed. I reached for the memory of the bonfire and the way I'd redirected the energy Tori collected.

Release.

Everything started to move again.

"Shit!" I reached out to catch the pen, reverting my attention to the original intention.

Stop, right now!

The pen stopped falling before it hit my hand.

Okay. It's okay. Try again. Maybe pick an actual song this time.

One of Mom's favorite 90s bands surfaced first. The Spice Girls. *Stop.* I let it play, humming along. *Do-do-do-something-something. Stop!* I didn't know all the lyrics, but it didn't matter. The chorus would do. Hopefully.

With the music playing on repeat in the back of my mind, I tried splitting my focus again. I directed a second intention to freeing Tori and Nora.

Nora blinked.

Tori almost lost her balance. She grabbed the table. "Whoa. What just happened? It was like there was a glitch and then —"

She stopped talking when she noticed the pen hanging in the air above my hand.

"What are you doing?" She glanced over her shoulder at the statues on the other side of the glass door. "Are they…?"

I experimented with mentally turning the volume down on the Spice Girls. *So far, so good.* I dropped my hand. The pen stayed where it was.

"Some things have changed since last we spoke, I think," said Nora, watching the pen hang in the air. "You found more than confidence."

I chewed my lip, bopping my head a little to the song playing in my mind. I could probably have let it go since Nora and Tori didn't need my intentions once I released them. I hadn't needed a song to hold things in the theater while I talked to Brian. But the old pop song was an earworm, and it wasn't going anywhere. *Ugh.*

The headache started. *How long can I hold this?*

"Yeah, so. I have a Gift. Long story, but I can manipulate time," I said.

Tori's eyebrows arched. "Seriously? It's not just telekinesis?"

"Check the clock," I said, tilting my head up a little.

She looked. "Okay, but that could still be telekinesis. Like, you're controlling the hands."

Nora pulled the pocket watch out of her skirt again. Its ticking echoed in the quiet room. She twisted something on the face, tapped it twice, and twisted it back. Nodding, she checked a dial, turned it again, and inhaled sharply. "Time in this room has indeed come to rest. It continues as usual outside, but you seem to have put a hold on most of this building."

"What kind of watch is that?" Tori asked.

It definitely told more than time.

Nora closed it, and it disappeared back into her skirt. "All witches have their tools."

"Sorry." Sweat formed in my hairline. "I know I said we have time. But I can't hold this forever."

"Nor should you," said Nora. "While I do appreciate this little show-and-tell, it changes nothing for the moment. We must finish the hearing to discover the hunter's intentions."

"So, you can just do this? Is this what you did at the beach? You can just stop time whenever you want?" Tori said.

She's making plans. Am I going to like them?

"I'm not—" I started. *Do I want her to know I've never controlled it before?*

"Can you go back?" Tori's dark eyes were bright, and I knew what she was thinking.

How many things would I change if I could reverse time? The only time I'd come close was back in Williamsburg when I somehow watched events roll back in Duncan's office. But it had been more like watching a movie than traveling through time. I'd been outside the bubble as it turned.

"We can discuss the limitations of Cate's Gift some other time," Nora said. "It would be prudent for us to return to the present before anyone notices they've lost several minutes of their day."

The blackouts I had in Queen's Creek.

My head ached.

"Let it go, my dear," said Nora.

Sighing, I released the energy. The pen hit the table.

A moment later, the door opened, and the administrator ushered in our new guests.

Tori's parents hugged her without speaking and pulled chairs to sit behind her. Tori's mother crossed her long legs, turning sideways to avoid hitting the table. Her father glared at the table like it had already bruised him.

They were both slender with graying hair. Tori's mother was as tall as she was without the platform boots. I tried to imagine Mrs. Walsh with goth makeup and found it wasn't a stretch. They had the same face, although faint creases framed her mother's eyes instead of black, winged liner.
Tori's father put his hand on his daughter's shoulder, guiding her back into her seat before he took his.

"Oh my gosh! Cate! What are you doing here? Did you hear about what happened at rehearsal? Oh. My. God. I thought we were all going to die!" Madi and Morgan spoke at the same time, their words tumbling over each other as they ran up to me.

Nora's eyebrows shot up, but I saw those same calculations running behind them.

"Ladies, if you could have a seat?" the administrator said, closing the door behind him just as the hunter slipped into the room.

I shivered. The temperature fell a few more degrees with his entrance, but none of the mundanes seemed to notice.

"Ah, yes, Mr. Wesson. You can take that one..." The administrator gestured to the last empty chair across from Mrs. Walsh. The one formerly occupied by Almond Milk Bro's friend. Beside me.

I coughed, my ears buzzing, barely aware of the conversations around the room. White noise started to take over like it had at my father's Reading when I'd wished to skip ahead, unprepared to hear the findings of the Watch and unaware of my Gift. *Not this time. Stay present.*

Morgan squeezed my arm, oblivious of the magical energy I fought to suppress, all prior anger apparently forgotten in the wake of yet another near-death experience.

"We'll catch up after," Madi whispered as they sat at the table where the bro and his advisor had been seated earlier.

I sank into my chair, making myself as small as possible to avoid any accidental contact with the hunter. Probably, his skin couldn't kill me. Probably, he wouldn't attack under minimal provocation. Still, I felt as though I'd stumbled into a lion's cage, and I didn't want to test him. My headache roared to life, almost drowning out the conversations of the administrator's staff as they circled back to their places.

The hunter ignored me. I should have felt lucky, but all my muscles tensed for the moment his attention might shift. My neck tightened until my shoulders rose toward my ears, and I consciously pulled them back down. Keeping him in my peripheral vision, I turned to see if anyone else in the room had noticed the dark cloud arriving with the new witnesses.

Only Mrs. Walsh looked my way. Her dark eyes moved slowly, measuring the distance between us before moving from one person to the next. When I tried to make eye contact, she looked away, her focus stolen by the scraping chairs at the conference table.

When the rest of the staff had resumed their seats, the administrator knocked on the table to call the meeting to order. His colleagues quieted, setting down their notes and giving him their attention.

"Although this council will await further information from the local police in the matter of the first violation, I believe those present are qualified to resolve the second," he said. He glanced from one sister to the other, settling on Madi after what looked like a quick mental game of Eeny-Meeny-Miny-Moe. "Miss Edwards, if you would introduce yourself, your sister, and your advisor to the room."

35

Madi cleared her throat. "My name is Madison Edwards. This is my sister, Morgan Edwards. And our uncle, Mr. Daniel Wesson is joining us for support today because our parents couldn't make it. We're from California and—"

"Thank you, Miss Edwards," interrupted the administrator. "Please explain the nature of your complaint against Miss Walsh, for the record."

"Umm. Sure. Okay. Yeah," Madi looked at Morgan, who nodded and held her hand. "So, ever since we met Tori, weird stuff has been happening to us. It's like she cursed us or something. We don't ever fight, and lately, that's all we do. And she gave something to Morgan that made her act like a psycho. And—"

The Walshes looked at the administrator, but he didn't interrupt. Tori's mother cleared her throat softly, taking a small mint pack out of her purse.

"I'm sorry, clarifying point—" One of the previously disinterested staff members raised his pen. "You're saying Miss Edwards, Miss Morgan Edwards, was it? She took some kind of substance from Miss Walsh that altered her behavior?"

The staff mumbled among themselves about drug use in the Greek houses and whether this constituted a second substance offense or if it should be rolled into the first violation if it were the same product.

Tori opened her mouth, but Nora stopped her before she could protest.

Madi's eyes widened. "Umm. I don't know what to say. We don't want to get in trouble. Someone from the board contacted us and asked if we would testify about something that happened at the beach, and—"

The administrator held up his hand. "We're not here to prosecute you girls today."

Madi didn't like how he qualified that statement, and it showed on her face. She sat back from the table.

Tori's mother snapped the mint tin closed.

The administrator sighed. "Please continue your testimony, but perhaps focus on the events you were asked about."

They didn't volunteer to be here. Somebody saw them on the beach and pressured them to come here today. I snuck a look at Mr. Wesson. *Madi said he came to support them, but maybe he'd encouraged them to come in the first place. Was he the man who'd chased us to Thomas's magic shop?*

The hunter watched the proceedings at the conference table as if they fascinated him. A witch with that much focus might be accused of attempting to manipulate the outcome. But I didn't sense any energy emanating from him. Like Tori said, he was a black hole, a negative space in the field. Even mundanes' auras reflected *some* energy.

How is he doing that?

He leaned forward, resting his arms on his knees as though entranced by whatever Madi was about to say. A small wooden amulet swung free of his jacket. It looked like a slice from a tree branch with the bark still edging it. Someone had burned a dark sigil into one side, but it had mostly worn away over time. The face was almost smooth from touch. I could just make out the shape of a hexenfoil—a flower made up of six overlapping circles.

A totem against magic.

I glanced at Nora, but she had her back to me at the table. I couldn't signal her without alerting the hunter.

"Umm. Okay. So, yeah. Umm. Like I said, we've been fighting a lot lately, and I really think it's because of this umm…supplement that Morgan's taking. It—" Madi said.

"It's herbal. Oh my God, Madi. Let it go. You're supposed to be talking about what happened at the beach. And anyway, that is not the reason I'm mad at you. Why is everybody blaming the tincture? It's practically tea. Like chamomile. It's soothing," Morgan said. "Unlike you."

Madi huffed. "Anyway. Morgan has been acting strange. And then I found a hex bag under my bed, and—"

"I'm sorry, you found what?" asked the staff member from before.

Madi smiled at him, apparently more than happy to elaborate now that she knew she had his full attention. "A hex bag. A small, cloth bag filled with a bunch of weird stuff that's meant to cause bad luck. She got it from her."

Madi raised an arm and pointed dramatically across the table at Tori.

When no one gasped, she pointed again. "Her. She gave Morgan a hex bag so she could curse me!"

Nora raised an eyebrow and turned to Tori, who shrugged, choosing to follow the administrator's directive to remain silent during testimony this time.

The staff exchanged looks that ranged from mild surprise to confusion and disdain. I guess drug use they'd expected, superstitious nonsense they had not.

Tori's parents frowned.

The administrator tried to get the hearing back on track. "Did Miss Walsh do anything to directly cause you harm? Perhaps after curfew? In a restricted area?"

He shuffled his notes, circling details as he found them, then looked up to see if Madi caught his hints.

Morgan whispered something in her ear.

Madi nodded and sat up straighter. "Yes. Yes, okay? She lured us out to the beach. In the rain. After dark. And there was a bonfire."

She stared at the staff, all big eyes and raised brows, but none of them reacted. Pursing her glossy lips, she thought for a few seconds and tried again. Madi leaned in like she had a secret, even though this performance was the main reason she'd come. She flicked her eyes back and forth from Tori to the staff members. Her stage whisper had not improved. "She was engaging in witchcraft with a bunch of other girls on the beach. The fire exploded, and we all got knocked out or something. I barely remember what happened. I have no idea how we got home. But when we did…there was blood all over my face."

At the mention of blood, the staff members huddled together around the table, conferring in low tones.

Madi sat back, crossing her arms in triumph. Morgan chewed her lip, avoiding eye contact with anyone in the room.

"This is outrageous!" Tori's father announced. He stood, facing the administrator. "Witchcraft? What kind of fly-by-night operation are you running here? Surely you don't believe our daughter hexed someone?"

If I'd been mundane, I might have believed his performance. It was certainly more authentic than anything Madi or Morgan had ever done, on stage or off.

The administrator cleared his throat. "Sir, you will be civil, or you will be removed."

A security guard I hadn't noticed before opened the door from the reception area. "Everything okay in here?"

"No, I will not sit here and listen to this slander," said Tori's father.

Her mother pulled on his arm. "Do sit down, dear. This is not our way."

Her tone sent shivers up my spine. Somehow, her quiet confidence scared me more than his open anger.

The hunter shifted almost imperceptibly to face the Salem witches. Their eyes met his, and he rubbed his chin, scraping the stubble with his fingernail.

The hair on my arms stood, but the hunter seemed unconcerned by the rising energy. *Can't he feel it?*

The administrator held up one finger to the guard, who stood ready to take probably the first active duty of his career. The other mundanes completely ignored the magical energy in the room, maybe putting it down to tension, the awkward silence before a fight broke out.

"Sir?" The administrator waited for a response from Mr. Walsh. So did the hunter.

"Fine, but know this. There will be consequences for the actions taken here today." Tori's father sat beside his wife, who kept her hand on his arm.

The hunter sat back in his chair, kicking one ankle over the opposite knee. *Mr. Casual. No intention of starting anything here.* But his fingers drummed a war song on his leg.

"That is the intention of this hearing, Mr. Walsh. To ensure that our students' actions have consequences," said the administrator. When Mr. Walsh only glowered at him, the administrator turned back to the girls at the table. "Miss Edwards, erm, Miss Morgan Edwards, do you have anything to add, or have you come only to support your sister?"

Morgan mumbled something and looked down, pulling on her shirt.

"Miss Edwards? Do you believe Miss Walsh to be a danger to herself or others on this campus?" the administrator asked.

Madi poked her, and Morgan jumped. Her eyes struggled to focus. *Did she dose herself before she came in here? Bold move.*

Morgan swallowed, cleared her throat, and looked at Tori. Her eyes wavered. "Yes. Yes, I believe she's dangerous."

The administrator nodded, making a few notes. "Thank you."

Tori's father leaned forward. "I think we've heard about enough. You have no evidence for the drug charge, and despite whatever these girls have been through, I've yet to hear anything that implicates my daughter in criminal offenses."

The administrator frowned. "Sir, your daughter will have a chance to answer these charges."

"It seems to me the girls should be able to work this out on their own. There's clearly been some kind of misunderstanding. No one here appears to suffer from any kind of serious injury," said Tori's mother.

"Be that as it may," he said, but he didn't finish the sentence. *He doesn't want to be here.*

"Oh, I don't think we need to waste any more time," said Tori's mom. She spoke softly but sternly. It sounded different than when Thomas pushed someone to follow their desires or when my mom used music to influence people. But I sensed something slipping into place. Like she'd tipped a domino and set a whole pattern in motion. She'd started lining them up the moment she entered the room.

The administrator checked his watch. "If you'll just be patient, ma'am."

"I believe one of the options with these hearings is to allow the students to agree on some form of restorative justice? Why don't we let them decide what would make them feel whole again."

The administrative staff exchanged looks, nodding and passing notes. The one who'd asked Madi the questions passed a sheet of paper to the administrator.

He read it quickly. "You all agree?"

They nodded in turn.

He checked his watch again. "Well then, Miss Edwards, Miss Edwards, Mr. Wesson, would you agree to a restorative conversation?"

Madi and Morgan looked at each other. They held a short, silent conversation of shrugs, nods, and eyebrow raises. Morgan looked over her shoulder to check in with her uncle before nodding their assent to the administrator. The hunter inclined his head only slightly as if this had been what he was waiting for.

The administrator continued, "If so, we'll let you all come to an agreement. It will have to be approved, of course, and if you would like one of us to mediate..."

"That won't be necessary," said the hunter.

The administrator's phone rang. He fumbled in his jacket, apologizing as he stood to leave. "I'm sorry, I have to take this."

He crossed the threshold without waiting for a response to his excuse. His colleagues followed.

36

The silence lasted long enough to make me question my hearing. Only the ticking wall clock assured me I hadn't spontaneously gone deaf. My heartbeat pounded in rhythm on my eardrums until I thought they would burst. Maybe Madi and Morgan were Believers, after all. Did they know their uncle was a hunter? Were they scions? Had I underestimated them?

Morgan coughed, and the air shattered. "Umm. What are we supposed to do?"

Nora smiled at the girl. Both sisters had taken her costuming class last year. "A restorative conversation is an opportunity for you to talk with Tori about how you feel she's hurt you and see if you all can come to an agreement about what it would take for her to make it up to you. It's an opportunity for all of you to make peace."

Tori frowned, studying her nails on the table.

"They didn't come here for peace," said Tori's father, his eyes on the hunter, who leaned back in the chair next to mine. Her mother squeezed his arm again. He covered her hand with his but didn't remove it.

"Let's just see what the girls have to say," the hunter said, folding his hands across his stomach. "And then the grown-ups can have our own conversation."

I couldn't stop my leg from shaking, so I scooted my seat a few inches to the side.

The hunter smiled.

I wanted to throw up.

Nora focused on Morgan. "Why don't you begin by telling Tori how what happened made you feel?"

Tori's black nail polish flecked off as she picked at her fingers.

Morgan swallowed. "I was afraid. I still don't really understand what you did, but umm…I feel like you took advantage of us? Like, umm, you tricked us somehow?"

Madi glared at Tori. "What did you do to us? Why can't we remember what happened at the bonfire? Why was my nose bleeding?"

Tori shot a furtive look in my direction. I wanted to melt into the floor. Everyone in the room probably knew what happened to those girls, except, apparently, the girls themselves. And if they hadn't figured out it was magic, there was no way we should tell them.

The hunter closed his eyes, committed to waiting for the girls to work it out on their own. *Did he care if they figured out his secret identity?*

Nora nudged Tori. They must have had some conversation before the hearing started because Tori pulled herself up straighter and made an effort to meet Madi's gaze this time.

"I am sorry for the pain I caused you," she said. "It was not my intention to do you any harm."

"But you did do harm, didn't you?" Madi said. Her tone wore away my sympathy. It wasn't like she'd never broken school rules. She'd probably caused worse injuries driving home from a frat party.

Tori's lips tightened. "I'm sorry."

"Thank you," said Morgan. She eyed the door. *She's not the one who chose to come here.*

"No, no. Sorry? That's it? She did something to us, and *sorry* will just make us forget it?" Madi said.

I mean, I'm pretty sure somebody in here could make you forget it.

"What do you want from me?" Tori asked. I wondered the same thing, but the adults in the room reacted differently.

Nora raised an eyebrow, and Tori sighed. Her parents whispered to each other. Then Mrs. Walsh tapped the back of Tori's chair. The girl twitched as if a mosquito had bitten her.

"I mean, how can I make this up to you?" she asked.

"I don't know if you can," said Madi, sitting back. *Brat.*

Morgan rolled her eyes. "Come on, Madi. You're fine. I'm fine. You wanted to report it. We reported it. Let's just go."

"No. Not yet. We haven't come to a, what was it? Restorative agreement," Madi said.

The hunter chuckled.

Tori's father looked like he might jump out of his chair again.

Nora's infinite patience approached an unexpected endpoint. "Madi, restorative conversations must conclude with an understanding all sides can agree to. What do you feel Tori owes you?"

Madi held everyone's attention as long as she dared, considering her options.

What could Tori give her that would make up for the energy she'd taken?

Ultimately, her gaze dripping with disgust, Madi met Tori's eyes. "You don't have anything that I want."

And that was when I realized our friendship had ended. She'd probably stopped considering herself my friend years ago. Not all friendships survived beyond freshman year. But I'd never seen her so openly hostile. And after the way

Morgan treated me during tech, I didn't need either of them in my life anymore.

I wouldn't write off all mundanes, as Tori did, but just because I didn't want to see her destroy them didn't mean I had to give these two any of my time or energy.

"So, you will both accept her apology, and we can all move past this?" Nora asked.

"God. Yes. We accept," said Morgan, standing. "Madi, come on. Accept her apology, and let's get out of here. We're going to be late for dress rehearsal."

At the mention of rehearsal, Madi jumped. "Oh! Right. Yes. Okay. We accept your apology."

She turned to the hunter as she pushed in her chair. "You coming, Uncle Dan? We can give you a tour of the theater."

He blinked his eyes open and sat up. "You go ahead, girls. I'll catch up. You don't want to be late for rehearsal."

The sisters didn't argue. They shouldered their purses and hustled out into the reception area. The lock slid into place on its own as the door closed behind them. A secretary poked her head out from the kitchen down the hall and waved, but the rest of the administrative staff must have returned to their offices. Once the girls stepped into the elevator, the space was empty.

"Cate, why don't you come over here, dear," Nora said, pushing on the chair beside her.

I jumped up so fast I got dizzy. Reaching to steady myself on my chair, I missed. The hunter grabbed my arm.

Everyone in the room shot to their feet.

I gasped.

His calloused fingers did not burn my skin. The cold feeling that surrounded him, the utter absence of energy, did not suck the life from me.

He didn't even stand up.

"You alright, there, miss?" he asked. He tilted his head,

letting his hair fall out of his mundane eyes.

He's just a man. The hunters are mortal, mundane, unmagical people.

I pulled my arm away.

He shrugged, smiling, and held up his hands. "I just came to talk."

I fled the three or four steps to put Nora between us.

"You have nerve coming here," said Tori's mother. She'd released her husband's arm and now stood beside him, her hands by her sides. Her fingers twitched. *She'd locked the door.*

"Hey now, I just came out here to visit my nieces. They're very excited about this show they're putting on. Imagine my surprise when I discovered not only is that theater a major safety hazard, but the whole campus is filled with... dangerous criminals." The hunter looked from Mrs. Walsh to Tori.

Nora put a hand in front of Tori, even though her student had made no move against him. "I believe you'll find the accusations against Miss Walsh have been dropped. There has been no evidence of wrongdoing on her part."

"Evidence is tricky like that, isn't it?" he said. "But I think we all know the risks associated with certain lifestyle choices. Some of these kids are playing with fire."

I didn't know what Tori's parents' Gifts were, but judging by the tension in their hands, if either of them had possessed a power of physical manifestation, the hunter's head would have exploded in that moment.

Nora held up a hand. The energy was rising again. As she spoke, my arms tingled. "No one here has been harmed. We have made this a safe space for all of our students. Threats against them will not be tolerated."

The hunter stood. "No threats. I just want to be sure we all understand things."

"What is it you want us to understand?" asked Mr. Walsh

through gritted teeth.

"I was sorry to hear about what happened to your other daughter," the hunter said. "Truly."

Mrs. Walsh gripped her husband's arm so tightly I thought his shirt would rip. The look in her eyes made it unclear whether she struggled to hold him back or to control herself.

A wave of heat emanated from Mr. Walsh. Something that sounded like "Bastard" escaped his lips. When the hot air hit the pocket of cold around Wesson, a shadowy vapor cloud formed.

Mrs. Walsh gritted her teeth. Something shifted in the air. A domino that set off a chain reaction. A quick flash of lightning dissipated the cloud, but its precision left no doubt who directed it. My eyes watered, and I blinked away dark afterimages. Tori had been right to warn us about her parents.

The hunter shook his head. His eyes flicked to the window and the empty reception space beyond. Satisfied, or possibly disappointed, that there were no witnesses to Mr. Walsh's loss of control, he continued. "But you should remind these girls to be careful of the company they keep. Someone here is pressing on the boundaries of regular folks' goodwill. There's a lot we're willing to overlook, but when their lifestyle starts to put others at risk, well, we can't have that, can we? Somebody might have to step in and put a stop to it. Permanently."

My head pounded, and my vision blurred. After exploding out of me in the theater, my Gift felt closer to the surface. I could hardly hold it down. *How much longer did he expect us to listen to this without doing anything? He knew what we were.*

He's provoking us on purpose.

It's a trap.

"The school can handle any safety concerns," Nora said.

"You know, I'm sure they do their very best," the hunter interrupted. "But some things just aren't in their jurisdiction, are they? And threats don't always stay on campus. Look what happened to this one's sister. Maybe she should have stayed in the dorm. City housing can be so…flammable. You'd think her friend would have seen it coming."

The scene in front of me doubled. A loud buzzing filled my ears. Nearly transparent shades of Tori's parents leapt forward, energy exploding out of them in flashes of light. Nora's shadow grabbed Tori's and pushed her down into her chair, shielding her. The hunter gripped his amulet and said something I couldn't hear. Darkness swallowed everything.

Then, it all reversed. The shadows faded. Everyone stood back as if nothing had happened. Because it hadn't. Yet.

"…seen it coming," the hunter said again.

"Stop it." The thought had barely processed when the words flew from my mouth. My fingers tingled, sparks of static hopping between them. Around us, the other witches froze. Statues.

The hunter smiled. "It'll be you then, will it? I thought it might be. It's always the quiet ones."

The clock had stopped ticking. *Why is he still free?*

I raised a hand, watching the tiny flashes between my fingers. The energy thrummed. I felt stronger than ever, but it wasn't enough to freeze one hunter.

The amulet.

"Tell me why you're really here," I said, hoping I sounded less afraid than I felt. "Are you going to kill us all?"

He tilted his head. "Now, why would I do that?"

"It's what happened in Richmond. With her sister. It was you. You burned down an entire building to murder two witches." Tears pricked my eyes, hot and stinging.

He rubbed his face, looking at the Walshes behind me. "No. That girl really was in the wrong place at the wrong time. I was only visiting the psychic downstairs. Checking something out for a friend. We had to know for sure. She might have been a fraud."

"But she wasn't. She'd still be alive if she'd been fake. You wouldn't have been so afraid of her," I said.

"Not of her. She was a wisp of a thing. What could she do? But the things she saw… She knew things that would change the world. She told me about you," he said.

My skin turned to ice, then fire. I couldn't breathe. My head pounded. "What did she say?"

He wagged a finger at me. "Nobody should know their own future."

The hunter wrapped his hand around the amulet hanging from his neck. His thumb traced a sigil carved into it. The energy we'd raised evaporated in seconds, replaced with that cold darkness we'd sensed when we first saw him.

I shivered, losing feeling in the tips of my fingers. My arms dropped to my sides, too heavy to lift. I struggled to maintain the time bubble. If I couldn't freeze him, at least I could keep him trapped here.

But he was the hunter, and he'd set his trap first.

The energy deserted me, and everything went black.

37

I woke briefly to the sound of raised voices. Sitting next to Nora, I propped my head on my arms and peered around the table.

The hunter had gone.

Tori wanted to go after him, but her parents wouldn't hear it. They told her to go back to her room and pack her bags. To let them handle it.

Nora argued against splitting up. "We're stronger together."

"This is our problem. We can't ask you to put yourself at risk. Look what's already happened. She needs you here." The Walshes used me as an excuse to leave on their own.

My head hurt more than it had after my first night back. Whatever he'd done, whatever that amulet did, was more draining than vodka. My eyelids refused to stay open. I slumped forward, my head cradled in my folded hoodie on the table.

The buzzing wouldn't stop. It drilled into my brain, scratching memories and pain all the way into the hidden parts where I didn't even know myself. My fingers vibrated. *No. Make it stop.*

But I didn't have to hold back my Gift. There was no energy left in the room to latch onto. I shook with cold instead of power. Magic is energy plus intention. No energy. Nothing to direct.

No skipping ahead this time.

The noise got louder, buzzing right in my ear.

"Cate, answer your phone. It's Adam." Tori's voice felt so very far away.

I tried to sit up, but any strength I had left with the energy I'd expended to trap the hunter. My lashes drooped over my eyes, and it felt like I was watching the world through bars.

The next time I woke, I lay on a lumpy mattress covered in ratty quilts. I rolled to the side, knocking the covers to the floor. A blurry black form faced me, but I couldn't judge the distance without my glasses. *Where are my glasses?*

"Are you awake?" Tori asked, morphing into her human shape as she came closer.

I rubbed my face and pushed myself up. The massive headache had faded, but I felt like I hadn't slept in days. How long had I been out? How did I get here? Where was here? This would be so much easier if I could see. "Glasses."

Tori pulled them from an end table by the futon, less than six inches away.

With my eyes back in place, I recognized Thomas's apartment. *No sign of my brother. He must be in the shop downstairs.*

Before I could ask any of the questions still fighting for dominance in my disordered mind, she shoved my phone in my hand. It wasn't ringing.

"Hello? Cate? Talk to me…" Adam's voice shook.

Had he been on the line this whole time? How long…?

Tori moved my phone to my ear with one hand while making puppet-talking gestures with her other. She leaned back a little to look into my eyes, her expression more like Dr. Bear's than the sullen student at the hearing.

"Cate," Adam said louder.

"I'm here." My voice felt old and disused.

"What's happening? Are you okay? Where's Thomas? Why did you give me this phone if you're not going to answer it?" A door closed on his side of the call, and rustling noises almost covered the last question. It sounded like he'd braced the phone on his shoulder to shift things around on his desk.

I took a breath. "I'm okay."

Neither of us believed me.

"Are you alone?" he asked.

"I'm with a friend," I said.

Tori smiled, but she still looked nervous.

"What happened? Last night, the map lit up so brightly it nearly burned the paper, and then just now, it flashed and turned black," Adam said.

I closed my eyes. "So, last night was me. And just now... Part of that was me, too."

"Cate—" I could feel the reprimand coming.

"There was a hunter."

"Where is your brother? He has the kynigolabe. He should have known—"

"He doesn't have it right now. He gave it to Tori." I opened my eyes, and she nodded. She still had it. That didn't answer the question of Thomas's location.

Please, Goddess, let Thomas stay in the magic shop and let those wards protect him. The hunter didn't come for him. He came for me.

"Are you safe?" Adam asked.

I couldn't lie to him. He'd sense it, anyway. A tear rolled down my cheek, and I swatted it away. "No."

Tori sank into Thomas's recliner, twisting her necklace around her finger.

"Show me where you are," Adam demanded.

I reversed the camera and panned the room, making sure he saw where all the furniture sat. When I got to the open space in front of the door, he blinked. Adam disappeared from the screen on my phone a split second before the call ended.

Then he stood in front of me.

My phone bounced on the futon. His arms folded around me, his face buried in my hair. He smelled like dew and freshly turned soil and the garden behind my mother's house. I cried into his shoulder until mine ached from heaving.

Adam sat back, his hands still on my shoulders. "You're okay."

It wasn't a question this time.

I sniffled. I was. I would be. I hadn't realized how badly I needed to hear someone else say it.

"So, umm. Hi," Tori said. "We met on the phone? I'm Tori."

Adam shifted on the futon so he could face her. His hand slipped from my shoulder to my knee. "Yes. Sorry about the sudden appearance. Normally, I would have tried to arrive on the other side of the door and knocked. But it's harder when I've never seen it."

Tori nodded as if this explanation of casual teleportation made perfect sense.

Adam squeezed my knee and released it. He stood and held out his hand to Tori. "Thanks for looking out for her. I'm Adam."

She grinned and leaned forward to shake.

"Pleasure, I'm sure," she said in her familiar, breathy voice.

Adam dragged a chair from Thomas's kitchen counter and sat in it backward. "Tell me about the hunter."

Tori and I explained the broad strokes of her hearing up to the surprise appearance of my former friends and their terrifying uncle.

"It was like all of the air was sucked out of the room. The temperature dropped out of nowhere. Was it like that at Shelley's?" I asked.

Adam shook his head. "No, but the hunters were gone when I got there. I just found what they'd done."

"You said they drew a sigil on the window? Would you recognize it again?" I pulled up the notes app on my phone and drew the shape I'd seen on the hunter's amulet.

He took the phone and tapped the screen, enlarging the image, turning it. "That could be it. It was a long time ago, and the windows were smudged, but yeah. That looks right. He was here?"

"He wore that sigil on an amulet around his neck. I think it made him immune to my Gift."

Adam's eyebrows shot up. "You used your Gift?"

The light twinkled in his eyes. He seemed torn between pride and concern. After all, he'd never actually seen me use my Gift since I released the mantle of the Gatekeeper, and I'd promised not to raise magical energy until we knew we were safe from the hunters. I wanted to tell him how it felt to direct the energy myself instead of acting as a conduit for my ancestors. The strength that flowed through me despite the pain it caused. *Maybe it would get easier with practice.* But there was more to tell, and the next part was harder.

"I froze time in that room," I said. "But it didn't affect him."

"Did he hurt you?" Adam gripped the back of the chair like it might escape as the hunter had.

I shook my head. "No. He wasn't there for that. Not this time. I think it was a test. A trap. He wanted to see what we could do. What we would do. He provoked us, but he was protected by that amulet."

"If he wasn't there to kill you, why is he here then? There's no way he missed the energy you all have been throwing around." He said it without judgment, but I still felt judged. I'd taken stupid risks since leaving Queen's Creek, but some of them were necessary.

Tori looked down at her fingers, wrapping and unwrapping the chain around them until her fingertips turned purple.

"He learned something from Shelley. Something about the future. Something about me," I said.

"He told you that?"

I nodded. "I think she had a vision before he killed her. Maybe it's why he killed her."

"We could ask her," Tori said.

"What?" I said. Adam met my eyes.

"How?" Adam asked, taking my hand across the space between us.

Neither of us had much experience having conversations with the dead. The shades we'd faced on the hill in Queen's Creek nearly overpowered him. The failing boundary spell weakened the veil between worlds, ours and the dead, ours and the fae, ours and who knew, really. But it was a one-time pre-magical apocalypse event. It didn't seem wise to tear new holes with magical energy so unstable.

Tori grinned and clambered out of the recliner. "One sec, I'm sure I saw it downstairs."

She disappeared down to the magic shop, leaving the door open and the beaded curtain swinging behind her.

Thomas's voice floated up to us, "Hey, what are you doing with that? You can't just—I'm going to expect payment!"

Tori emerged with a beat-up board game, still wrapped in plastic. "See? I knew he'd have one. We'll use this. Don't they have Ouija where you come from?"

We did not, but I'd seen the board before. One of my freshman-year hall mates had pulled it out almost every night in October. There'd been a scary movie night that featured it as well. I was pretty sure the girls pushed the planchette themselves.

Tori unpacked the board on the low table in front of me and sat cross-legged behind it.

"Have you done this before?" Adam asked.

She raised an eyebrow. "Sure. You haven't? It's a staple in Salem. Every sleepover ends in a séance. Don't you guys come from, like, a whole secret town full of witches? And you don't talk to the ancestors? No wonder you have such bad luck."

"We talk to the ancestors," I said, though our rituals tended to be one-sided, an offering exchanged for signs and portents. Our relationship with the dead was much more formal than a board game.

Adam picked up the planchette, turning it in his fingers. "And they answer you? You can have a complete conversation with anyone who's passed?"

Tori plucked the game piece from his hand. "Almost anyone. Sometimes, the spirits don't respond. I don't know why. Maybe they're too far from this plane." She looked down, setting the planchette in the middle of the board.

Has she talked to Grace? Is that how she recognized the hunter?

Adam rubbed his face, casting me a sidelong glance.

"Come, sit down here." Tori patted the floor beside her.

I wanted to say, "What's the worst that could happen?" But I didn't want to know the answer. Plus, I could hear Nyla and Angel screaming about curses from the back of my mind.

"Is it safe?" I asked instead.

"Of course," she said. Then she looked around the room. "Actually..."

She walked into the kitchen, pulled out a drawer, and took

out five tea lights. *How long had she been here before I woke up?*

Tori arranged the candles in a circle around the board and lit them, calling the quarters. "There. A protective circle. No runaway spirits. Satisfied?"

Adam and I sat across from her.

"So, you want to call the girl the hunter killed, right? She's the one he was going after when my sister died?" Tori's demeanor changed when she made the distinction. She adopted a distanced tone.

"Can you do that?" I asked.

"Do you have anything of hers? Or anything she touched?" She looked meaningfully at Adam.

"No," he said, rubbing my back. "How will you make the connection?"

She thought for a moment, looking around the room. Then she shot up and grabbed Dr. Bear from her bag.

I raised an eyebrow. "Wasn't that…?"

She settled back down, fluffing the bear in front of her so its feet touched the board. "He belonged to Grace. But she lived in the same building. It's the closest thing we've got."

Adam spoke softly. "If it belonged to your sister, won't it call her instead?"

Tori's lips tightened, smearing the black lipstick so the pink underneath showed through. Her eyes glistened. "Maybe."

38

Before we started, Tori propped her phone on a sugar skull pop socket, pointing it at the board. "So we don't have to stop to take notes. Ruins the flow."

We each placed two fingers on the plastic triangle.

"Open yourself to the universe," Tori whispered. "Let its energy flow through you. Concentrate on the person you want to reach, but don't pull. Let them come."

She took a long breath and rolled her head around, batting her lashes closed. "Close your eyes."

I peeked at Adam. He shrugged and closed his eyes.

In the darkness behind my eyelids, I watched floating specks cross my vision. I tried to make shapes of the patterns the candlelight drew. *Concentrate on the person you want to reach.*

But I'd never met Shelley.

I really wanted to talk to my dad, but he wasn't dead. I wouldn't find him on the other side of the veil. He was somewhere else. I'd heard his voice in Queen's Creek, spoken with him in the Gatehouse, although he wasn't physically there with me. If I went back to the time stream, could I reach him again? Brian's Einstein-Rosen bridge theory. Bending time around a gravitational field. Brian didn't think it was possible to control gravity that way, but he hadn't seen everything magic could do. The will-o'-the-wisps that fed on magical energy. The storms that shot purple lightning. The way Mrs. Kirk lifted the creek from its bed or the way Adam manipulated the land, raising the hill without making the earth quake.

No wonder the hunters feared us.

Feared me.

What had Shelley told Daniel Wesson that made him think I would change the world? I'd already fulfilled Alice's prophecy by bringing down the Gate. What more could Fate ask of me? Who was I? Prophecy Girl?

The planchette rattled.

I nearly lost my connection when it zoomed across the board. My eyes popped open. The pointer crossed the entire alphabet before returning to the letter M. It hovered there for a moment and took off again, dragging our fingers with it.

The red light on Tori's phone stayed lit. Hopefully, it would catch the message. Whoever moved the planchette went too fast for me to read.

Tori kept her eyes closed, her fingers lightly but firmly planted on the game piece. Adam's eyebrows pinched together in concentration, but he kept his eyes closed as well, following the rules as always. He would know if she lied about moving the planchette afterward.

The invisible force dragged the planchette across the board one more time before falling still.

"Is it done?" Adam whispered.

"Yes." Tori snapped open her eyes and leaned back to grab a notebook and a pen from her bag. That thing had to be charmed. It didn't look big enough to hold all of that.

"Now what?" I asked.

"Now we play it back and read the message." Tori grabbed

the phone, pushed in the pop socket, and laid it flat on the board where we could all see it. She swiped to the camera.

The video showed us all sitting down and reaching for the board. At first, nothing happened. Then, just like it had a few minutes ago, the planchette leapt to life. I saw myself jump at the unexpected movement. In the video, Adam twitched, raising his head a little, but his eyes stayed closed. The little triangle circled the board, whirling fast until it circled the same three letters. It stopped above the M.

We had to stop and start the video several times to work out the whole message, but eventually, Tori squinted at the page she'd written, added a few slashes, and dropped it on the board facing Adam and me.

"M A G I C / W A S / N E V E R / M E A N T / T O / B E / CONTAINED"

I'd heard that before. My father's last letter.

"Who was the message from?" I asked, struggling to slow my racing heart. "Was it your sister?"

Tori tapped her pen on the notebook. "I'm not sure. It didn't feel like her. Did you concentrate on someone? Were you specific?"

"Yes," said Adam.

"I tried," I said at the same time. But had I, really? My heart stumbled at the possibility of making the connection I'd dreamed about for the past two weeks. *What if that was my father?*

What if it wasn't? I didn't believe in demons, and I couldn't think of a reason any of our ancestors would purposefully mislead us or do us harm, but wasn't that how all of those movies started?

How did this thing really work, anyway? We sat there, directing our energy through the veil, calling to people who'd crossed over. How did the magic, the energy, the universe know who to reach? It didn't feel like a direct line. More like a message in a bottle. A flare in the darkness. How could we possibly know for sure who answered?

They were watching me. *Get control of yourself.* "I'm sorry. I never met her. There wasn't much for me to hold on to. Can we try again?"

Adam looked at the bear. "What if we focus on Grace this time? Can we ask her to lead Shelley to us?"

Tori considered it. "I think this will work better if I give you something to ground you to her."

She reached for her bag again, pulling out a picture I'd seen before, where she and her sister smiled together. She handed it to me, then sat down and plopped Dr. Bear into Adam's lap. "Here. You guys hold those, and I have my necklace. Focus on the object and try to imagine meeting the person it represents."

She twisted the necklace with her fingers, rubbing a smooth spot with her thumb.

Adam made eye contact with Dr. Bear, then turned him a bit to the side, taking in the details of his white jacket and the embroidered emblems on his fuzzy feet. The small burn mark on one paw. "How long have you had this?"

"My parents gave him to me after the funeral. He was a graduation gift for Grace when she decided to go pre-med," Tori said. "I guess they figured they could get a two-fer out of it. Still going to have a Dr. Walsh in the family."

"There's something inside," Adam said.

Tori raised an eyebrow. "What? Oh, yeah, he's probably got one of those heartbeat things in there. I let the battery run out. It was creepy."

Adam gently pulled off the doctor's jacket. "No, it's something else."

He ran a finger down the seam in the bear's back.

"It's his Gift," I explained. "Adam's element is earth. He's always been good at finding things. He sees what's beneath the surface."

Tori's mouth quirked to the side. "Okay, but I'm telling you. I've had that guy for three years. There's nothing in there but a little glowy heart thing and a battery pack."

"Do you mind if I?" Adam asked, prizing the Velcro seam apart.

"Go ahead," she said.

He pulled out a battery pack first, and Tori nodded. But the heart that came out next didn't look like the plastic ones from the toy shop. Tarnished silver covered a locket almost the size of his palm. He rubbed a thumb over the carved design.

"Okay, that is not what I thought was in there," Tori said, reaching for it.

Adam held it out, his palm open, but his eyes never left it.

"Does it look familiar?" I asked.

"No," said Tori. She held it up to the light from the candles.

"Yes," said Adam. "It was Shelley's."

The sadness in his eyes almost broke me. *Should I be more jealous because of what her loss has done to him? Or was I being unforgivably cruel to feel bitterness over someone he'd cared about? I believed him when he told me nothing happened between them. So why did I feel this way? If this was how Jasmine felt about me, I might need to show her more sympathy.*

"What's it doing in Grace's bear?" Tori said. She ran a fingernail around the edge of the locket until something popped. The heart opened, and a small slip of paper dropped out. Swirls of writing covered the tiny page.

"Maybe we don't need to try the board again," I said. "Shelley found another way to send us a message."

Adam picked up the paper and flattened it on the board in front of him. Four lines of shimmering text flickered in the candlelight. The glittery ink smeared in a few places, but he read out the words:

*"True… something… freedom shall be found
when the… Witch no more is bound.
For through her strength shall others rise,
a sister's love will bind the ties."*

"It's another prophecy," I said.

"What does it mean?" said Tori.

"How did it get in the bear?" Adam wondered.

Something the hunter said…

"She saw it coming," I said. "She must have. Maybe not soon enough to stop it, but soon enough to save this. To hide it."

"They found him under her bed," Tori said. "That's why he didn't burn. Grace crawled under there with him. She would have survived, but the roof collapsed. She couldn't get out. It was the smoke that took her."

"Shelley must have thought she'd be safe there," Adam said.

"Yeah, well. She was wrong, wasn't she?" Tori said.

"She must have been terrified," Adam said.

It would have been terrifying for both of them. Would it be worse to face your enemy and burn or to hide, slowly suffocating as much from the fear as the smoke? My throat tightened.

"I can't hide anymore," I said. "They came for her because she saw a future of freedom for witches. But I'm the one they'll come for next. I have to be strong now."

For a split second, I expected some kind of dramatic underscore to emphasize my lines. Maybe I'd spent too much time around Madi at the theater. I didn't get a spotlight for my moment of realization. Not even a comic lightbulb effect.

"It doesn't have to be you this time," Adam said, but doubt deepened his voice.

"Why would it be you?" Tori asked. "There's nothing

wrong with your Gift. This says *when the witch no more is bound,* so, like…it's got to be somebody who's been through a binding."

"She was," Adam said. "Her parents bound her Gift years ago. She only got it back about a week ago."

"Okay…and what did you mean about *this time*? It doesn't have to be her *this time*? How many prophecies have you enacted?" she asked.

"Just one," I said. "Or, I guess, two now."

"It doesn't have to be you," Adam said again.

"Have you been bound?" I asked.

He looked away.

I turned to Tori, "Have you?"

She crossed her arms. "I'd like to see my parents try that."

I turned back to Adam. "Who else has recently freed a bunch of incarcerated witches? We gave Queen's Creek their freedom, but if we don't stop the hunters, they're not going to keep it."

Tori squinted at me. "Maybe you are the Chosen One."

"Again." The weight of the world descended back to its usual place on my shoulders.

39

nd the hunters already know. That's why they came here. Somehow, they've already heard the prophecy," Adam guessed.

"So, how do we stop them?" said Tori.

"Did you bring the compass? Where are they now?" I asked.

Tori pulled the compass out of her bag. It popped open on its own, glowing red like it had at the hearing. The arrow spun.

"Shit. What does that mean? Are they here?" I asked.

"Where's Thomas? Are the wards in place?" said Adam.

As if summoned by the mention of his name, my brother pounded up the stairs. The beaded curtain cascaded into the walls. "Good, you're awake. We've got trouble."

"What's going on?" I looked past him, but no one followed.

Thomas put his hands on his hips and bent forward to catch his breath. "A guy outside says he's from the state fire marshal's office. Says I'm overdue for my annual inspection."

"Are you?" *Please let the easiest explanation be the right one.*

Thomas straightened, his eyebrows knitting together. "I am

a model citizen, thank you. But I need to show him the report from last year, or he won't go away."

He went to a drawer in the kitchen and started sifting through delivery menus and junk mail. "These guys have the worst timing, honestly. I just got the last customer out of there. I was going to start barricading the place."

Tori looked down at the sidewalk from Thomas's front window. "He's not going to go away, no matter what you show him."

Adam and I joined her at the window.

Daniel Wesson looked up and waved. *Mother-maiden-and-crone, how did he find us again?*

"Guess those threats at the hearing weren't so idle after all," I said.

"What am I missing?" Thomas asked, coming around the counter to see what we were looking at.

I shoved the compass into his hands, and the color drained from his face.

"Him?" Thomas said, looking down at the guy. "But he's so…obvious."

"I know, right? Like, if there was a lineup of dudes, and you had to say which one was most likely packing a shotgun full of rock salt in the back of his vintage American-made muscle car…" Tori waved back at the guy.

"What do you want to do?" Adam asked.

"Well, I clearly can't invite him in to do a fire inspection, can I?" Thomas mumbled. He did a double-take. "Oh, hey, Adam. When did you get here?"

I rolled my eyes.

"I wasn't asking you," Adam said a little harshly, but he'd never had much patience for my brother.

"Excuse me?" Thomas said.

Adam put one hand on the wall beside the window and leaned forward to keep an eye on our visitor. "You had one job, man. I gave you the kynigolabe so you could watch out for her. We knew there would be trouble. But somehow, the hunter completely evaded your notice until he literally appeared on your doorstep. So, I'm sorry, but I'm not asking you what you want to do next."

"He's not a vampire," Tori said.

"What?" Even Adam turned to look at her.

"Thomas said he couldn't invite him in. But he's not a vampire. He doesn't need an invitation. He's going to come in whether you invite him or not."

"There are wards all over the store. Won't let in so much as a shoplifter," Thomas insisted.

"He's not here to steal from you," Tori said.

The amulet. "I'm not sure the wards will be enough. He has something charmed to dissipate magical energy."

"Is the door locked?" Adam asked.

"Shit." Thomas leaned his forehead on the window.

A bell rang downstairs as the door opened. The hunter disappeared from view.

"Okay. So, you're going to stay up here, and Thomas and I will chat with his new customer. Maybe he can *encourage* the guy to shop somewhere else," Adam said.

I grabbed his arm as he headed to the stairs, turning him to face me. "What are you going to do? There's an awful lot of cement between you and the earth. Even if you manage to access your Gift, it won't last long. He wasn't affected by my time bubble, and when he was ready to go, he took all my energy with him. I'm still hungover from whatever he did with that amulet."

"You're the one he's here for. We're not just going to hand you over. *Through her strength shall others rise.* That doesn't sound like a solo mission, Chosen One. Stay here. Make a plan. Let us do this." He squeezed my arms and kissed my forehead.

I leaned into him, wishing we could spend time together without the threat of imminent danger. *Maybe after graduation.*

"Besides, I'm Commander of the Watch. My Gift isn't my only defense." Grinning, he stepped back and pushed my brother toward the stairs. "Let's go."

"Sure, sure. I'll take point," Thomas said. "As long as I have the Guardian at my back."

"I've got you," Adam said, slapping him on the back.

Thomas looked back over his shoulder and shot me a slightly shaky thumbs-up before they disappeared through the beaded doorway.

Tori picked up Dr. Bear, stuffing the battery pack in and putting his coat back on. She sat cross-legged on the futon and hugged him. Her body shook, rattling the frame under the thin cushion. "What are we going to do?"

"We need a plan that stops the hunters from coming for us," I said. Assuming Thomas and Adam get this one out of the magic shop, and the other one isn't already waiting someplace nearby. Nora said *a pair of hunters.* Where was Daniel Wesson's partner?

"We need to wipe them out." Tori's face flushed. The shivers I'd taken for fear transformed into barely contained rage.

He killed her sister.

"If we kill them, we're no better than they are," I said, parroting my lessons from home. Every witchling in Queen's Creek eventually asked why we had to hide. Why we lived in isolation when we had Gifts that made us stronger than our adversaries.

Tori squeezed the bear in her arms, leaning forward with bright eyes. "I don't care about being better. Why do we need to be better? What has that ever gotten us? Look at the prophecy. It doesn't say anything about being better. It's about strength. We have to be stronger than they are."

"We have to think of the greater good," I said. "We don't know how many of them are out there. Who's waiting for this guy to come back? They could be anyone. We can't start a war, especially when we don't know who our enemies are."

"I know where you could start," Tori said. "Those girls at the hearing. They said he was their uncle."

"Madi and Morgan? They came to your coven meeting. You really think they know he's a hunter?" But I'd had the same thought. It led to darker suspicions I didn't want to think about.

Tori didn't have the same reluctance. "Maybe they're spying for him. How did he find us so quickly?"

"I don't know. Nora says they have some kind of energy detectors. EMFs or something. What do you want to do?"

"They have to pay for what they've done. They brought the wolf to our door. Who knows what they'll do next." The gleam in her eyes grew more intense.

"We can't just go around destroying people who might be dangerous. That's what hunters do. We can't sink to their level," I said, channeling the moral imperatives espoused by Mrs. Kirk, the former Speaker of Queen's Creek. I disgusted myself, but Tori's vehemence both frightened and tempted me. It felt so good to give into the energy on the beach. What could we do if we had more? What would it cost? I had to convince both of us to take a more reasonable approach. "It's beneath us."

"The only thing beneath me is my sister's grave."

"Tor—"

"No. We're done. We could have done this together. It would have been so much more fun. But my sister's killer is downstairs right now, and I can't let him get away. If you don't want to help me get justice for Grace, maybe you should just wait here like your boyfriend told you to." Tori stomped past me.

"Wait!" I raised my hands, but I hadn't built up enough energy to call my Gift. *How much had that amulet taken from me?* My fingers twitched, the static between them hardly more than I could have created by rubbing my feet across Thomas's rug. "Please, just wait. We need a plan. His amulet —"

Tori spun around. Her eyes flashed. When she lifted her arms, the practiced motion raised the energy in the room almost immediately. "Oh, now you want to help? Thanks, Cate, but there's only one thing I need from you."

Her hands rolled at the wrists, pulling and twisting something invisible through the air. Her fingers flexed, and I gasped. My heart raced like it had at the beach. The energy I hadn't been strong enough to raise myself flowed through my body, rushing from my toes up my legs, through my torso, to the tips of my fingers and the top of my head. Goosebumps pricked my arms. I tried to hold on to it, but Tori tugged, and the energy escaped. Light radiated from my fingers, drawn along an invisible thread between us. Tori's black nails glowed as each new pulse connected. I couldn't catch my breath. My legs gave out, and I sank to the floor, lightheaded and weak.

"You don't have to do this," I said, but the words might have been only in my head. It was hard to tell with the blood pounding in my ears.

"Get some rest. I'll handle *Uncle Dan*. You weren't strong enough on your own, and maybe that amulet will protect him from my magic, too. But I'm getting justice for Grace today. No matter what it takes," said Tori, leaving the apartment. The floor vibrated with each step she took.

40

I groaned, rolling to my back. I had to get downstairs. Even in her power-boosted state, Tori might not be strong enough to overcome the charm on the hunter's amulet. *Three against one should be good odds, but who knows what other weapons he might have? I doubt he came to the shop unarmed.*

Something crashed in the magic shop. Raised voices argued, muffled by the distance between us and the ringing in my ears. Another rumble and something slammed against the wall. The vibrations rattled the dishes in Thomas's sink.

I pushed myself to my knees, hanging my head until the dizziness subsided.

Someone screamed.

My muscles refused to obey my command to stand, so I crawled to the doorway and used the frame to brace myself. The beaded curtain knocked against my face. I gripped a handful of the dangling jewels and ripped them down. They spilled over the floor, rolling down the stairs ahead of me. Too late, I berated myself for booby-trapping my own exit.

Downstairs, glass bottles rattled and crashed to the floor. The front door slammed shut, setting off the tiny bell. Soft thuds became groans.

Something exploded.

I coughed before I recognized the smell of smoke.

Gripping the handrail, I began my descent. With each step, the light changed. First darker as the electric overhead bulbs shattered and went out. Then, a flash of something warmer, flickering and growing. Shadows danced on the narrow stairwell.

I stepped on a bead and nearly fell when my ankle rolled with it. The handrail saved me, and I clutched it for dear life.

Click. Clack. Click. The bead bounced harmlessly ahead of me. So loud for such a small thing.

I shouldn't be able to hear it.

I held my breath. The crashing sounds had stopped, replaced by a soft crackle.

I shoved through the curtain at the bottom of the stairs and was hit by a wave of heat that fogged my glasses. Flames traced the counter of the magic shop. They licked their way up the walls, smacking the antique books on their shelves. The air hung heavy with smoke, a sickly sweet mixture of burning paper and herbs. The plastic packaging on Thomas's inventory melted into sticky film. One of the displays had fallen across the entrance, blocking the door.

My heart pounded. I'd worried so much about the amulet that I failed to recognize the obvious danger. *Hunters don't need magic to fight us when mundane methods are just as lethal.*

The smoke darkened as the fire grew, making it harder to see and almost impossible to breathe. I backed up against the wall.

"Thomas!" I called. "Adam! Where are you?"

Maybe they already got out. Maybe they blinked themselves out to the street.

Maybe Tori stole their energy, too, and they passed out under a pile of fallen crystals.

Sweat and tears rolled down my face. Everything hurt.

"Cate! What are you doing? We have to get out of here!" Thomas grabbed my arm and dragged me to the stairs. "We'll never get out this way. There's a fire escape from the back of my apartment. Go!"

"Where's Adam?" I pushed against my brother, and he pitched backward, rolling on one of the loose beads from the busted curtain.

I reached out to grab him, but he bounced back up again, propelled by a force from behind. I stumbled back, bracing myself on the doorframe. Thomas fell past me onto the stairs.

In his place, Adam appeared out of the smoke, soot staining his face and blackening his hair. He put a hand on my shoulder, pushing me after my brother.

"Move!" his voice rasped, and his eyes watered. He kept his hand on my shoulder, grabbing the opposite side of the doorframe with his other. His chest heaved.

Ahead of me, Thomas righted himself. Standing one step above me, he wiped his hands on his pants and reached for Adam's arm. "Come on, big guy. Cate, grab his other arm."

I blinked at the reversal. The Guardian clutched my brother's arm as if he might fall to the floor without it. Thomas shone in the firelight, his fair skin glistening as if it repelled the ash and smoke in the air. *Of course. He's in his element.* Even if the hunter used the amulet to dissolve his energy, as soon as he torched the place, he gave Thomas a new source.

I scanned the wreckage for Tori.

"She's gone," Thomas said, dragging Adam's arm over his shoulders. "I mean, she's not here. She got out. Come on. We've got to go now!"

The thought of what Tori might do next knotted my stomach, overthrowing any relief that she survived.

Working together, Thomas and I helped Adam up the stairs

and back into the apartment. By the time we got there, the smoke made its way up the stairwell and started to pool across his ceiling.

"Stay low," I said, pulling them to the floor. We crawled toward the glass door that led to his fire escape. He'd been using it as a balcony, so once we got through the door, we still had to maneuver around illegal furniture and awkwardly positioned potted plants.

I pulled myself up to stand at the rail, gasping for breath. Smoke billowed out behind me. Adam rolled onto his back on the grating, his feet still braced on the doorway from pushing himself out. Thomas unhooked the ladder, dropping it down to the sidewalk.

"Unless you want to have a real uncomfortable conversation with some mundane firefighters, I suggest we vacate the premises," Thomas said, already dropping through the hole he'd opened in the grate. He paused. "We're not coming back here, are we?"

I watched his apartment fade out of focus as the smoke overtook it. "I don't think so."

Thomas's tongue stuck out the corner of his mouth for a second. He blinked and disappeared.

In my weakened state, I thought he'd fallen. I fell to my knees, peering through the hole. "Thomas!"

"Does Adam have the map?" My brother's voice came from back inside. He coughed. Something rattled. A door opened and closed. Clattering objects hit the floor.

"Are you insane? Get out of there!" I yelled. The temperature in the doorway rose as the fire climbed the stairwell.

"Does he have it? Check his pockets!" Thomas called back.

Adam groaned when I crouched over him. Under the grime, his face had a green tinge, whether from bruising or smoke poisoning, I couldn't tell. His eyes were rimmed with red. But he was still breathing, which was more than I would be able to say for Thomas if he didn't get out of there soon. Gift of the fire element or not, he still needed oxygen.

"Adam, I'm so sorry. We have to go. Do you have the map?"

He didn't have his coat on, so there weren't many pockets to check. Maybe he left it in Queen's Creek?

His eyes fluttered. "Have it...here..."

He stretched, pulling himself up to sit. Reaching behind him, he dragged the folded paper from his back pocket and handed it to me.

The map nearly burned my fingers, but I couldn't stop to check which addresses lit it up this time.

"I've got it! Get out of there!" I yelled to Thomas.

His head appeared at the door, more smudged than before but otherwise safe. "Can you get down on your own?"

I glanced at the ladder. It seemed sturdy enough, but Adam didn't have the strength to climb down, and I didn't see how either Thomas or I could manage it with him.

"Can you climb it?" Thomas asked again.

I nodded. "Yes, but— "

"Good. Go." Thomas grabbed Adam's ankles and blinked. They both disappeared this time. The fire really had strengthened him. I'd never seen him take a passenger before.

By the time I climbed down, Thomas had propped Adam against one of the trees lining the street. He sat in the dirt square cut from the sidewalk, leaning back against the trunk.

"Is he okay?" I knelt beside him, wiping his hair back from his warm face.

Adam turned his face into my hand, then lifted his own to hold it in place. "I'm okay. Just need a minute."

Thomas looked down the street toward the sound of sirens. He adjusted the strap of a bag across his shoulders. "Do what you gotta do, man. Touch grass or whatever, but we need to move as soon as you feel your feet again."

Adam sighed and closed his eyes, releasing my hand. He dropped his fingers into the dirt on either side of him. With each deep breath, some of the color returned to his cheeks, soft pink overtaking the sickly green hue. Some of the redness faded from his eyes, but one of them was badly bruised.

A moment later, he stood, still a little shaken, and leaned against the tree. "Where do you want to go?"

They both looked at me.

Although they'd each recovered some, whatever happened in the magic shop before it explo ded had taken a lot out of them. I probably didn't look much better. My head ached and my stomach threatened to dredge up my breakfast.

I could only think of one place close enough to walk to where no one would question our appearance or bother us while we caught our breath and came up with a plan.

When we got to the café, I pointed the guys to a table in the back and placed an order with the barista. He barely blinked at the grime I tracked in and handed me the bathroom key without waiting for me to ask for it. I'd worked with him before, but Brian and Morgan had the day off for the play (*bless the goddess for small favors*—I had no idea what they would do when someone noticed I was missing). Once I had the drinks in hand, the barista lost interest.

Adam and Thomas took turns washing up in the bathroom, and both looked almost normal once they'd cleaned up. *Must be nice to have an elemental Gift whose element was so easy to access.* According to the census we found in the former Speaker's office, my Gift came from elemental spirit, whatever that meant. How did you channel that? *Why couldn't I have earth, air, water, or fire like every other Gifted witch in Queen's Creek?*

I spread the map out over the table. Tiny lights sparked all over it, but none so bright as the Midwest. Adam pulled at the edges of the map, and it grew, giving us a closer look at the brightest spot. Chicago. *Of course.*

This time, a white light glowed near the beach.

<h1 style="text-align:center">41</h1>

It's Tori. She's going to go through with it," I said. "She's gathering her mundane coven so she can pull energy from them."

"She's what now?" Thomas asked.

"It's her Gift. She's like a goddess-blessed magical energy vacuum. That's why I'm still so wiped. She took everything I had left. What happened when she got downstairs?" I asked.

"You were right about the charm. It's that amulet, right? It felt like the air went out of the room. There was no energy to draw from," Adam said.

Thomas nodded, "I tried, you know, giving him a nudge that there were other places he'd rather be, but either he really didn't have any doubts about why he came in, or that piece of jewelry gives him immunity to all magic."

"Might have been both," Adam said. "This guy knew what he came here to do."

Thomas rolled his eyes. "Do you think he practiced that monologue in the mirror first?"

They laughed. I'd have been glad to hear it if I weren't so worried about what the hunter planned to do next. *Did he wait around to see the shop burn? Did he know we escaped?*

I pushed my coffee to the side. "Guys. You didn't get those bruises from a monologue. What happened? Where did he go?"

"Sorry," Adam said. "So, your friend came downstairs at top speed. I think she was going to throw him across the room or something."

"Yeah. That's what it looked like. She was all—" Thomas held up his hands, fingers spread like witches in the movies. After a few dramatic gestures, he dropped them. "But, obviously, no magical energy, no magic. So she just kind of looked like a lost mime."

"She didn't like that," Adam said.

"No, that pissed her right off. She started throwing stuff. I really hope the Holloways have good insurance. Some of that stuff was one-of-a-kind," Thomas said. "Anyway, she has terrible aim."

He sipped his tea and pointed to Adam's black eye. "The hunter didn't do that. He took a crystal ball to the cheek."

"Shit," I said. "Are you okay? Did she at least give him the same kind of injury? What did he do?"

"I'll be fine," Adam waved off my concern. "I think she hit him in the shoulder? He lost his balance for a minute. So then he just skipped to the end, I think. Threw out a handful of some kind of powder and ignited it with a lighter. Anything it settled on went straight up in flames." Adam shook his head at Thomas. "That place was a tinderbox. Did you never dust in there?"

Thomas glared at him. "Are you seriously blaming my housekeeping skills for an arsonist attack? I had a fire extinguisher. It wasn't big enough."

"Guys," I said.

Adam gulped some water before continuing. "Right, so I tried to go after him, but some of that powder landed on my arm, and it took me a minute to get it to go out. Meanwhile,

Tori ran at him. I guess she was going to claw him to death with her fingernails. She jumped on him, but he shoved her back and took off. When she fell, she knocked that big display over between us and the front door. I don't know what was in those jars, but they shattered when they hit the floor, and the whole thing was just a wall of fire. She was stunned, but she got out. I couldn't follow her."

"She took an athamé," Thomas said. "Earlier. When her magic didn't work. She grabbed a knife from the counter."

So, she's armed and angry. Great. I mean, good for her. She'll be safer if he finds her again.

"Where is the hunter now?" I asked.

Thomas dragged the bag out from under the table.

I recognized the Medusa head screen print. "Is that Tori's bag?"

"Yeah," he said, reaching his arm deeper into the bag than should have been possible. "She left it up there, and I figured we might need a few things."

He started dumping supplies on the table. A candle, matches, some cloth, a large bell. Then, the compass. He popped it open, and we watched the arrow spin. It slowed but didn't stop, unable to get a reading.

"What does that mean?" I asked.

"Nobody's actively hunting us right now, I guess," Thomas said.

Maybe he thinks we're dead.

"So it won't tell us where he is?"

"Not unless he makes a move. It's meant to be a warning, not a tracking device," Adam said.

The little light on the map flashed. *Tori, what are you doing?*

"We have to stop her. She's going to drain those girls and go after the hunter herself," I said.

Thomas put the compass on the map, covering the glowing dot at the beach. "I just want to see…"

The arrow spun faster, then stopped, pointing south of the beach.

I looked at the map. Tori's light shone the brightest, but it wasn't the only dot in the city. With a shaking hand, I dragged the compass over a fainter light on campus. Maybe we could triangulate his location.

The arrow spun, landing in a completely different direction.

"Does that mean he's moving again?" I asked.

"That's not our guy," Adam said.

"What do you mean?"

"Look where it's pointing. There's no way he got to the other side of the city already," said Adam. He pulled the compass back over the beach. The arrow pointed south again. He slid it back over the campus, and the arrow spun away.

"There are two of them." Nora said a pair of hunters were close enough to be here by the end of the week. What had this other guy been up to?

What if it was someone we already knew? Back at the scene shop, I felt like someone was watching. Maybe it wasn't just Angel's poor taste in music.

Adam looked at me. "Have you seen him already?"

I bit my lip, flipping through a mental file of everyone I'd encountered since I came back. A few angry customers. A frustrated classmate. No one who showed the kind of disdain for my life that Wesson did. Except maybe…What if it wasn't a *him*? "Brian's girlfriend came into the café the other day. She said something…"

Thomas raised an eyebrow. He must have met her once or twice, as often as he came into the café last year. "Look, I get that you're all paranoid and on your guard right now, and honestly, you probably should be, but not everybody who's mean to you has an evil plan to murder you. Some people just suck."

"You haven't seen the way she looks at me." It was a weak argument, but I couldn't shake the way she made me feel, even if I couldn't pinpoint the reason for it.

"Sure. But that doesn't make her a hunter, just an asshole." He stared hard at the map as if it would tell us more than it already had. The same lights glowed.

Adam leaned forward, resting his elbows on the table. "Still, we need to be cautious. If you see her today, you run the other way."

From its position over the college, the compass arrow shivered. The hunter was no longer on the way there. He (or she?) had arrived. What were they after?

Nora. She told us to hide, but her very existence drew enough magical energy to appear on the map. Would their mundane tools pick it up, too? Or was Tori right, and Madi or Morgan was spying for the hunter? Had they told their uncle about their witchy costume professor?

I grabbed Adam's hands over the table. My heart raced, and my fears tumbled out of my mouth all at once. "He came for me. He followed Shelley's prophecy, looking for a witch who'd been bound, and somehow found out about me. He went to the magic shop because my brother works there. Is he going to the theater because of my advisor? Tying up loose ends?

"Goddess, if he's tracing my steps, did he go to the dorm first? Do you think Nyla's okay? She's mundane, and she doesn't know anything. Would that matter to him?"

"He got information out of Shelley. If he gets to Nora…she knows about the other witch communities. She has contacts all over the country. If they get her, they get everyone."

"They won't get to her. We'll stop them," Adam said.

"How? What about Tori?" I said.

Thomas smirked. "Let Tori handle that guy. I like her odds."

"What if that hunter has an amulet like Wesson's? She'll drain those girls for nothing. He'll negate all the energy as soon as he gets to her," I said. "We can't let her do that to them."

"You think you can convince her to stop? Hide out somewhere until we figure out what kind of charms he carries?" Adam asked.

I shook my head. She was so angry. She wouldn't stop until she got vengeance for her sister, and she didn't care who she hurt.

Thomas agreed. "She's not going to let you talk to her. If you try to stop her, she'll just vacuum up all your magical energy again."

"Too bad we don't have one of those amulets," Adam said. "If we could neutralize her Gift for a little while, we might be able to save her…and those mundane girls."

Thomas tapped the side of his cup, not looking at me. "You're not going to like it, but you know what we have to do." He reached into the bag again and pulled out Dr. Bear. "We can bind her."

"What? No!" I said. "Then what? She'll still want to go after the hunters, and we'll have blocked her best defense." Adam pulled a hand away from me and rubbed his chin. He met Thomas's eyes. "Can you…encourage her to wait a little? If we can get past her Gift?"

"I can't inspire her into anything she doesn't want to do," Thomas said.

"We can't do this," I said. *I can't do to her what my parents did to me. No matter how dangerous she is.*

We all stared into our cups as if the ripples would clear things up for us. My coffee was less forthcoming than the water I'd used to scry on Adam a few days ago. I still hadn't asked him about what I'd seen, but now wasn't the time for petty jealousy.

Adam broke the silence. "If this hunter has an amulet like the other one, it won't matter if she has a Gift or not. Binding her won't make her any weaker."

"What if he doesn't, and she could have taken him out?" I said. She might be stronger than any of us. Nora had practically said as much.

"We won't leave her to face him on her own," Adam said.

"So, what? You want to bind her and then charge in like the cavalry to save her from a danger we caused? Who else is going to get hurt?" How many times had I broken my promise not to do magic over the past few days? How many things had I done to draw the hunters' attention to the people I was supposed to protect? I came here to warn the other witches, and all I did was put a target on their backs.

Thomas coughed on his tea. "You want to keep it down? Somebody's going to think we're plotting a kidnapping over here. And anyway, we didn't cause this. The hunters did. We just want to live our lives. If the mundanes are going to side with them, they aren't worth saving."

Nobody looked our way, but I lowered my voice. "I'm sorry, but the hunters are coming for everyone we care about, and you're talking about disabling one of our allies."

"Is she an ally, though?" Thomas asked. "After what she did to you?"

My whole body ached with what she'd done to me, and I couldn't deny part of me—maybe most of me—thought we'd be better off if we let the hunters catch her. But the thought shocked me. No matter what she'd done, she didn't deserve to face her sister's fate. Besides, we might need her strength beside us when we confronted them. I pushed my anger down. "The hunters killed her sister. She just wants justice. Can you blame her? We can't desert her and let them burn her, too."

Thomas slid the compass back over the dot on the beach.

The arrow spun once, stopping in the same direction it had before. It looked so calm compared to the red flashes and vibrations it made when the hunter showed up at the hearing. "We've got time. This one's not moving very quickly. Maybe he doesn't know exactly where she is."

"What about Nora?" I said.

He shook his head. "If he were there, the warning light would have gone off."

Adam snapped the compass closed and tucked it back into Tori's bag. He folded the map slowly, tapping it on the table. He addressed Thomas with his Watch Commander tone. "I think we have to split up. We'll go to the theater since we know Wesson has an amulet. Maybe we can get Cate's adviser out of there before he arrives. You go to the beach. Try and beat the hunter there. Maybe you can *talk* to him if he doesn't have the amulet. But let's do the binding first. I don't want you to have to fight both of them at once."

"I don't like all the ifs and maybes in this plan, Commander," Thomas said.

I grabbed Dr. Bear, hugging him to my chest.

"*Stop,*" I said, gathering any energy I could from the caffeine I'd just inhaled. "I don't think you're hearing me."

They froze.

42

round us, the noise of the café continued. I closed my eyes, taking in a deep breath. The tension in my head lessened. If Thomas could recharge his Gift through his proximity to fire, and Adam pulled energy from the earth, where could I pull the energy to power my Gift?

How did someone replenish energy from the spirit?

It's part of me. The energy comes from my spirit, so it has to be there, always. How do I reach it? *To know thyself is the beginning of wisdom.* Some ancient Greek said that. One of my professors hung it on the wall and pointed to it whenever someone made an excuse about forgetting an assignment. *Lack of preparation on your part…* How do I prepare?

I couldn't let Adam and Thomas do to Tori what our parents had done to me. The loss of my Gift had affected my entire life, even when I didn't know the cause. That hole inside—it was almost unbearable.

But I hardly had the energy to make them wait a few minutes while I figured out how to convince them not to bind her. And to make an alternative plan to keep her from attacking us if we tried to stop her.

Just breathe.

The air flowed in through my nose and out through my mouth. I paced myself, forcing my arms to loosen around Dr. Bear, concentrating on slowing my heartbeat. The black and white specks behind my eyelids danced. I pictured myself back in the Gatehouse. Not the real one where the Speaker had almost condemned me to live out the rest of my days. The bright Gatehouse of my vision when I crossed the Creek looking for my father. A mental palace, comforting and safe. It was the last place I felt at peace before we confronted Mrs. Kirk on the bridge and opened the boundary.

Sunlight streamed in through the windows. Even in my imagination, no one had replaced the curtains I used to stop Elspeth's bleeding. I stood at the window facing the water, the path, and the woods that led home. Light flashed off the ripples in the Creek, and insects chirped on the banks. Somewhere down that path, my mother and brothers went about their lives. Did they know how close the hunters were to finding them? I had to protect this place.

Turning, I went to the opposite window, the one facing into the forest that ringed our home. Shadows clung to the trees, but they were thinner than I remembered. Construction on the new development continued not far away, and the noise from the machines echoed off the Gatehouse walls. Less and less stood between Queen's Creek and the world of the mundanes.

My Gift grew stronger in this timeless mirror of the real place. The energy reached out for me, begging for direction. As long as my actions aligned with my spirit, it would come when I called. A small voice whispered, "In peace of mind, your freedom find." What choice could I live with?

I opened myself to the meditative state, letting thoughts, dreams, and whispers pass through until my mind cleared. Out of the silence came a voice I'd never heard before.

Breathy, like Tori's but softer around the edges.

"True peace and freedom shall be found
when Salem's Witch no more is bound.
For through her strength shall others rise,
a sister's love will bind the ties."

Salem's witch.

I held my breath. *It's not me.*

We thought we understood it, but the smears on Shelley's note hid some very significant details.

Stupid, cryptic prophesies.

It's not me this time.

Tori is the Chosen One.

In the distance, the voice whispered its assent.

Thank you, Grace.

The beginning of an idea formed. My heart raced again, but excitement fed it instead of fear this time. That had been the problem all along. We allowed our fear to lead. So did the hunters. The power of our magic didn't make us dangerous. The fear of it did.

I couldn't control their fear, but maybe I could do something about ours.

I sent a question through the veil, so close in my meditative state. *Will you help us?*

Grace answered for the ancestors, sending a rush of strength through my veins so powerful my eyes popped open, and I gasped for breath.

My fingers shot out to grip the table, and it rocked, knocking into Adam, who winced.

Dr. Bear tumbled from my lap.

Thomas caught him and set him back on the table. He did a double-take. "What did you just do?"

Adam ran a hand through his curls, his eyes darting

around the room, taking in everything that changed while he was frozen. When he got back to me, he raised an eyebrow. "Glad to see you got your energy back. But if you're going to be using your Gift on me, we're going to have to have a conversation about consent."

Thomas nearly fell out of his chair laughing.

"Now, who's drawing attention?" I said.

But the customers who looked only saw a few college kids hanging out in a coffee shop and shrugged off a little strange behavior.

"I'm sorry about that," I said to Adam, hoping to convey as much sincerity as possible. I'd used my Gift in panic and frustration, but the temporary pause had given me the guidance we needed to move forward. "You're right. We have to bind Tori. But not for the reasons you think."

"What do you mean?" Thomas asked.

"I think it will protect her from the hunters. They can't use the amulet to negate her magical energy if it's already bound. If we bind her now and help her get away, when we release the bind, she won't be weakened like we were when we faced him at the magic shop. It's her strength that's going to bring freedom to witches. Her sister's love. The prophecy is about Tori, not me." I sat back in the chair with my coffee and waited for them to argue.

They didn't.

"*A sister's love will bind the ties,*" Adam said. "More than one. What ties? How many binding spells do you think it means?"

"I think Grace will help us with that part," I said.

Thomas looked back and forth between us, then raised his hand. "Uh, guys? Not to be the bearer of bad news, but... Tori's sister is dead, remember? How is she going to help?"

"I spoke with her."

"You what?" Thomas rubbed the back of his neck.

"So, remember how I contacted the Gatekeepers at the Creek?"

"Through the time stream? When I had to rescue Gabe from Martha?" he asked.

"Yeah. I don't really understand it," I admitted. "But somehow, when I use my Gift, I'm still connected. I can reach people in other times. I think they might be other realities. I can reach through the veil." Maybe Brian could help me figure out more about how these spaces worked. As long as I could connect with my Gatehouse, the one aligned with my spirit, it felt like I could reach others. Other worlds.

I might actually get my father back. I just had to figure out which world he was in. Maybe I should try the Ouija board again. Get him to guide me. If that really was him moving the planchette...and not another wayward spirit or vengeful ghost. How did it work? What was really out there?

"My sister talks to dead people," Thomas said.

I sighed. It was so much more complicated than that. Tori might have used the board all her life, but she hadn't explained what gave her confidence in its results. At least when I used my Gift, I heard their voices. Maybe we could use Adam's Gift to verify it somehow.

Thomas and Adam waited for me to elaborate. *Probably didn't want to get frozen again.*

I straightened, pulling my cup closer on the table. "Point is, I think Grace can help. Tori's Gift allows her to borrow and use energy from others. I think Grace's amplifies magical energy. I felt stronger as soon as I started talking to her."

"Cool. Then what do we need Tori for? Why don't you just ask ghost sis to power us all up and then we'll go give the hunters a reason to fear us," Thomas said.

"They'd just send more after us," Adam said.

"Right," I said. "And I don't think Grace can reach beyond the veil anyway. I can't connect her to you."

"But she gave you a boost," Thomas said.

"Only because I can go to where she is. And it won't be enough to stop the hunters."

"But you think Tori can reach her," Adam said.

"I think it's possible. She contacted her through the Ouija board before. They're related. There's already a blood connection there. If I can guide her…"

"You want to let Grace boost her energy-stealing power? How does that help us? It just makes her a threat to other witches," Thomas said.

"She's not going to connect them so that Grace can amplify Tori. She wants to let Tori borrow Grace's Gift," Adam said. "She'd be able to strengthen others and transfer their energy. What's your plan, Cate?"

I described the way Tori pulled energy from the girls on the beach, the way she'd talked about connecting them all, linking their life sources together. "What if we get her to do that with everybody in Queen's Creek? The Source of magic is the people. If we link all the witches together, they can carry that Source wherever they go. No more weakening when witches are on their own or depending on the unstable energy we released when the boundary came down. They'll always have each other's backs."

"Like an energy share plan. Long-distance spellcraft. Unlimited magic minutes." Thomas crossed his arms and rocked back in his chair.

"Sure," I said.

"Just to be clear," said Adam. "We're going to bind Tori to protect her magic from the hunters who want to destroy it and her. Then we'll unbind her and help her contact her sister from beyond the veil so that she can take her sister's energy-amplifying Gift and use it to perform a mass binding spell on the entire population of Queen's Creek?"

"Yes? And then the witches from other communities as

well, if it works. Do you think they'll go for it?" I asked.

"Mrs. Kirk is going to have a heart attack," he said.

"But Mrs. Kirk isn't the Speaker anymore," I said. "Your father is."

"You want me to go back and talk to him."

"Please?" I asked.

"Your sister's crazy," he told Thomas.

My brother shrugged. "That's what we love about her."

Adam smiled. His eyes shone. "True."

My cheeks burned. "You better get going. Thomas and I can handle the binding spell."

Adam tucked the map into my fingers. Then he stood, leaning across the table to kiss me. His lips landed just beside my ear. "Be careful. You might not be chosen by the prophecy this time, but you'll always be my Chosen One."

I groaned. We were really going to have to talk about his choice in pet names.

Adam disappeared from the café, blinking out in a dramatic exit worthy of my brother. Clearly, Thomas was a bad influence.

An older woman at a nearby table stared at the spot where Adam had stood. She pulled off her glasses and wiped them on her shirt. When she put them back on, she saw me watching her, and her confused frown turned to an embarrassed smile. She looked away, probably already convincing herself she needed an eye exam. No one else seemed to have noticed. *I know I said I didn't want to hide anymore, but are we ready to reveal ourselves to the world?*

43

In case the hunters were watching for energy spikes like the one Adam caused when he blinked out, and to avoid pushing our luck with the unobservant mundanes at the cafe, Thomas and I walked back to campus. We took the reverse route from when we fled the beach, watching for suspicious shadows, nosy neighbors, or any other strange behavior. Honestly, our hypervigilance probably alerted a few people on the sidewalk.

I didn't want to get too close to the beach and risk Tori sensing us, so we ducked into an alcove of the church near where I'd left my bike that day. We sat on the cold cement and Thomas dumped most of the bag between us. I pulled Dr. Bear and a black velvet ribbon from the pile. Thomas grabbed a candle, a lighter, and a bottle of water. He reached into the landscaping along the edge of the sidewalk and dug out a handful of dirt, piling it in front of him.

We called on the earth and the air that surrounded it. Thomas dripped some of the water over the dirt as we called on that element. He lit the candle, and his features glowed in response to his Gift's elemental source.

I held the ribbon over Dr. Bear's eyes and wrapped it

around his head. *I'm sorry. This is the only way.*

With each pass around his head, we chanted the binding spell. "We bind you, Tori, from using your Gift. From pulling the energy of other witches, from doing harm. We bind you, Tori, from using your Gift..."

Before we closed the spell, I added one last piece: a time lock. She wouldn't be bound forever. And her release wouldn't be dependent on our survival or even on our loyalty.

I hope this works.

As I tucked the end of the ribbon under the pieces that wound around Dr. Bear's head, I blew across it, whispering a command with my Gift. "Freeze. You're on break, Dr. Bear. For the next hour, no time will pass."

Thomas frowned, but when I said, "So mote it be," he echoed the words. The spell was complete.

I set a timer on my phone to track it.

"An hour?" he said. "You don't want to do like, until midnight? Or better yet, until you release the ribbon or until the candle goes out?"

A helpful breeze made the flame flicker. A second extinguished it completely, saving me that argument.

"An hour is enough to get her out of here if you go now. I'll bet you don't even need that long if you give her a little push," I said.

"Where are you going to be?" Thomas packed everything back into the bag, carefully pressing Dr. Bear down on top. He handed me the compass, and I tucked it into my pocket.

"I've got to warn Nora at the theater. The show opens tonight. There will be so many people...it'll be easy for Wesson to slip in if he tells them he came to see his nieces perform. They probably already got him a ticket." What would he do if he found her? My stomach turned at the idea of someone yelling "fire" in the crowded theater. Maybe the building really was cursed.

"I'll come back for you once I get her to the Gatehouse," Thomas said. "Keep your phone on you."

I hugged him. "Be well."

With my bike out of reach, probably still parked in front of the office for the hearing, I had to sprint across campus on foot.

A crowd already blocked most of the main entrance, friends and family coming to see the production. I wove between them and ducked around the side of the building.

Please let Nora be in her office.

Students usually covered the front of the theater duties, ushering our patrons in, checking their tickets, and helping them find their seats. The professor only needed to step out on stage for a minute or two to welcome them and introduce the director before starting the show. Then she could go to her office at the back of the building. Or go home, really. She might watch from the control booth at the back of the theater or sit in the audience for the first run, but her classes had most of the work handled. After tonight, the student director would take over any announcements before showtime.

Bet he'd love to start a day early. This will be the biggest audience.

The light from her office peeked around the door, casting a line across the hallway and up the wall on the other side. Crackling static and muffled conversation from the backstage radios drifted out from the monitor on her desk. I pushed the door open, knocking and calling out as I skidded to a stop.

"Nora! We have to go. The hunters—"

My brain glitched and for a minute, I stood there, my mouth open like some kind of sitcom spit-take. Because the person waiting in Nora's office, sitting on her desk next to a bag of takeout, wasn't my advisor.

"Hi, Cate," said Jasmine, smiling.

Nora's computer speakers crackled, muffled voices from the stage coming through the backstage monitor.

What's she doing here? How do I explain what I just said to the mundane girlfriend of the one unmagical friend who knows my secret? Did he tell her?

I need a minute.

Pulling magical energy to me, I let it tickle my fingers as I set my intention, trying something new.

Rewind.

"What are you doing?" Jasmine crossed her legs and leaned back, bracing herself on the desk. She didn't freeze. Time did not reverse, not even in a holographic playback like I'd seen when I met Duncan. The energy faded from my fingertips.

I shoved my hands into my pockets. The room felt cold, like when Wesson arrived at Tori's hearing. But the hunter wasn't there. *Overactive air conditioning? Please, let it be an upgraded a/c. But then, why can't I direct my magic?*

Jasmine's eyebrow arched. Time didn't freeze, and she had asked me a question.

She couldn't be... but what if she was?

My stomach twisted. *I was right!* Something like vindication battled with my panic. Because this would explain why she hated me so much. It would justify my distrust of her.

Jasmine smiled, waiting.

Shit. Now what?

Answer her. Adam told me to run, but I didn't feel like running. I stalled. "Umm. Nothing. I'm looking for my advisor. Have you seen her?"

"She's making an announcement. I'm sure she'll be back soon. Why don't we wait together? Are you hungry?" Jasmine sat up and lifted the takeout bag, unloading French fries and burgers onto the desk. She popped a fry into her mouth, then sucked in a breath. "Hot!" Her charm bracelet tinkled as she fanned her mouth.

"You brought dinner for Nora?" I stepped closer. She didn't have an amulet around her neck like Wesson's, but that bracelet…

Jasmine laughed, a high bell-like sound that sent shivers down my spine. "No. You did. I was never here."

"What?"

She slid off the desk and covered her face. When she raised her eyes, they shone with tears that didn't fall. "I just heard the news. It's awful. She was so loved. Did you know they fry these things in peanut oil?"

Wow. She's better than Madi. The chill in the air grew stronger, and I crossed my arms, tucking my fingers under my elbows to stop them from shaking.

"Nora doesn't have a peanut allergy." *Did she?* In all my years in this department, had she ever joined us for a meal? My mind went blank.

Jasmine pulled a little packet of white powder out of her pocket and sprinkled it over the fries. Holding the packet with the tips of her acrylic nails, she dropped it into the trashcan by the desk. "Doesn't she? Oh, well, this will make it seem like she does. Such a shame she didn't tell anyone about her sensitivities. You think you know someone," she said, stepping closer, "but you never really know what secrets they're hiding."

My head started to ache. "I guess not. I knew you were a bitch, but I never would have imagined you were a murderer."

She wiped her eyes and glared at me. "Don't call me that."

"What? Bitch?" *Way to antagonize the crazy person. This is going to end well.*

Jasmine huffed. "I've never killed anyone. This?" She threw an arm behind her, gesturing to the potentially fatal fries. "This isn't murder. It's self-defense."

"What's Nora ever done to you?" *Seriously.* Had any witch actually done anything to merit this vendetta? Or were the hunters honestly still working off the paranoia of two centuries?

"You know what she is," Jasmine said. "What you are."

Paranoia, then.

"I'm not a murderer." I rubbed my temples.

"No, you're worse." Jasmine pulled herself up to her full five-foot-two and narrowed her eyes. "Witch."

The confidence and disdain of her judgment would have been funny if I didn't feel myself growing weaker the closer she—and that charm bracelet—came to me.

"Where?" I feigned surprise as I took a step back into the doorway and looked down the hall for anyone I could call for help. But everyone was in the theater on the other side of the building. I gripped the door frame.

She rolled her eyes. "You should probably sit down. You don't look well."

"No thanks. I'm good here." *I might throw up, but I'm good. Definitely not coming back inside to see how much damage that charm can do.*

She stepped toward me again.

My phone vibrated. Saved by the bell. I'd have to thank whoever was on the line for buying me more time. *Oh, the irony. If she didn't have that charm, I'd have all the time in the world.*

Taking a breath to steady myself, I channeled Madi's attitude. I even smiled. "Sorry, can you just hold on a second? I have to take this."

The hunter raised an eyebrow but waved her hand, excusing me. She obviously didn't think I had the strength to run away. She wasn't wrong. I stepped into the hallway, leaving the door open so I could keep an eye on Jasmine.

Brian had texted: Where are you? The show's about to start.

Do I tell him his girlfriend is a psycho who's trying to kill me and our professor? Probably not in a text message.

I texted back: Is Nora on stage?

Brian sent me a picture of my advisor talking to the stage manager in the wings.

What do I tell her? Run? Cancel the show? Evacuate? We're probably safer if the mundanes stay put. Isn't that why the hunters go after witches in the first place? To protect mundanes?

The show must go on. But a little chaos might not hurt. Keep everyone distracted.

I texted: Tell her I said Good Luck.

Superstitions exist for a reason.

His quick response: You mean Break a leg?

Me: No TIME. Tell her Cate says GOOD LUCK!

What do I expect him to do with that clue? Brian and I haven't exactly had a chance to build a secret code for talking about magic yet.

I closed my eyes, willing my friend to trust me, even if it turned half the crew against him. *Please, please, please. I'm sorry, Brian. I'll make it up to you. Just say it loud enough for the Believers backstage to hear.*

"She did not!" The stage manager's voice roared from the monitor on Nora's desk. Something fell backstage, and the ensuing argument became hushed as the crew tried to stifle the noise before the audience noticed.

Jasmine grabbed my arm and dragged me back into the office, slamming the door. I tripped over a stack of books on the floor and fell back against the desk.

"What did you do?"

"If this is going to be my last show, I want it to be memorable," I said, reaching behind me to grab anything I could use as a weapon. My hand closed around something smooth and cold.

"Oh, I think you've made an impression," Nora said from the doorway. She wasn't even out of breath. If we survived this, the mundanes were going to have questions. "Miss Mitchell, how nice to see you again. Are you here to see Brian? He's in the control booth."

Jasmine looked from Nora to me. The weight of being surrounded settled heavily. She bit her lip, fidgeting with her bracelet again. The clasp snapped, and it fell to the floor.

"Hey, Jasmine, catch!" I threw *Hamlet*'s skull at her. It wasn't very heavy—probably plastic—but her dancer's reflexes kicked in, and she reached out as it flew through the air.

Nora scooped up the bracelet. "What a lovely piece," she said. "Antique?"

"It was a gift from my grandmother," she said, turning over the skull and frowning at the Made in China label on the bottom. She dropped it on a pile of files and held out her hand for the bracelet as if Nora might just give it back. *Her grandmother? Did she take it off one of their victims? Force a witch to craft it at matchpoint?*

"Oh, dear." Nora stepped back. "You seem to have broken the clasp. Here, let me see if I can fix it."

She winked at me as she walked behind her desk. I swept Jasmine's meal delivery into the trashcan and moved out of the way, putting more space between us and the hunter. Jasmine rubbed her wrist where the bracelet had been, panic growing behind her eyes.

Nora held her hand out flat at eye level. "Let's see here…"

She covered the bracelet with her other hand and murmured something I couldn't hear. Light flashed, energy releasing. It reminded me of Nora's tarot card, the warmth that came before the image shifted. She had a Gift for creating charms, maybe she could break them, too.

Jasmine jumped.

When Nora opened her hand, the dusty remnants of the silver charms sparkled. She tilted her hand, letting it drift to the desk. Not dust, dirt. *She's an earth witch, like Adam. That's how she always knows things. No one can hide their secrets from her.*

"Oops," Nora said. "I'm so sorry about that."

The hunter tensed, tightening the muscles along her arms and up her neck.

She's afraid.

She should be.

"You think that means you've won? That your magic makes you better? Stronger?" Her voice shook behind the brave face.

"Oh, I know we're stronger. But it's not the magic that makes us better," I said. "You are unarmed, but you're still alive. When the roles were reversed, your partner left me to burn."

Jasmine swallowed hard, then lifted her chin. "No matter what you do to me, this is not the end. Your dark magics will not prevail. You are evil, and I'm not alone."

"Neither are they." Brian stepped into the doorway behind her.

44

B rian!" Jasmine turned, her voice softening. "I've been looking all over for you."

He looked at her like they'd never met before. She'd kept this side of herself well hidden. *Better than I'd hidden my magic.*

"What are you doing here?" he said. "Are you threatening Cate?"

"It's not what it looks like," she said.

Brian looked around the room but found no clues. "Then, what is it?"

"You were saying?" I said to the hunter. "Some kind of vague intimidation. We're evil, you've got friends, or whatever? My brother says you hunters like to monologue. Don't let us interrupt your performance."

"Your brother," she said, and an uneasy smile crossed her face. "Have you spoken with him lately?"

"You mean since your friend burned down his apartment? We all got out of there. Thanks for your concern," I said.

Brian's eyes bulged.

I sensed another *Are you okay?* coming. And I really thought I was. It wasn't *my* girlfriend who turned out to be a secret assassin.

Before I could reassure him, Jasmine spoke, and my stomach dropped. "You might want to make a call."

Brian closed the door behind him, dragged the chair in front of it, and sat, leaning forward to watch us all.

Keeping an eye on the hunter, I pulled my phone out of my back pocket.

Nora stacked her cards back up, releasing a sharp static pop, and went back to shuffling them. "Put it on speaker."

Thomas's phone rang five times before he answered. My heart rate doubled every time.

"Hello?" His voice sounded far away, like someone else held the phone.

"Thomas? Where are you?" I would not ask if he was okay. There was only one acceptable answer, and we were better off assuming he'd give me that one.

He coughed. "Not sure I can answer that just now."

I didn't like the smile that crept across the hunter's face, much more confident than the last one.

"Are you…" I faltered but wouldn't give Jasmine the satisfaction. "Are you alone?"

Thomas chuckled, hiding the strain in his voice. "Nope. Turns out that fire marshal got a call about a bonfire at the beach, and he's very dedicated to his work. Shame he's missing his nieces' play, though."

Wesson had gone after Tori. According to my timer, she wouldn't be back at full strength yet. Anyway, he still had that amulet. Even if we hadn't bound her, he was protected. Thomas's magical influence wouldn't work on him either.

They could be dead by then.

No, hunter or not, he was still mundane. And wherever they were, it was two against one.

Wesson's voice came on the line. "That's enough. Stay where you are. I think I should have a word with your sister, hmm?"

"No problem. Just watch where you point that thing, okay? We're at your mercy here. No need for anybody to get hurt," Thomas said. He sounded so tired. How much energy had he tried to use before he'd accepted what the amulet could do?

Then, the meaning of his words caught up with me. *He's armed.*

My hands shook. We had one hunter right in front of us. We'd stopped her. But now Wesson had Thomas and Tori. Had they been tracking us since we left the magic shop? Maybe the fire was never meant to kill us. Just to flush us out. "Hey, there's no reason for anybody to get hurt here. That fire could have been an accident. We're all okay. There's no reason to—"

"Let me talk to Jasmine," he said.

The hunter held out her hand.

I gave her my phone, and she tapped the screen to switch off the speaker. *What I wouldn't give for Caleb's Gift.*

"Yeah, okay. No, it's fine. You can stay there. I'm sure they'll cooperate now that they know where we stand," she said. She handed the phone back to me, carefully avoiding Brian's eyes.

"Where do we stand, exactly?" I asked Wesson, tapping the speaker back on. "What do you want?"

The hunter sighed. His breath through the phone made my skin crawl. "Look, I don't have anything against you, personally. I'm sure you're a lovely young lady," he said. "But your kind is a danger to the rest of us, and we can't have you coming into spaces that ought to be safe and putting our children at risk. I don't like the *influence* you've already had on my nieces. And if that witch in Virginia was right, you're the harbinger of your kind. Some of my friends down there have been getting real strange readings on their EMF detectors. Great big energy spikes where there used to be nothing but cell towers. Got me thinking there's something out in those woods. Maybe something that's been there all along. And then I come to visit my nieces and catch some spikes of my own. Right when the kids are coming back from Spring Break. Imagine my surprise when the frequency I'm capturing matches what's coming out of the woods in rural Virginia."

He knows about Queen's Creek. How many friends does he have out there? I have to warn Adam. They're closer than we thought.

"You were right, he does like to monologue." Brian stood, stepping closer to the phone but keeping a distance between himself and Jasmine.

"It took me a minute to find you," the hunter's voice continued. "You don't seem the type. Not like your friend here, the vampire."

Tori made a noise of protest in the background, but he kept talking.

"But after your little display at the hearing, I had my friend, the bursar, look you up for me. You grew up down south, didn't you? Just outside Williamsburg. I wonder how long your family has been there. They must miss you, now you're away at school, huh? Might be you should go back where you came from and let everybody else there know they're better off staying home, too."

"What about Thomas? Where are you? How do I know you'll let them go?"

"You want to see your brother again? Go home. Wait for us to contact you." Wesson ended the call.

"You'll let us go? Just like that?" I looked at Jasmine. It couldn't be this easy. *Hunters who tried to burn us to death are just going to let us walk out of here, pop back home and regroup?* I envisioned an army of hunters and scions lined up at the Creek, preparing to invade. But if they had numbers like that, why hadn't they done it already?

She shrugged. "Like I said. I'm not a murderer. I just don't want you here." Her eyes shot to Brian, pleading. Whether for forgiveness or understanding, I wasn't sure.

"What happened to you?" he asked.

"I'm doing this for us," she said. "Did she tell you what she can do? It's—"

"Amazing," said Brian.

She shook her head. "Evil. Against God's will. Just being in the room with them is dangerous." She backed up to the door and held out her hand to him. When he didn't take it, a tear trickled down her cheek. Brian hadn't seen her earlier performance, but this one didn't sway him. She sucked in a breath and swiped the tear away, swinging the door open. With her hand on the knob, she looked up at me. "You should do what he said. Go home. No one has to get hurt."

"Oh, sure. We were just about to call a truce. What's a little arson and poisoning between friends? I mean, we did destroy your charm instead of letting it siphon our energy. Shame about such a lovely antique. We're probably even now," I said, gripping the desk to steady myself. My arms and voice shook as anger and fear threatened to get the better of me. "Forgive and forget. As soon as your friend releases his hostages."

"This is insane," Brian said, the danger finally overcoming his excitement.

"Find me. When this is over and you see reason. Find me before it's too late." Jasmine took off down the hall.

"Wait!" Brian ran after her.

I might as well have been frozen by my own Gift. What would she do if he caught her? What would he do? Did she know where Wesson was keeping my brother? What had Wesson done to him?

A moment later, the fire alarm went off. Down the hall, people started yelling. The doors to the theater slammed open, and the crowd surged out of the building.

"Go," Nora whispered, jolting me out of my panic spiral more effectively than the blaring alarms. I raced around the desk and across the small office. The hallway was packed, but I could see two figures weaving through the crowd ahead. There were too many people between us. I wasn't sure I could hold them all with my Gift. My head still ached, and the energy felt very far away. I didn't dare risk losing them to do a meditation reset. *Find a shortcut. Get ahead of them.*

Dodging the crowd, I pulled open a side door and cut through the backstage hall. The air grew colder the closer I got to the shop. I swallowed back nausea as a wave of pressure rolled over me. The garage door to the scene shop was open. It should have been empty during a show. I slowed, listening for voices.

"Don't move," said Wesson.

"That's a fire alarm," said my brother. "You, of all people, should know what that means."

I leaned on the wall, my heart thumping. The door was only a few feet away.

"I said stay where you are." Wesson's voice pitched lower, barely audible over the siren. Something clicked.

The wheeled platform that held the dressing room set stood between me and the people in the shop. Nyla and Angel had managed to fix most of it, but one side still showed cracks where it had been hit by the drop. An electric screwdriver on the floor told me they'd been working on it between scenes. *Hopefully, they left with the rest of the crew when the alarm went off.*

My phone vibrated.

It buzzed again. I backed against the wall to pull it out without the light giving me away. The alarm I'd set for Tori's binding. It had two minutes left.

Cool. Thanks. A lot of good that did us when the hunter in there had an amulet that negated magical energy. Binding her had been a mistake. I thought we'd been protecting Thomas, but we'd just made them both more vulnerable. When the bind released, she'd be back at full strength, but Thomas wouldn't have any energy for her to pull from. Then the amulet would nullify her Gift too.

Where did the energy go when that black hole activated? Energy cannot be created or destroyed. I'd read that somewhere in Dad's notes. So, for that amulet to remove magical energy, it had to be storing it somehow or sending it somewhere else. Could it be overloaded?

The hunter didn't know Tori was bound. He probably thought both his captives were under the influence of the amulet. *But Tori's Gift is safe. For the next two minutes, anyway. How quickly can she activate it once the bind breaks?*

My Gift had been strong enough to contact the ancestors in the Gatehouse almost as soon as we broke the bind. The energy had exploded out of me. But I'd been bound much longer than an hour. Would Tori even feel it when the bind released? I had to prepare her somehow. She'd used telepathy at the beach. Maybe I could send her a message, if I could get her attention. My Gift responded almost subconsciously during the hearing when Tori's parents had already raised the magical energy in the room. Would she feel it if I raised it now? The skin on my arms pricked with cold. How close could I get before the amulet sapped my energy?

This is a stupid idea, but I don't have any others.

I stepped around the corner into the room, keeping the platform between me and the hunter. Tori sat on the base of the tower ladder. Thomas rested one arm on a low rung, leaning against the frame as if he had nowhere else to be.

Less than two minutes. My fingers tingled. I called to the energy in the room, raising my magic, even as the amulet tried to pull it away from me. My head throbbed against the pressure. A chill raised goosebumps on my arms, but I took a breath and pulled the energy closer. Sparks flashed between my fingers. I closed my eyes.

"Watch out!" Thomas yelled.

<h1 style="text-align:center">45</h1>

Jasmine bolted in through the exterior door across the room, with Brian right behind her.

I stepped back, but Wesson had already seen me. The hunter stood with one foot on the front of the platform, his opposite arm outstretched, a gun trained on my brother. He had a nasty gash on his arm.

"Well, hello, Cate. What are you doing here? I thought we understood one another. Did you get lost trying to find your way home? Why don't you just come around and join us over here? Maybe I can point you in the right direction." He flicked his wrist with the gun in his hand, gesturing for me to stand with Thomas.

I lifted my hands, my magic still crackling around my fingers. Widening my eyes, I feigned surprise, an impression of the ingénue Morgan played on stage. "What's going on back here? Is that a gun?"

The hunter smirked. He tapped the amulet and the charm's pull increased. The lights dancing between my fingers faded. "Silver bullets...got 'em for werewolves, but they'll probably work just as well on you."

"Pretty sure silver bullets would kill just about anything," I said. "Seems like overkill for a few witches. Especially when you've got that amulet collecting all our energy."

"I'm willing to test that theory." He pointed the gun at my chest.

"No!" Brian skidded past Jasmine, coming to a stop between the hunter and me. He raised his hands. "Don't shoot!"

"Brian!" Jasmine screamed. "Don't hurt him! He's an innocent."

"Control your boyfriend, Miss Mitchell. I'd hate for our first mission to have civilian casualties. Might affect your future with the league. Even if you are a legacy." He lowered his weapon but didn't put it away.

Jasmine held out her hand to Brian like she had in the office. "Please, let's just go now. This has nothing to do with us."

"I'm not going to let him murder my friend," Brian said.

Wesson sighed, raising the gun again. "That's unfortunate. Looks like he's made his choice, my dear."

"No, saving people is the whole reason we came here. He just doesn't understand. Let me talk to him." She stood beside Wesson and put her hand on his arm.

He glanced down, noticing her missing bracelet, then turned his attention back to Brian. "What happened to your charm? Did he convince you to take it off?"

"No. He knows how special it was to me." She glared at me. "She and the professor destroyed it."

He waved the gun at each of us. "Well, that was awfully rude of them. It was a family heirloom. Your grandma will be very disappointed."

"She doesn't really need it anymore, though. Does she?" Thomas asked. "Not when you've got your own occult jewelry. How many of those do you have back at league headquarters? Stocking up on enchanted equipment for your battle against magic?"

"You aren't worried about having such a powerful magical object around your neck? Where does all the energy go?" I asked.

The hunter frowned. "Go? It doesn't go anywhere. I'm keeping it safe, right here, where you can't use it against me."

"You're stealing energy from all the witches you've attacked?" I asked.

Something crossed Jasmine's face like she hadn't considered it that way before. Her eyes drifted to his amulet.

"You didn't know that?" I asked her. "Your partner here is murdering people for using magic, but he's keeping the energy for himself. Is that your holy mission?"

She shook her head, frowning at Wesson. "That wasn't the plan. The energy…the powers they have…it's evil. If you use it, you'll be corrupted."

"I'm disarming my enemies," he said. "So they can't do me harm."

The same words Thomas and I had used to bind Tori, and for the same reason, when you got down to it. Fear was more dangerous than magic.

The timer on my phone went off. Facing Tori, I mouthed, "I'm sorry."

Her ankh necklace glowed. Then the light flashed and faded, absorbed into her chest. For a moment, she looked confused. Maybe she'd blamed the amulet for her weakness.

Then, louder, I said, "I release you."

Tori's eyes widened in understanding, and she stood. The dark look she gave me almost made me regret setting the time limit on her bind. But she shifted her attention to the hunter.

Wesson smirked. "Oh, you do? I'm the one with the gun, sweetheart."

He cocked his weapon, and the small sound set off a chain

reaction.

Brian took a step forward, still standing between me and the hunter. Jasmine pushed down on Wesson's arm, pointing the gun at the ground. He shoved her away.

Tori used her unbound Gift to reach for the hunter's amulet, drawing the energy it held. The pendant pulled away from his chest until the strap snapped and the amulet flew through the air. Lightning flashed between Tori and the amulet, and the wooden disk glowed orange and red.

Wesson shielded his eyes, cursing.

Jasmine screamed as she fell back, and Brian lunged to catch her.

The hunter staggered, swinging the gun around to Tori. "Freeze!" he yelled.

The same word flooded my mind, and the next few seconds seemed to happen in slow motion.

The amulet exploded, shattering splinters in all directions. The energy it released knocked the wind out of me, surging to replace what the amulet had taken. I directed it at the hunter, the gun, and the silver bullet racing for the young witch.

The world stood still. Silence. Wesson hung in the air halfway across the room, blown backward by the force of the explosion. The bullet floated in the air. Brian and Jasmine fell to one side. Tori stood, arms flung wide, in front of the tower ladder. Thomas knelt a few steps away, shielding his face from flying debris.

My skin buzzed, and I couldn't tell if it was from the energy release or its return. I bent double, catching my breath, dizzy from the cycling energy. In. Out. Breathe. The air ruffled the hair in front of my face. More than my breath. Time catching up again, slipping through my fingers. I lost my grip. The fire alarm blared.

My head.

"Get down!" Thomas yelled, freed from the time bubble by my weakness. I sensed movement around me as the others were released.

Stop. The quiet returned, like someone twisting the dial on the shop's ancient stereo. Raising my head, I took stock of the space. The bullet had moved from where I first froze it, hanging in the air on its way to Tori. The hunter's intention must have driven some of the energy she'd released from the amulet. From his position in the air, it never would have flown so straight on its own.

But Brian and Jasmine stood between the bullet and its target, twisting to protect themselves from the force of the explosion.

The energy thrummed in my veins. I straightened, breathing hard with the effort of controlling it. *How should I direct it? I might only get one chance.*

I stumbled forward. My vision blurred, and my heart roared in my ears. I'd felt this way before. In a realtor's office back in Williamsburg. A translucent image overlaid the scene in front of me. Not memory. The future.

Ghostly images of the people in the shop separated from their mortal forms, slowly inching forward. I caught my breath as the shadow of the bullet burst through Brian's chest, over Jasmine's shoulder, and lodged itself between Tori's eyes.

"No!" I gasped for breath, and the play-through stopped. The overlaid images shimmered and faded, leaving the frozen forms in their original positions. Almost. They had shifted slightly while I watched the preview, each of them a few inches from where they started.

And the bullet still moving toward them.

It crept through the air against all my intentions. Maybe it had intentions of its own, or it had been traveling too fast, or my energy was too depleted by the amulet.

I forced myself to my feet and staggered across the room. Such a small thing, moving with such force. I grabbed a two-by-four from a pile of scrap wood and slammed it down on the bullet. It barely moved.

It didn't make sense. Brian had moved the crew before the drop fell.

People moved through space with less force than a bullet. I controlled time, but my Gift didn't come with super strength. Focus on the things you can change.

My turn to feel like the Flash.

I dropped the two-by-four and stood beside the bullet. My vision doubled again and I followed the shadow-bullet, marking its trajectory. When it got to Brian, I closed my eyes, letting it clear. Opening them, I put my hands on his shoulders.

The energy glitched like it had in the days before the boundary came down in Queen's Creek. His eyes widened. "I'm sorry," I said, shoving him sideways as hard as I could. He stumbled, grabbing for my arm as he lost his balance. A second later, my Gift reasserted itself, catching him mid-fall.

My breath shortened and sweat beaded on my forehead. I couldn't hold them all. The energy was too chaotic. Even as I tried to choose my next move, time glitched again. Brian fell a little further. Jasmine twitched, tripping over his leg. The bullet passed over them.

I shifted the direction of my Gift, releasing Thomas and letting the hunter crash to the ground as I gathered the energy and focused it all on the bullet.

Tori remained frozen in front of it, held by Wesson's intention. How much magical energy had he stored in that amulet? Thomas jumped to his feet and tackled Tori, but her arrested momentum shifted his trajectory. They slid toward the bullet.

"Stop!" I yelled, releasing any energy I had left. They froze.

I backed up and got a running start, then slammed into my brother, sending him and Tori sprawling just as I lost what little control remained. Time rushed back, everything hurtling back into place, fast-forward to make up for the pause.

I collapsed to the floor. Every inch of my body ached from the vibration of holding them in place.

"Get off of me!" Tori yelled, though her voice was muffled under my brother's weight.

I rolled to the side so he could get up, then pushed myself to my feet. I paused halfway up, head down, hands on my knees, letting the dizziness pass. It would have been so good to sit back down and meditate, test out my theory on recharging my Gift from my spirit, but the irony was that without it, I didn't have time. I took a deep breath and straightened on the exhale.

The hunter groaned behind me. I crawled back to him and kicked the gun out of his hand, sending it spiraling across the floor. It slid toward the paint frame, teetered on the cut-away edge, and fell through the hole in the floor, dropping down to the storage space beneath the shop.

The fire alarm cut off, but the ringing continued in my ears.

"A thank you might be nice," Thomas said, giving Tori a hand to stand up. Blood streaked his cheek.

Another inch to the right. Another second of indecision. I almost lost my brother forever.

I threw my arms around his neck.

He patted my back, whispering into my hair, "We're okay."

Even though he had to feel as drained as I did, the words worked like magic. My heart started beating again, and my breath smoothed. I stepped back. *What do we do now?*

Thomas offered Tori his hand again.

Tori slapped it away and stood on her own. "Thank you? For what? Nearly getting me killed?"

When he didn't answer, she stomped across the room to

where the hunter lay dazed on the floor. She bent down and dragged a dagger out of the hunter's boot. "Thanks for holding that for me, but I'll take it back now."

"Actually, that athamé came from my shop," Thomas said, following her. "It's not meant to be used as a weapon."

Tori stood over the hunter, spinning the knife in her hand.

46

Jasmine's eyes grew wide. She and Brian had landed in a tangle a few feet away. He groaned, cradling his arm. His head was bleeding.

Tori cocked her head, considering the prone hunter. The athamé shimmered in the fading light from the window.

"Unless you're going to stab him with that, could you just put it away?" I asked. "They came for us because we scare them. Threatening them with ritual knives will not improve their impression of us."

"Maybe I am going to stab him with it," Tori said. She raised the knife. Part of me wished she would go through with it. But Wesson hadn't lied when he said he wasn't alone. How many more waited for us to give them a reason to destroy us? How many mundanes would give into their fear if we became what the hunters told them we were?

"And then, what?" Jasmine said, shaking. "Are you going to kill us, too?"

"Don't tempt me." Tori nudged Wesson with her boot.

"She's not the one who killed your sister," I said.

"She's one of them. What difference does it make?" She pushed the toe of her huge shoe over the gash on the hunter's arm and pressed on it until the hunter moaned.

She's one of them. Morgan had said it at the café when Tori's potion made her paranoid. Maybe she wasn't completely oblivious to her uncle's activities.

Do our allies outnumber our enemies? Nora said it was time to find out. She was right.

"The difference is that's not who we are," Thomas said. "We can't overcome our enemies by becoming them."

"She tried to help. It doesn't make up for the other things she's done, but if she hadn't tried to disarm him, this might have ended differently." I nodded my thanks, and Jasmine inclined her head to accept it. "We should consider that truce now."

Tori lowered the knife, but it could have been as much because her arm was tired as it was because of what we said.

"The fire department will sweep the building when they get here, if they're not here already. We shouldn't stick around unless you want to explain his injuries," I said.

Jasmine helped Brian to his feet, careful of his arm, and the five of us made our way out of the shop, leaving the hunter behind.

Outside, the late day sun burned my eyes after so much time in the backstage darkness. Thomas called out to someone ahead of us. An EMT materialized from the fire department ambulance.

"There's someone inside. He…fell. Hit his head when we were evacuating. Might have a concussion." My brother put a hand on the guy's shoulder to encourage him to hurry without asking questions.

The young man waved to his partner, and they ran into the building with a stretcher.

A small crowd of theater patrons and college students milled around, waiting to see what kind of emergency had canceled the show. They gasped when the door swung open and the EMTs wheeled out the stretcher. Wesson lay with an arm across his eyes to block the evening sun.

Tori, Thomas, and I stepped back to let them pass, but the crowd pressed too close for us to slip away.

Something moved in my peripheral vision. Wesson pushed himself off the stretcher and lunged at Tori. My hands came up automatically, freezing him in place.

"Uh, Cate? What are you doing?" Thomas asked through gritted teeth. He smiled and waved at the confused mundanes who stood closest to us. Most of the crowd was oblivious to the new statue in front of the theater, but the EMTs definitely noticed the change in their charge.

"He's not going to stop. It wasn't enough to take down the Gate and let magic out. We have to be able to use it," I said. "I won't play the victim anymore. No more hiding."

Thomas looked from me to Wesson to the gaping mundanes standing nearby. Then he started to whistle. I'd never stopped to think about what a muse with a power boost could do. It became immediately obvious which of the students outside had secret dreams of starting a band. Humming grew to a chorus. People stomped their feet and clapped their hands. A mini parade of improvised instrumentation wove around the edge of the field. It drew as much attention as the frozen hunter.

And then it drew more.

As students danced down the sidewalk, theater patrons joined them until the parade headed deeper into campus. Soon, we stood almost alone with the immobilized Wesson.

"Well, here you are," came a voice just behind me.

"We've been looking all over for you. Where have you been? Are you packed?" said a second voice. Tori's parents stood beside me. She mumbled a response I couldn't make out.

"Pleasure to see you again, dear," said Mrs. Walsh, as if our last meeting had been a social event rather than her daughter's disciplinary hearing.

"We'll take it from here if you don't mind." Mr. Walsh flicked a finger, and a breeze ruffled my hair. It flowed around me, cooling my face.

"I can't let go," I said. "He's the one who…"

"We know who he is," Mrs. Walsh said.

I risked a glance at her face. Her dark eyes never left the hunter.

"He will meet justice," Mr. Walsh said. A twist of his wrist intensified the breeze until a funnel of leaves raced around the frozen hunter.

I couldn't hold him if I couldn't see him.

"Let us handle him this time," Mrs. Walsh said. "It's our turn. Besides, you are needed elsewhere, I think."

One last breath. *I release you.* My legs gave out, and I fell to my knees.

"Time to go," Thomas said, reaching for my hand. "Close your eyes."

47

Duncan lived in a small three-bedroom Cape Cod-style home near the military base in Williamsburg. As a real estate agent, he would tell people it was an ideal starter home for young families. As a witch, he'd made several improvements that wouldn't show up on a home inspection.

For instance, the room Thomas and I blinked into did not appear on the blueprints and would have been difficult for guests to find despite the house's small footprint. When we stepped over the threshold into the house's main hallway, the door we'd come through vanished into the side of the stairwell.

Duncan called out from down the hall. "Thomas? Is that you? I'm in the kitchen."

My brother led the way. A turn behind the staircase opened out to a chef's kitchen that had no business in a house this size. A young man with long, dark hair and Native American features stood behind a stove that faced out into the eating area. It took me a second to recognize Duncan Scott, a witch from Queen's Creek who'd used a glamour to disguise himself as realtor Luke Williams for the past several years.

"Cate! You're back!" He came around the island and wrapped me in a hug.

Thomas slid a bar stool behind me, and I sank into it, still catching my breath from our instantaneous travel. Did it always feel like this? No wonder Thomas crash landed into his bedroom so often.

"Be right back," Thomas said. He leaned across the counter to kiss Duncan's cheek before he blinked out again.

"Your mom's going to be so happy to see you," Duncan said, flipping a large grilled cheese sandwich on the stove. "This has all been really stressful on her."

A loud thud shook the small house. Duncan sighed. "Your brother could crash land in an empty airfield lined with pillows."

"Sorry!" Thomas called from somewhere near the room where we'd arrived. He walked around the corner with Tori casting a shadow in his wake. As she came into the room, Duncan cut the sandwich in half and dropped a plate in front of each of us. Thomas pulled a Gatorade from the fridge and chugged half of it before grabbing two more bottles for us.

"Blessed electrolytes," he said with a wink. "Just the thing when you've expended more energy than your body can keep up with."

I was too dizzy to argue. The meal disappeared like magic, and Thomas was right about the electrolytes. Tori must have agreed because she said nothing as she sat beside me, munching her grilled cheese.

"Thank you," I said. "And please don't take this the wrong way. I'm so happy to see you, and I'd love to catch up and get a tour of the house, but if I don't talk to Adam soon—"

"The keys are on the hook," Duncan said, nodding to a quaint catchall shelf by the side door. "I'm impressed you made it this long. Drive safe."

"Thank you," I said again.

Duncan's house wasn't far from the office where I'd first met "Luke." I followed the same route I'd taken the last time I left Queen's Creek, managing not to miss the final turn-off this time. The paved road gave way to gravel, then dirt, as I approached the Creek. I parked the car in a small clearing at the end of the road and jogged the rest of the way in, zipping up my hoodie against the early evening chill.

The air lightened near the Creek as if a storm had just passed. Tiny lights flashed in the trees. Lightning bugs and will-o-the-wisps playing some kind of game. A soft glow peeked out of the Gatehouse window.

If I hadn't known the structure had mostly burned down after being struck by lightning a few days ago, I'd never have guessed it. The cottage that sat on the edge of the Creek appeared to have settled into the space a hundred years ago or more. Ivy traced the gingerbreading, and the bright paint colors had faded into natural tones.

The door opened. A tall figure in a cloak stepped out, holding a star torch ahead of him. Its warm light chased away the shadows from his face. Adam smiled.

I recognized that smile. I'd seen it in my cup back at the dorm. *I'm so stupid.*

This is why we don't drink and scry. Goddess, I'm a fool. I spent so much time being jealous of myself. My Gift had started to emerge, freed from the bind that held it and strengthened by the energy we released from Queen's Creek. But I had so little experience with it I didn't recognize it when I asked to see Adam. I'd focused my intentions on Adam at the Gatehouse, and the magic had shown me Adam at the Gatehouse. But I hadn't simply looked across space. I'd looked across time.

"I was starting to worry," he said.

"About what? If anything had happened, you would have known how to reach me."

He laughed.

But there was sadness in his eyes.

Something rustled in the trees above us, and Adam looked up.

I crossed the space between us and threw my arms around his neck. "I'm sorry for making you worry."

His arms tightened around me. "Never do it again."

"I promise."

The next morning, the witches of Queen's Creek gathered on the banks. The hunters we faced in Chicago had been arrested, but Wesson said they were not alone, and I believed him.

We'd given them no reason to hate us, but they didn't need one. *How do you protect yourself from someone else's fear?*

Inside the Gatehouse, the reconstruction efforts outshined the natural beauty of its exterior. Alice's single chair and simple rug gave way to a new sitting room. It had become a space to welcome visitors rather than house the keeper of a Gate that almost never opened.

Tori and I sat together with Dr. Bear between us. He looked much happier without the ribbon across his eyes. We each placed a hand on the bear and called out to Grace across time and through the veil. Our eyes closed, and I showed Tori the Gatehouse I'd visited in my mind. As it came into focus, her sister sat in Alice's chair.

"I've missed you," said Grace. She held out her arms.

Tori's eyes filled with tears. She had grown taller than her sister, but their features were almost a mirror. *They're practically twins now, the same age until Tori's next birthday.*

"I'm so sorry, Gracie. We stopped him, but I can't bring you back. I tried...I wasn't strong enough. I couldn't reach you," Tori whispered. "And I can't stop more hunters from coming. Forgive me."

"You've never needed my forgiveness. It's time to forgive yourself. As for the hunters…let me help," Grace said.

When they embraced, the energy rose around them. Tori's Gift pulled gently at the edges. Grace released her own energy, an amplifying power that glowed as it grew.

Afterward, Grace smiled, brushing a dark hair from her sister's eyes. "Be well."

Grace stepped back, and the room faded around us.

We opened our eyes in the new Gatehouse.

"I just need a minute," I said.

Thomas took Tori to meet the elders.

Alone again, I faced the space that would have been my home and my prison if we hadn't found a way to release the energy that hid it from the rest of the world. The consequences of that already reached so much farther than Queen's Creek. I let magic out into the world, and the world would have to change because of it. That scared some people. But I felt stronger now, and I knew how to protect my people. The choice was no longer between hiding together or going it alone. Once we completed the new spell, no witch would have to face their enemies alone again.

But it still didn't undo the mistakes I'd made. The losses we'd suffered. I was no closer to finding a way to bring back my father.

Inhale. Exhale.

I closed my eyes again. Focused my intention. Unraveled time.

Maybe the veil would always be thin near the boundary, or maybe the time stream my ancestors harnessed all those years ago clung to the Creek even without the boundary spell to hold it there. In my mind, I watched the Gatehouse change, shifting through generations of designs, something a little different for each keeper who'd lived here.

Where is he?

"I will always be with you." My father's voice still sounded too far away.

I pressed forward and back along the timeline, watching the Gatehouse shuffle through the years.

A form flickered in and out in front of me. Somehow, I was always too far forward or too far back.

"Dad?"

"I will always be with you," he said.

"I'm going to find a way to get you back," I said. "Forgive me."

"Always."

I reached for him, but he was gone.

The energy that held me to the time stream faded with him. I opened my eyes to the present.

48

Outside, Adam and his dad guided our families and neighbors into a ritual circle. Tori stepped into the center with them.

"Friends, I'm so grateful to you all for your continued support," said Giles Parker, former Commander of the Watch, now Speaker of the Covens. "Over the past two weeks, we've faced a lot of changes in our community, and I'm sure we all understand that there will be many more to come. My son, your new Watch Commander, has recently been in touch with members of covens like ours who've managed to survive without the security of a Gate."

The people in the audience murmured various opinions about the risks of such a lifestyle but quieted when Giles raised a hand. He dropped his hand to Tori's shoulder.

"This young lady grew up in one such community. She assures me that they find safety in each other. But they've had generations of practice in dealing with the mundanes, and even they have suffered losses at the hands of the hunters."

The mention of the hunters sparked louder exclamations. We'd been taught to fear them for so long that they'd become almost mythical figures of imminent destruction. As a result, some younger witches didn't believe they existed at all.

Adam and Duncan spoke to the crowd about what they'd experienced on their Wakenings. Duncan's testimony, in particular, held sway because his disappearance three years ago had been a catalyst for many families to cancel their children's experience outside the Gate.

Thomas, Tori, and I talked about the lives we led among the mundanes, answering questions about everything from how to make breakfast without magic to how to recognize and avoid danger. We left out some of the details of Thomas's abduction.

"We're not here to convince you to leave," Thomas said. "That's not why we came back. Queen's Creek isn't going anywhere, and this will always be our home. But for those who want to go out and see the world, we want to help you do it safely. And for those who wish to stay behind, the Gate is down. It will only be a matter of time before our community starts to show up on mundane maps around the world. The location of our home is no longer a secret. *We* are not secret."

I took a breath and spoke to the crowd. "We need a way to protect ourselves that doesn't imprison us. The magic has never been tied to this place. The ability to direct energy toward our intentions is inside all of us."

"Witches are strongest together," Tori said. "But just because we may be physically far apart doesn't have to mean we lose that connection."

"Tori can help us. Her Gift allows her to sense and manipulate energy even at a distance," I said, leaving out the part where she could draw it out of me against my will. I also glossed over the bit where we contacted her late sister to pull her Gift across the veil. But Grace's Gift for sharing and enhancing energy complemented Tori's, and we needed both for what we were about to do.

"When we left here, the farther we got, the less we interacted with each other, the faster our Gifts seemed to fade. It became more difficult to call the energy. The magic we could do was weaker," Thomas said.

"If you let me, I'll link you all together, so the energy flows through all of you, no matter where you go," Tori said.

After taking a few questions, we had to admit we didn't exactly know how this would work or if there were limits to how far a witch could go before they lost the connection or felt pulled to return. But the people of our community had grown up sharing what they had with others and making sure that we all found the things we needed. Most of them stayed.

We called the quarters, opening our arms and faces to the sky. We welcomed the sun, the water of the Creek, the air around us, and the earth beneath us. The energy of the space combined with the energy of the people, all of us focusing our intentions on the greater good, on sharing our strength, on something greater than ourselves. Tori pulled the energy to the center of the circle, a glowing beacon brighter than the bonfire she'd built on the beach. She held it there, flashing above her fingertips. She wound threads of energy from each person into the ball of light, weaving it together like her fishnet sleeves.

And then.

"I release you," she said, casting out the net over the crowd. The zig-zagging lines linked neighbor to neighbor and disappeared into the sunlight.

49

You're packing again," Adam said.

"School year's not over yet." I'd borrowed a bag from home to take a few more of my dad's notebooks back to Chicago. They lay spread out on my childhood bed with a few of the folders and photos I'd found in the attic. None of them glowed or shivered or spoke out loud to guide me. Now that Brian knew about magic, I hoped he'd help me find whatever I'd missed. Assuming he was still talking to me after I nearly got him killed.

"Want some company?" Adam leaned against the doorframe, crossing his arms. Mr. Casual.

I put the bag down. "What happened to *they need me here*?"

He smiled. "That was before the Chosen One came back and freed them all. Again."

"It wasn't me this time." Tori could have all the credit for ushering in the next phase of Queen's Creek's history. Her spell brought our community a sense of connection that exceeded any bind. And no one had to stay trapped in town to maintain it.

Adam pushed off the wall and stepped into the room. "Who found her and brought her here?"

I stuffed the notebooks in the bag and yanked the zipper. It stuck. "We did that together."

His hand closed over mine, guiding the zipper along its track. "Let's do this together, too."

"Do you even know what this is?" I looked up at him without raising my head, heavy under the weight of the question and all of its possible interpretations. I didn't know the answers to any of them.

"We're going to find your dad. It's time to bring him home."

Thank You!

I hope you enjoyed catching up with Cate and learning a little more about the world she's helping to build. I'm so excited to share this story with you, and so appreciative that you've chosen to join me!

Please consider leaving a review if you liked *Unforgivable.*
You can help this book find its audience (and earn my eternal gratitude!) by typing a sentence or two.

Also by Jenn Lessmann:

Unmagical

Coming in 2025:

Unbelievable, the final novel in
the *Cate Corey's Unmagical Life* trilogy.

Can't wait that long for more news from Queen's Creek? How about a FREE bonus story that covers the first three chapters of *Unmagical* from Thomas's point of view?

In Street Muse, Thomas Corey has twenty four hours to convince his twin sister to come home before the Gate closes, and she's locked out of his life forever. Unfortunately, Thomas's Gift is...unpredictable, and he's about to find himself the unexpected center of some very unwanted attention.

Subscribe to the *Queen's Creek Chronicle* to get access to this story and other bonus content, author updates, and witchy book recommendations: www.JennLessmann.com/Thomas

Acknowledgments

Many thanks to all my readers, particularly those brave souls who read this book in its early stages. My Ream and Vella followers, who were there for some of the early chapters that didn't make the final cut, you make me excited to write new stories. Beta readers, especially Davida, Kristin, and Bethany, your feedback was invaluable in making this story flow and keeping the characters' behaviors consistent and relatable. Thank you Janae, Wendra, and Anneli for helping me reach finish line when I need accountability and for sharing your stories with me.

Big appreciation to Karryn Nagel and Louisa West who manage the Cozy the Day Away sale and Witchy Bookworms promos with efficiency and care. The communities you've built for authors and readers are a tribute to your warmth and professionalism.

Thanks to J.E. Marriott and the members of the Book Witch Discord servers. I could not ask for a more supportive group of author/publisher/marketers.

Chrishaun, thank you for sharing your lens, your knowledge, and your friendship.

Thank you to Kat, for putting up with an endless stream of "what if…" and "does this make sense?" and for generally being an awesome critique partner and friend.

All my love and gratitude to George and the kids, who make this creative life not just possible, but a source of pride and joy. That's real magic.

About the Author

Jenn Lessmann is the author *Unmagical* and *Unforgivable,* the first two books in the *Cate Corey's Unmagical Life* trilogy.

A former barista, stage manager, and high school English teacher with advanced degrees from impressive colleges, Jenn continues to drink excessive amounts of caffeine, stay up later than is absolutely necessary, and read three or four books at a time. She lives in Virginia with her husband and their two boys and writes snarky paranormal fantasy whenever their dog will allow it.

In her spare time, Jenn runs a podcast about what it means to live a creative life - as a business owner and creator - with bestselling author and game designer Chrishaun Keller.

Catch their conversations on Building the Creative Life, now on Spotify.